W9-BCG-544

PILU
>>>>>> *of the* <<<<<<
WOODS

AN ONI PRESS PUBLICATION

PILU

>>>>>> *of the* <<<<<<

WOODS

WRITTEN, ILLUSTRATED,
COLORED, & LETTERED BY
MAI K. NGUYEN

EDITED BY
ROBIN HERRERA

DESIGNED BY
KATE Z. STONE

PUBLISHED BY ONI PRESS, INC.

JOE NOZEMACK, FOUNDER & CHIEF FINANCIAL OFFICER
JAMES LUCAS JONES, PUBLISHER
CHARLIE CHU, V.P. OF CREATIVE & BUSINESS DEVELOPMENT
BRAD ROOKS, DIRECTOR OF OPERATIONS
MELISSA MESZAROS, DIRECTOR OF PUBLICITY
MARGOT WOOD, DIRECTOR OF SALES
SANDY TANAKA, MARKETING DESIGN MANAGER
AMBER O'NEILL, SPECIAL PROJECTS MANAGER
TROY LOOK, DIRECTOR OF DESIGN & PRODUCTION
KATE Z. STONE, SENIOR GRAPHIC DESIGNER
SONJA SYNAK, GRAPHIC DESIGNER
ANGIE KNOWLES, DIGITAL PREPRESS LEAD
ARI YARWOOD, EXECUTIVE EDITOR
SARAH GAYDOS, EDITORIAL DIRECTOR OF LICENSED PUBLISHING
ROBIN HERRERA, SENIOR EDITOR
DESIREE WILSON, ASSOCIATE EDITOR
MICHELLE NGUYEN, EXECUTIVE ASSISTANT
JUNG LEE, LOGISTICS COORDINATOR
SCOTT SHARKEY, WAREHOUSE ASSISTANT

ONIPRESS.COM
FACEBOOK.COM/ONIPRESS • TWITTER.COM/ONIPRESS
ONIPRESS.TUMBLR.COM • INSTAGRAM.COM/ONIPRESS

@OHMAIPIE / MAIKNGUYEN.COM

FIRST EDITION: APRIL 2019

HARDCOVER ISBN: 978-1-62010-551-1
PAPERBACK ISBN: 978-1-62010-563-4
EISBN: 978-1-62010-564-1

PRINTED IN CHINA

LIBRARY OF CONGRESS CONTROL NUMBER: 2018940556

10 9 8 7 6 5 4 3 2 1

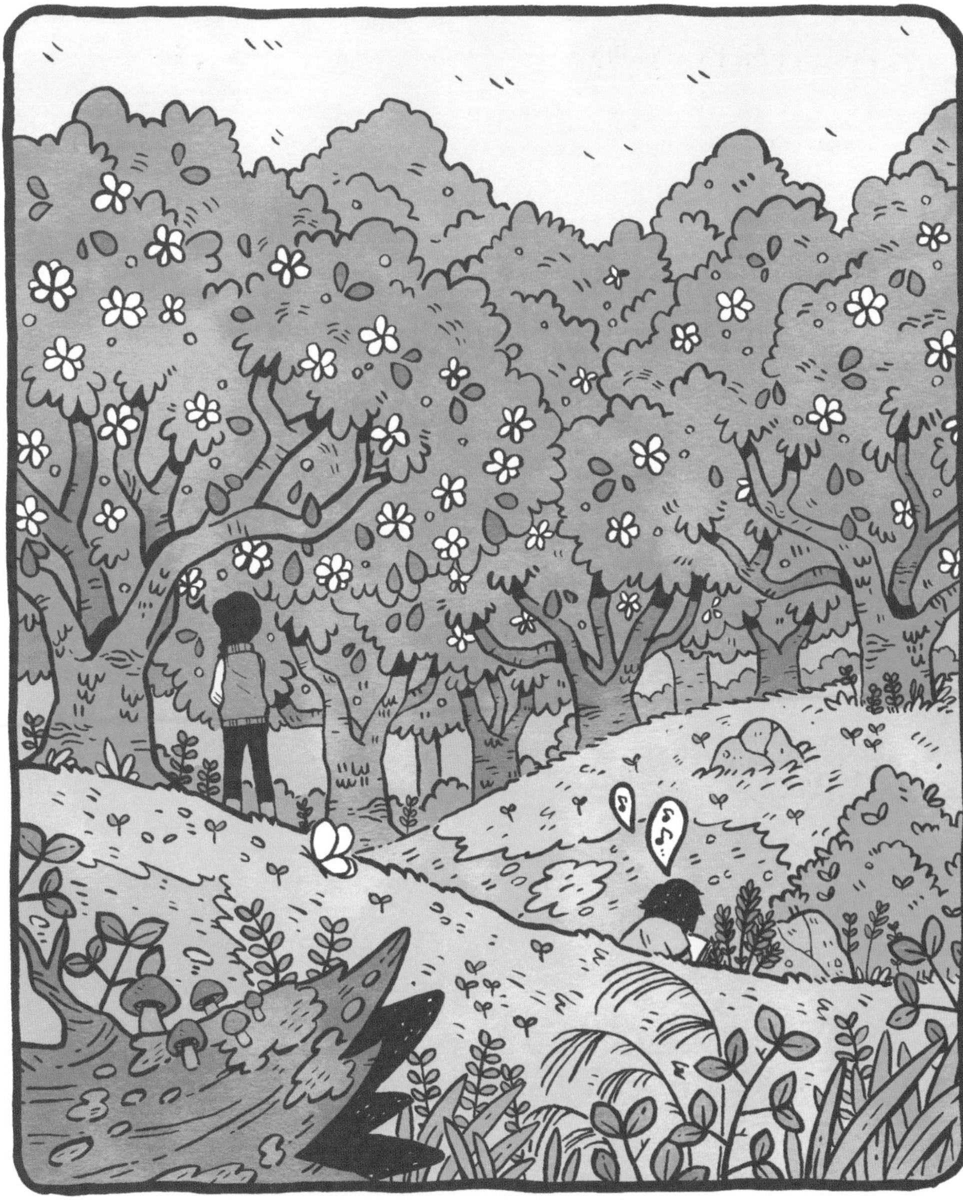

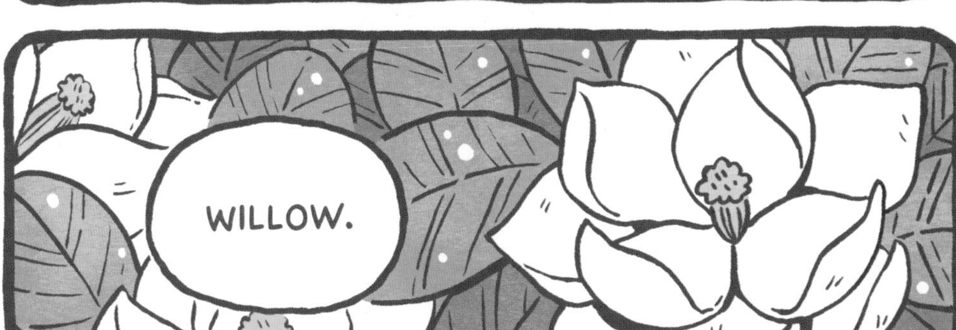
WILLOW.

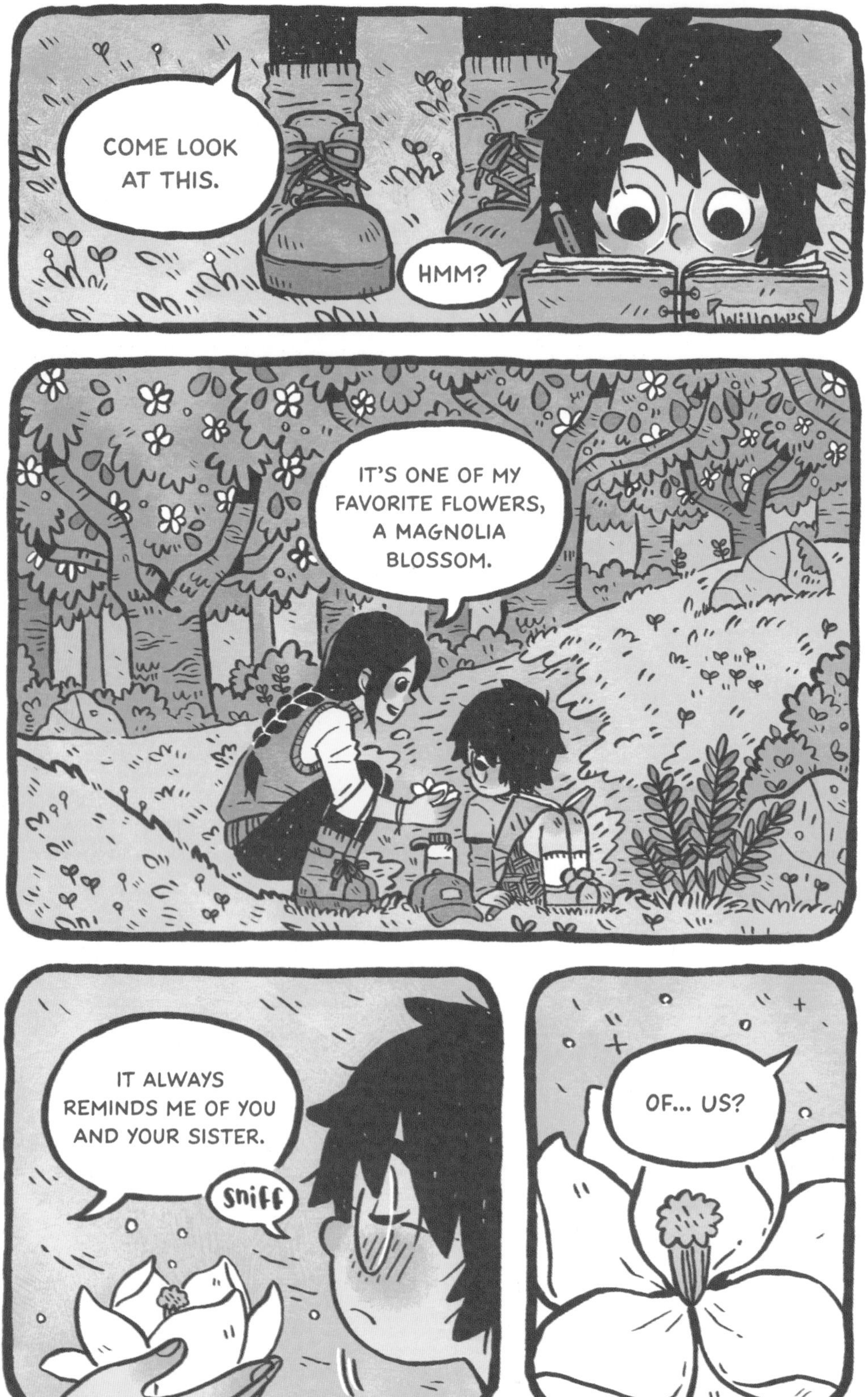
COME LOOK AT THIS.
HMM?
WILLOW'S
IT'S ONE OF MY FAVORITE FLOWERS, A MAGNOLIA BLOSSOM.
IT ALWAYS REMINDS ME OF YOU AND YOUR SISTER.
SNIFF
OF... US?

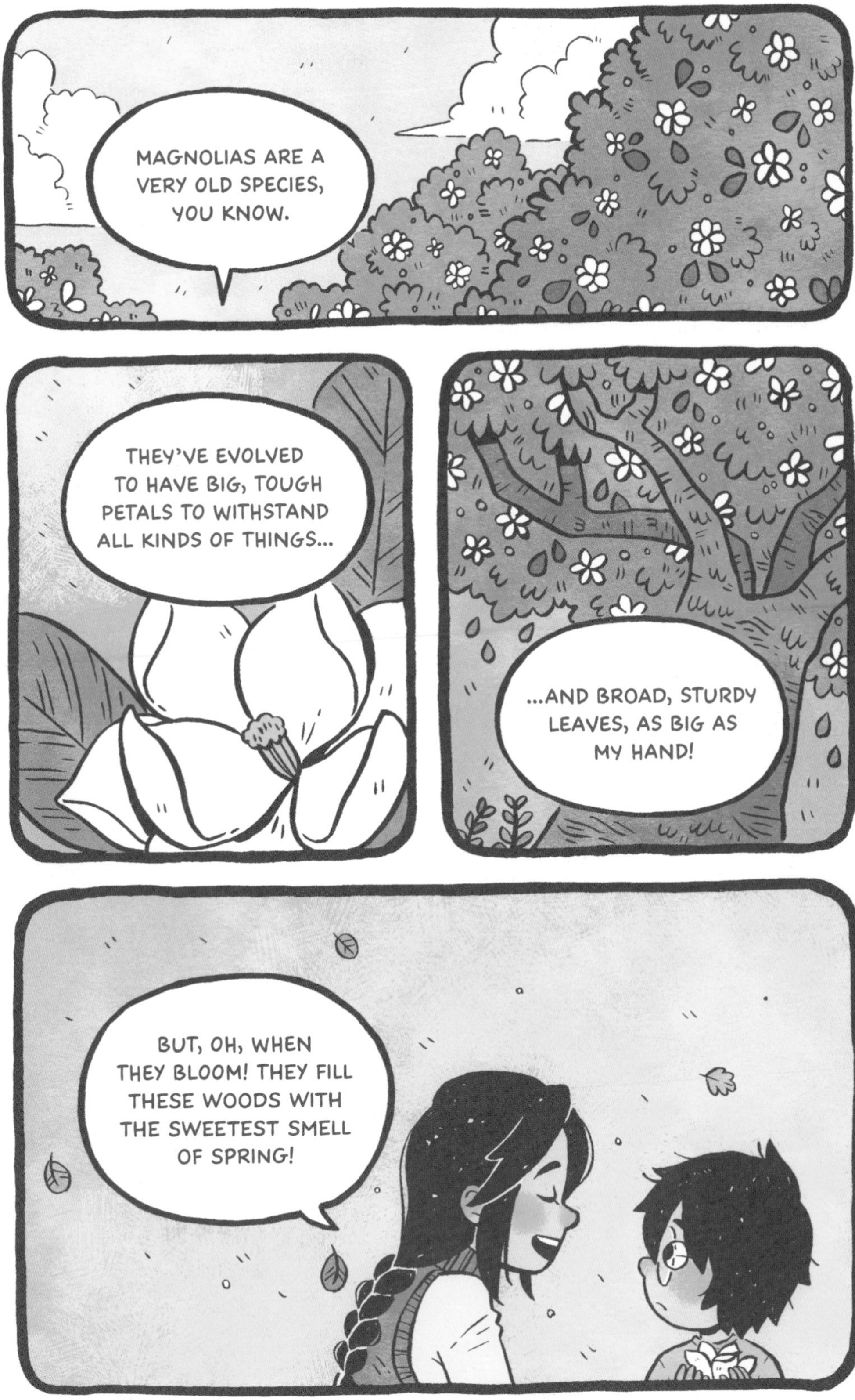
MAGNOLIAS ARE A VERY OLD SPECIES, YOU KNOW.
THEY'VE EVOLVED TO HAVE BIG, TOUGH PETALS TO WITHSTAND ALL KINDS OF THINGS...
...AND BROAD, STURDY LEAVES, AS BIG AS MY HAND!
BUT, OH, WHEN THEY BLOOM! THEY FILL THESE WOODS WITH THE SWEETEST SMELL OF SPRING!

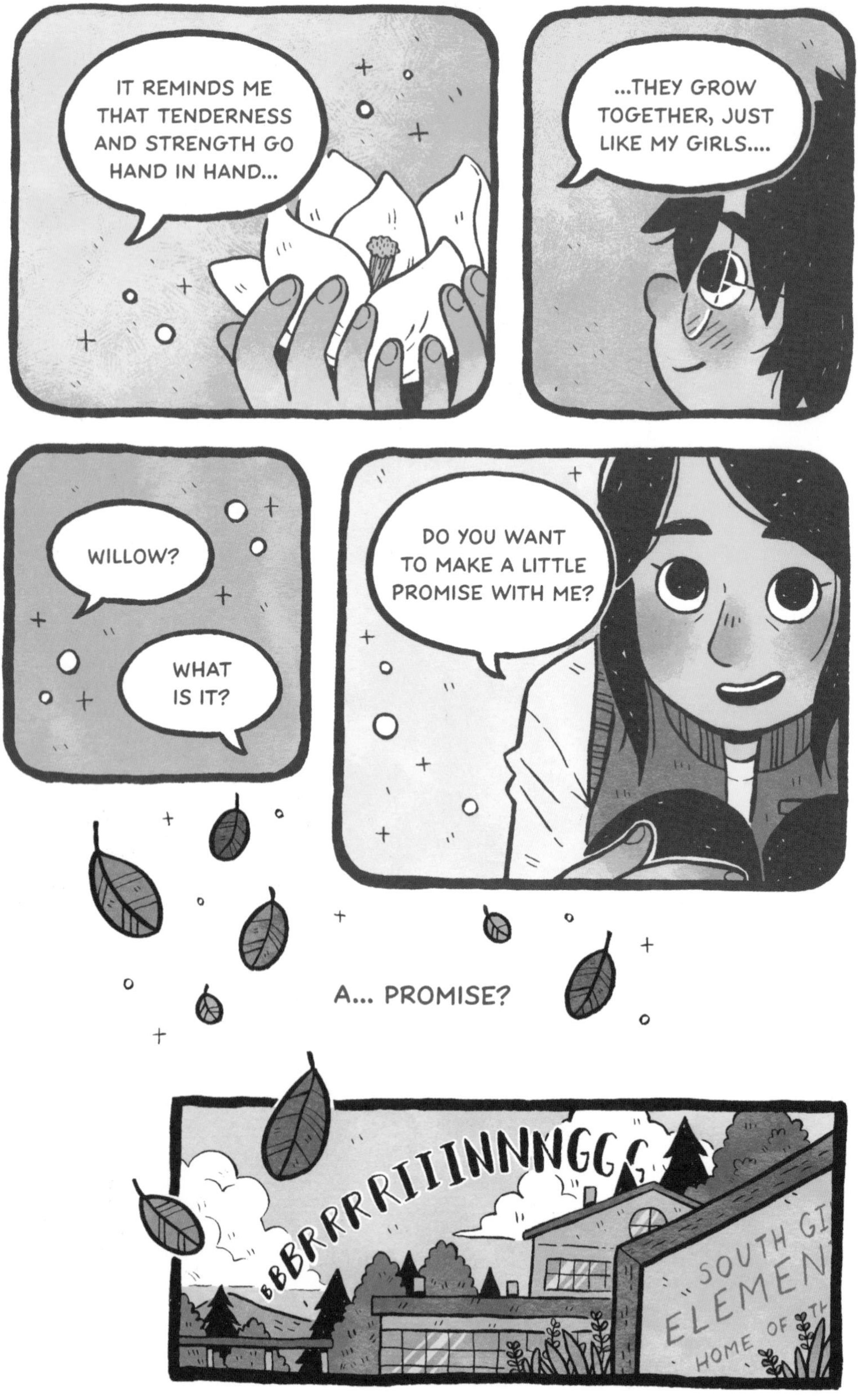
IT REMINDS ME THAT TENDERNESS AND STRENGTH GO HAND IN HAND...
...THEY GROW TOGETHER, JUST LIKE MY GIRLS....
WILLOW?
WHAT IS IT?
DO YOU WANT TO MAKE A LITTLE PROMISE WITH ME?
A... PROMISE?
BBBRRRRIIIINNNGGG
SOUTH GI
ELEMEN
HOME OF TH

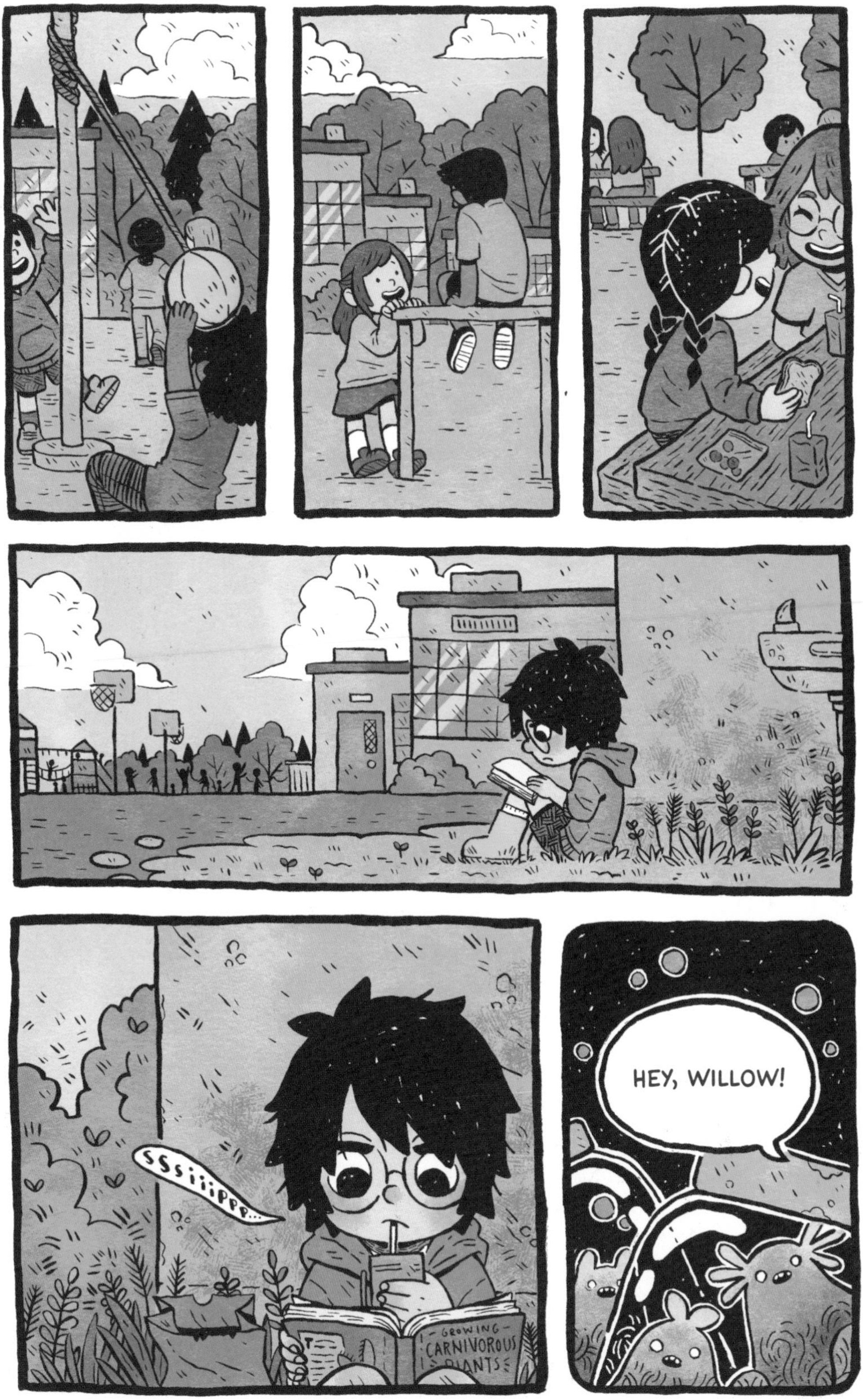
GROWING CARNIVOROUS PLANTS
SSsiiiPPP...
HEY, WILLOW!

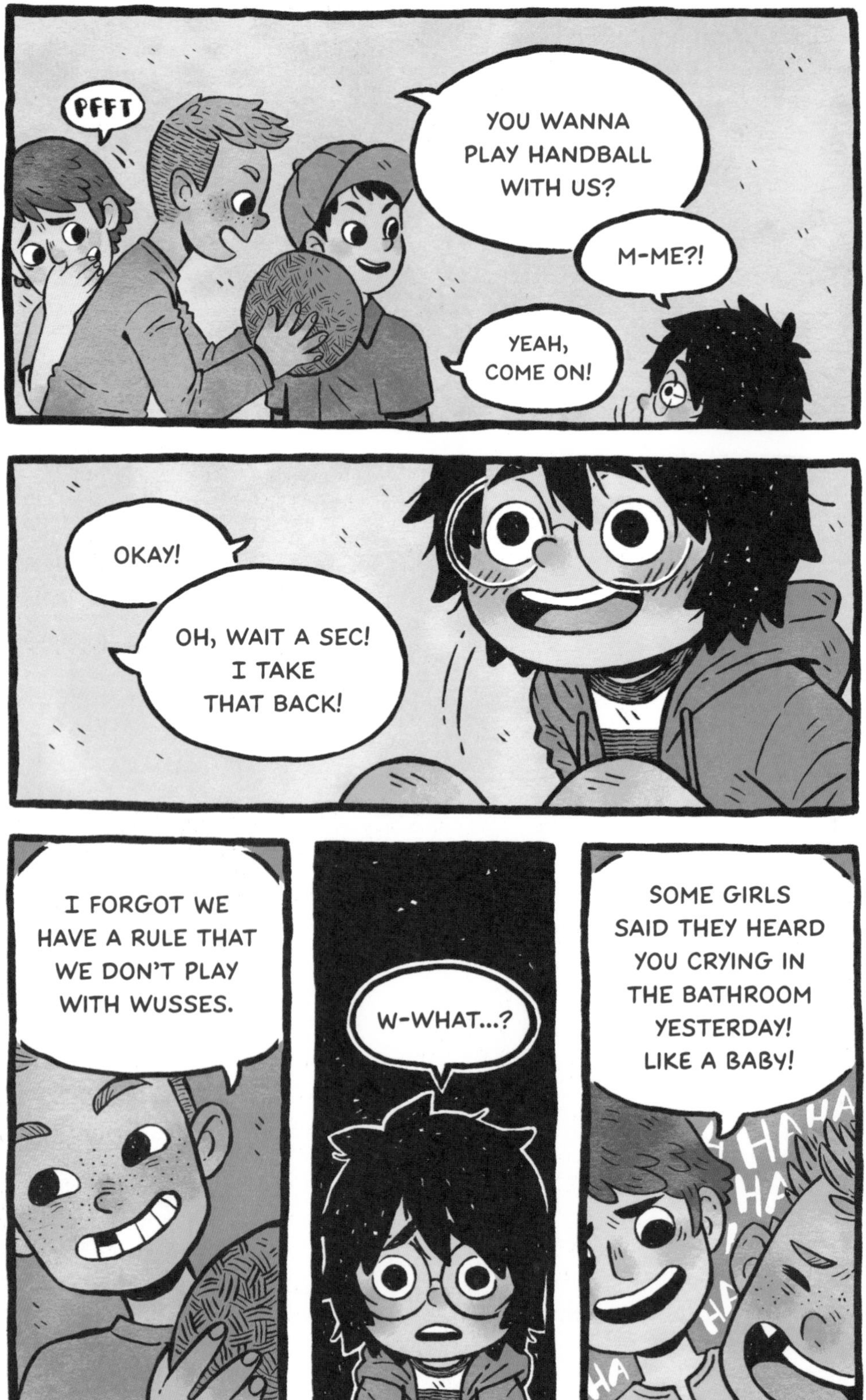
PFFT
YOU WANNA PLAY HANDBALL WITH US?
M-ME?!
YEAH, COME ON!
OKAY!
OH, WAIT A SEC! I TAKE THAT BACK!
I FORGOT WE HAVE A RULE THAT WE DON'T PLAY WITH WUSSES.
W-WHAT...?
SOME GIRLS SAID THEY HEARD YOU CRYING IN THE BATHROOM YESTERDAY! LIKE A BABY!
HA HA HA HA HA HA

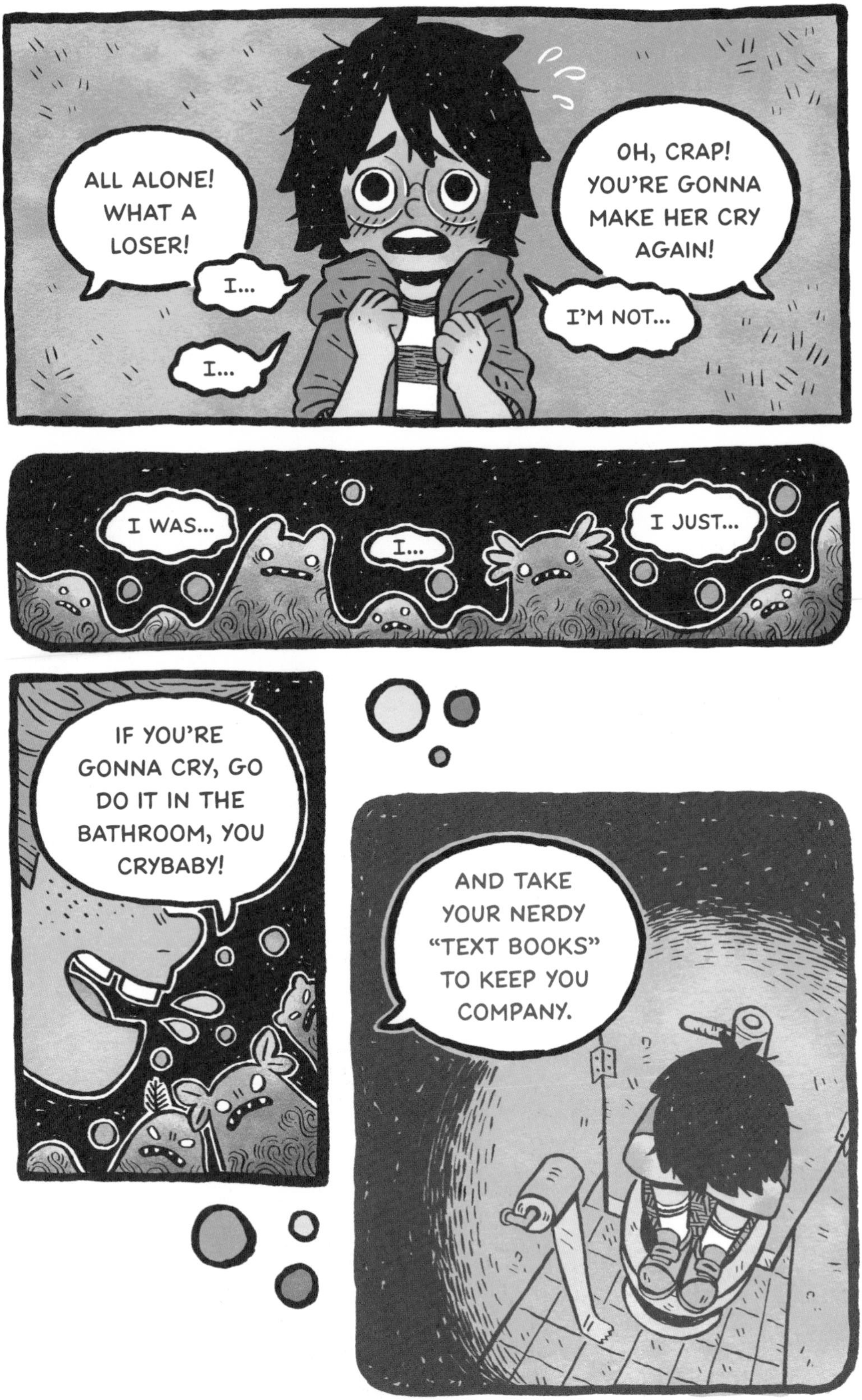
ALL ALONE! WHAT A LOSER!
I...
I...
OH, CRAP! YOU'RE GONNA MAKE HER CRY AGAIN!
I'M NOT...
I WAS...
I...
I JUST...
IF YOU'RE GONNA CRY, GO DO IT IN THE BATHROOM, YOU CRYBABY!
AND TAKE YOUR NERDY "TEXT BOOKS" TO KEEP YOU COMPANY.

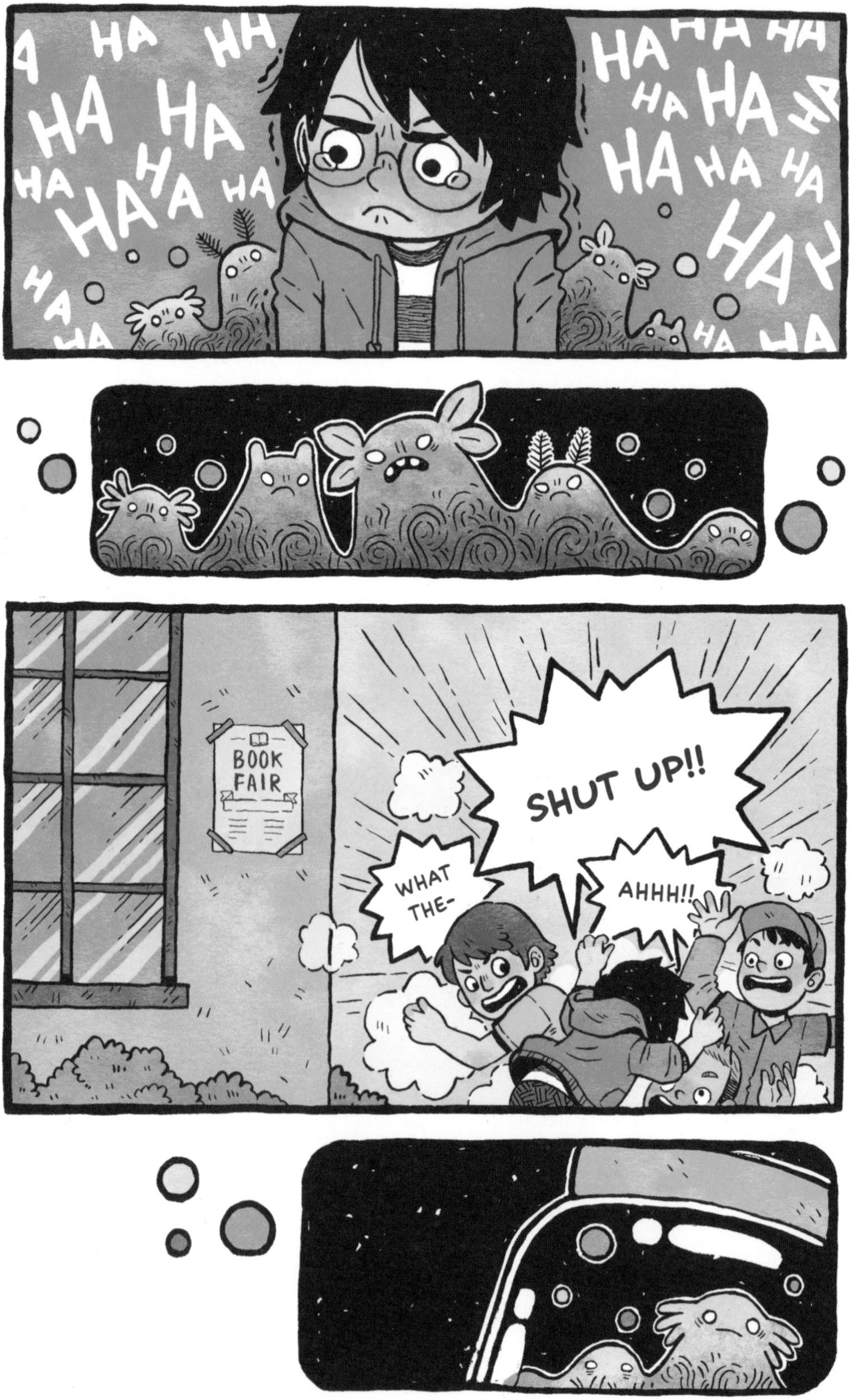
HA HA HA HA HA HA HA HA HA
HA HA HA HA HA HA HA HA HA HA HA
BOOK FAIR
SHUT UP!!
WHAT THE-
AHHHH!!

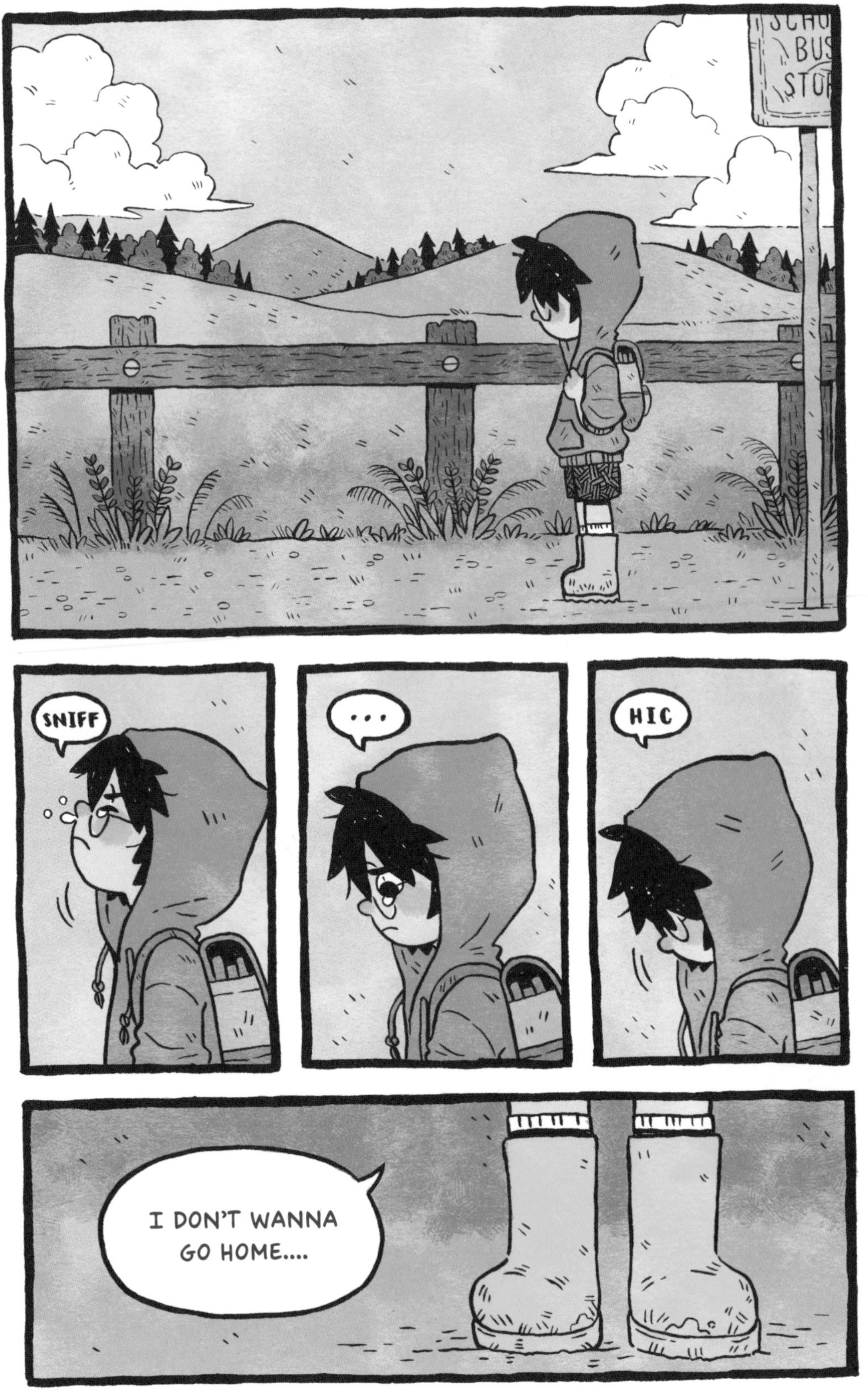
SCHO
BUS
STO
SNIFF
...
HIC
I DON'T WANNA GO HOME....

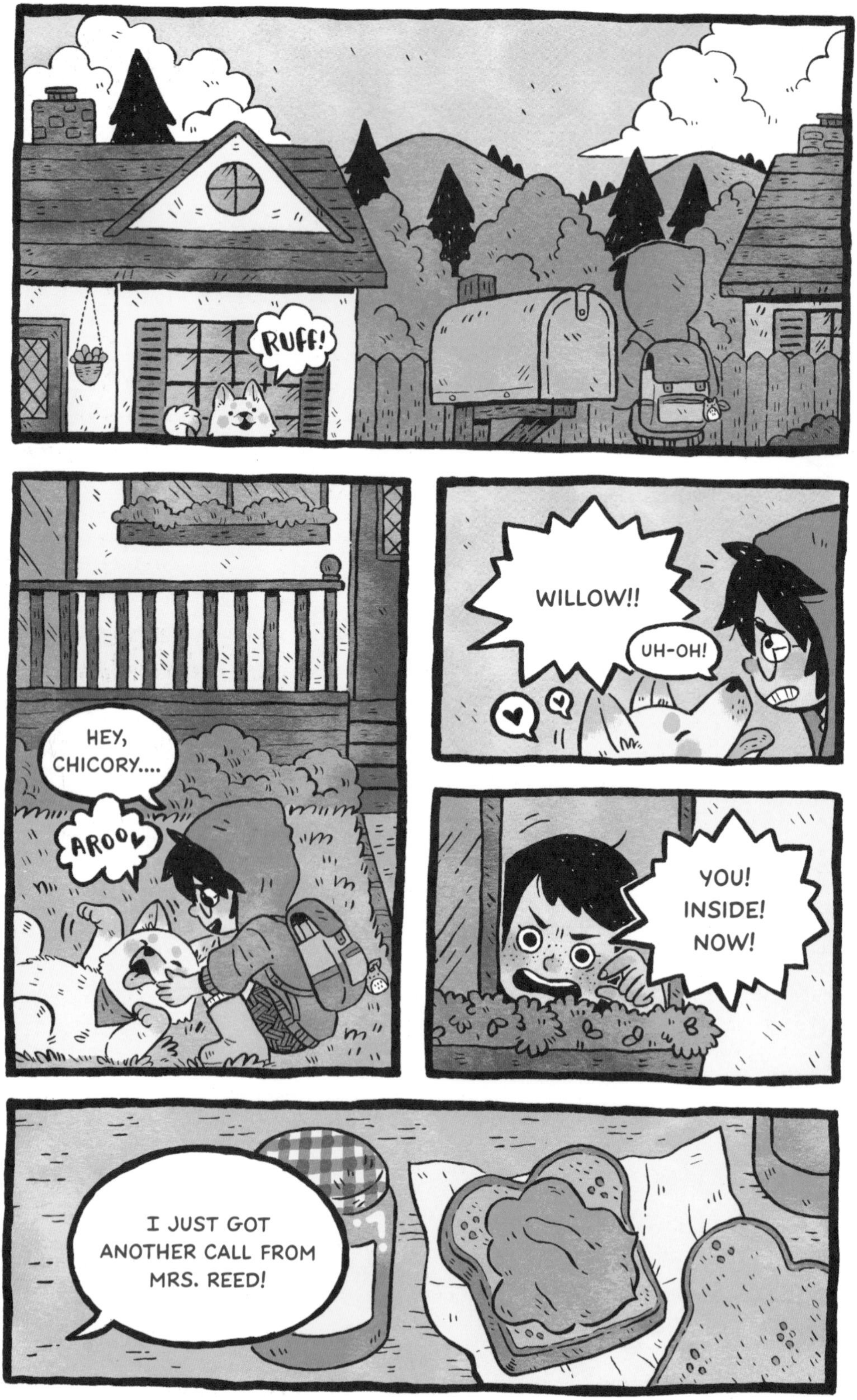
RUFF!
HEY, CHICORY....
AROO
WILLOW!!
UH-OH!
YOU! INSIDE! NOW!
I JUST GOT ANOTHER CALL FROM MRS. REED!

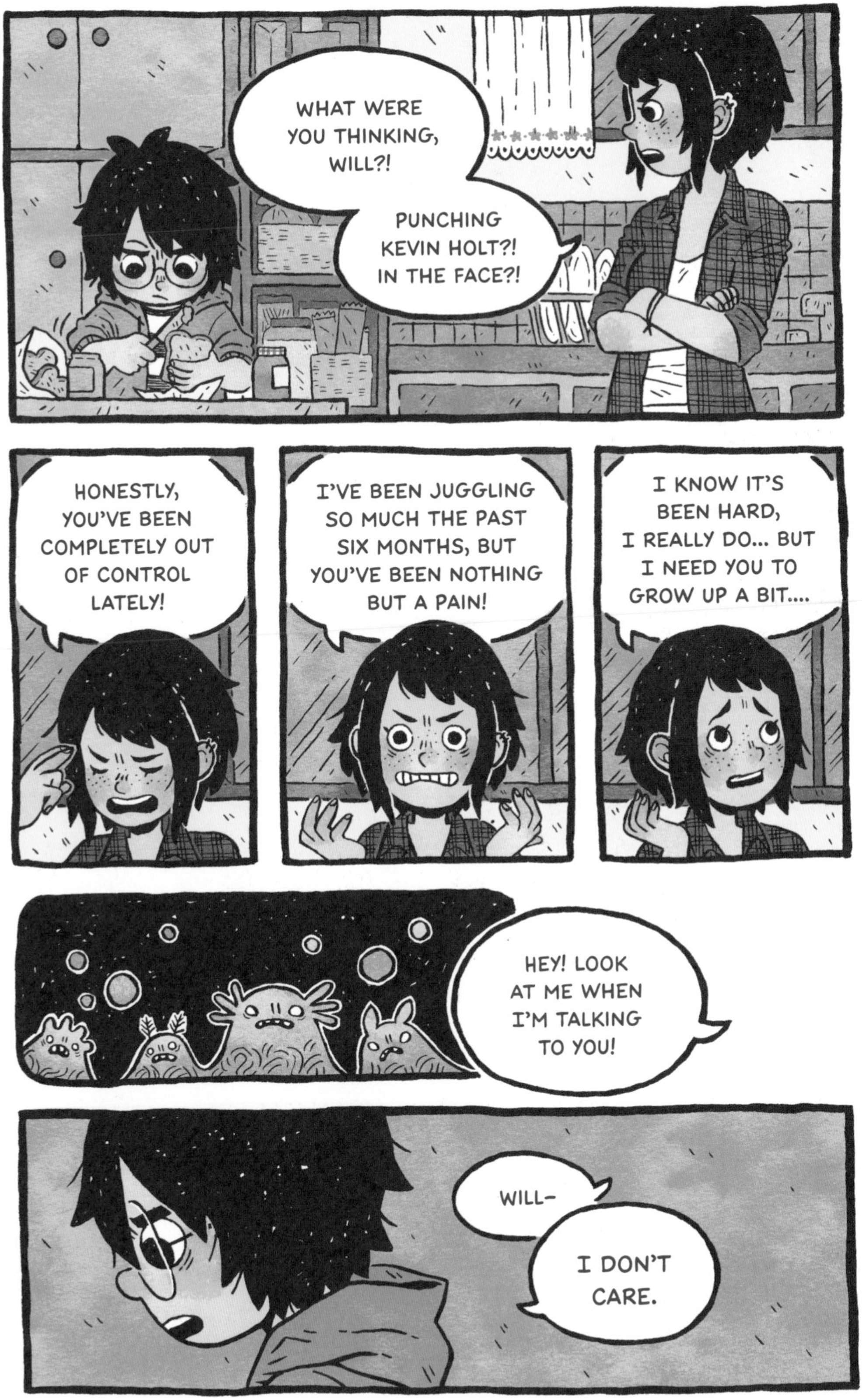
WHAT WERE YOU THINKING, WILL?!
PUNCHING KEVIN HOLT?! IN THE FACE?!
HONESTLY, YOU'VE BEEN COMPLETELY OUT OF CONTROL LATELY!
I'VE BEEN JUGGLING SO MUCH THE PAST SIX MONTHS, BUT YOU'VE BEEN NOTHING BUT A PAIN!
I KNOW IT'S BEEN HARD, I REALLY DO... BUT I NEED YOU TO GROW UP A BIT....
HEY! LOOK AT ME WHEN I'M TALKING TO YOU!
WILL–
I DON'T CARE.

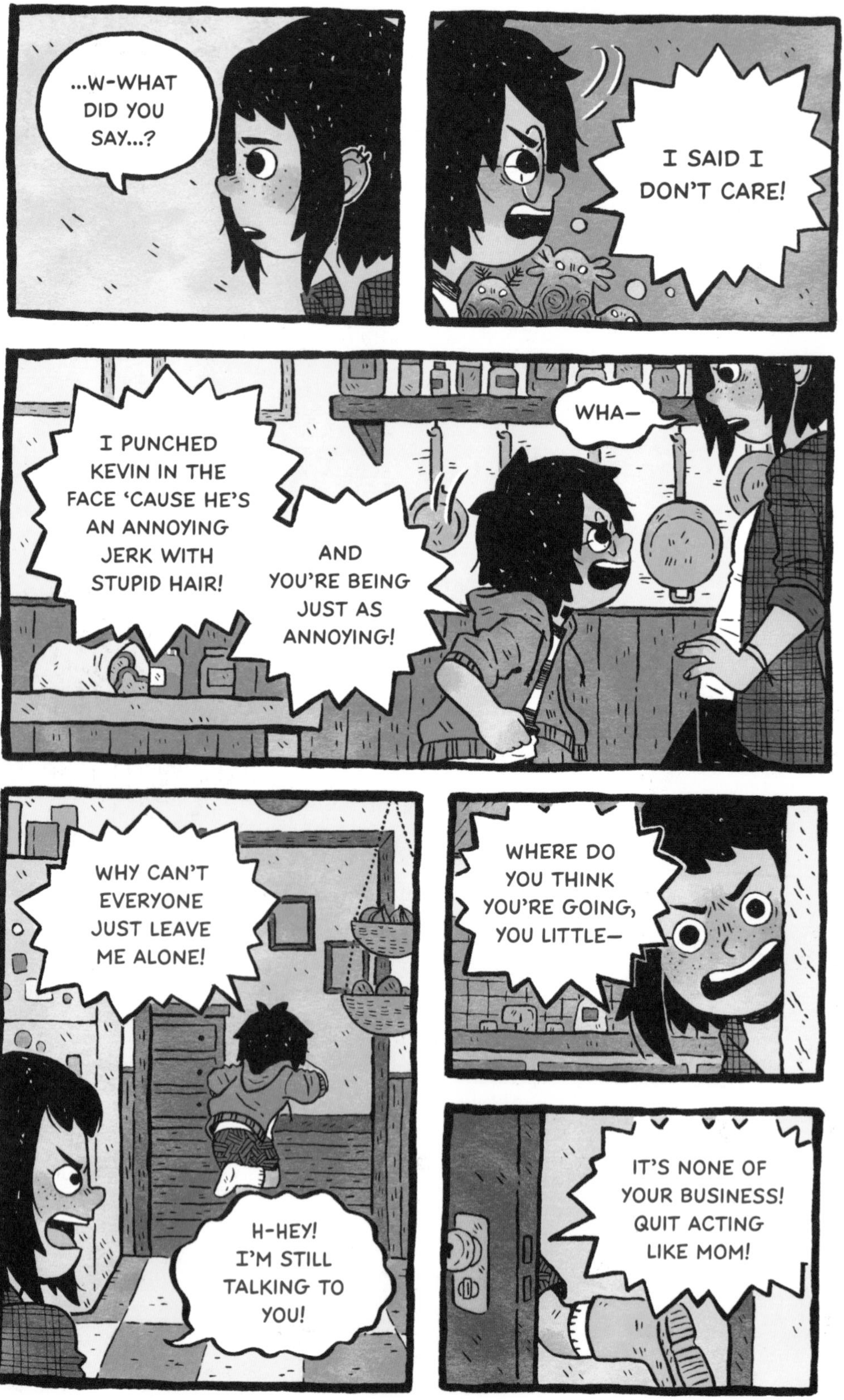
...W-WHAT DID YOU SAY...?
I SAID I DON'T CARE!
I PUNCHED KEVIN IN THE FACE 'CAUSE HE'S AN ANNOYING JERK WITH STUPID HAIR!
WHA–
AND YOU'RE BEING JUST AS ANNOYING!
WHY CAN'T EVERYONE JUST LEAVE ME ALONE!
H-HEY! I'M STILL TALKING TO YOU!
WHERE DO YOU THINK YOU'RE GOING, YOU LITTLE–
IT'S NONE OF YOUR BUSINESS! QUIT ACTING LIKE MOM!

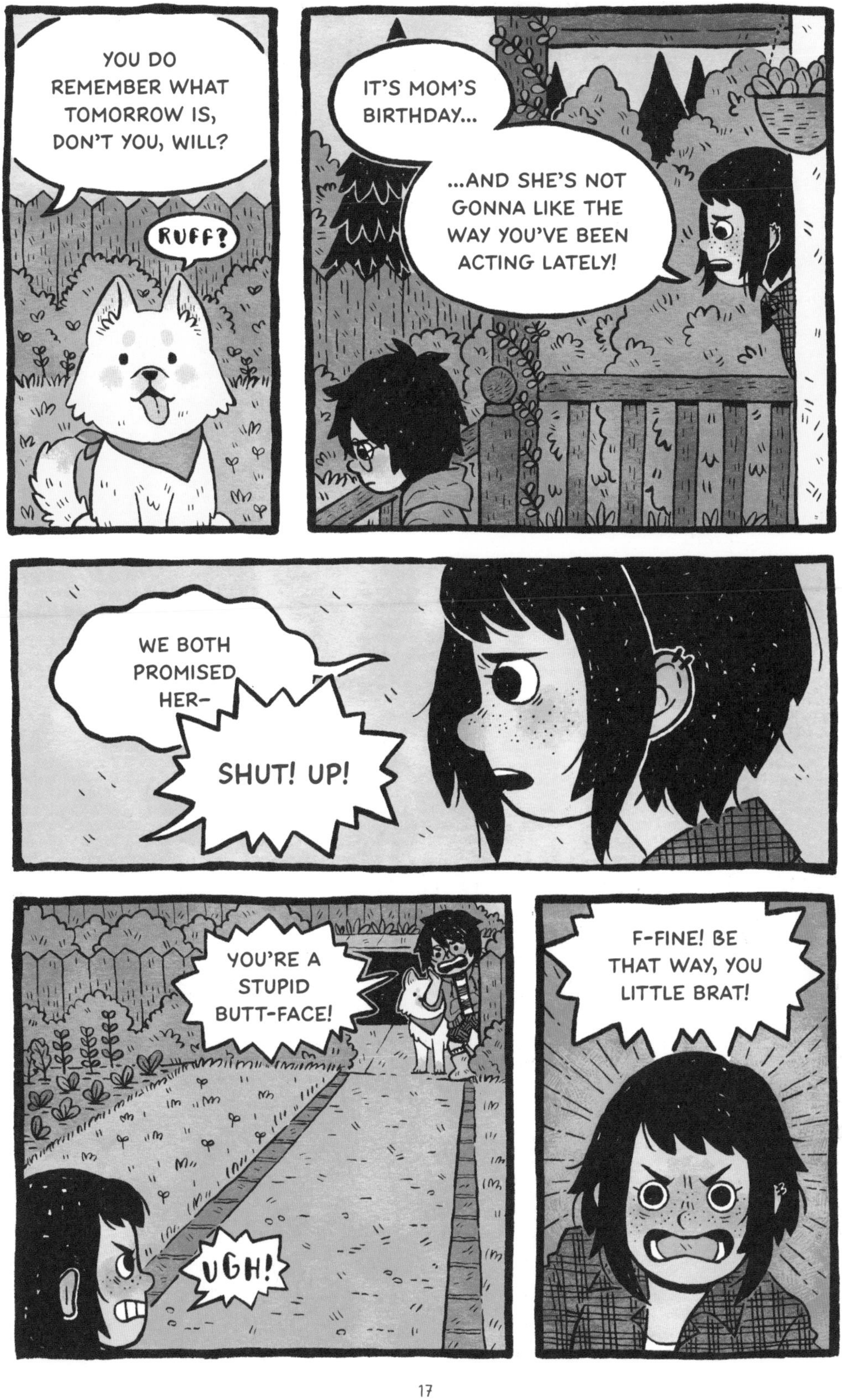
YOU DO REMEMBER WHAT TOMORROW IS, DON'T YOU, WILL?
RUFF?
IT'S MOM'S BIRTHDAY...
...AND SHE'S NOT GONNA LIKE THE WAY YOU'VE BEEN ACTING LATELY!
WE BOTH PROMISED HER–
SHUT! UP!
YOU'RE A STUPID BUTT-FACE!
UGH!
F-FINE! BE THAT WAY, YOU LITTLE BRAT!

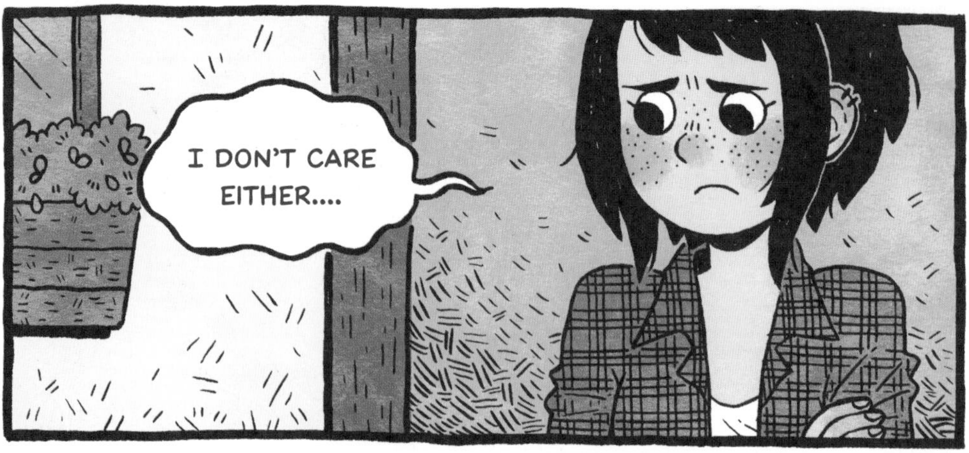
I DON'T CARE EITHER....

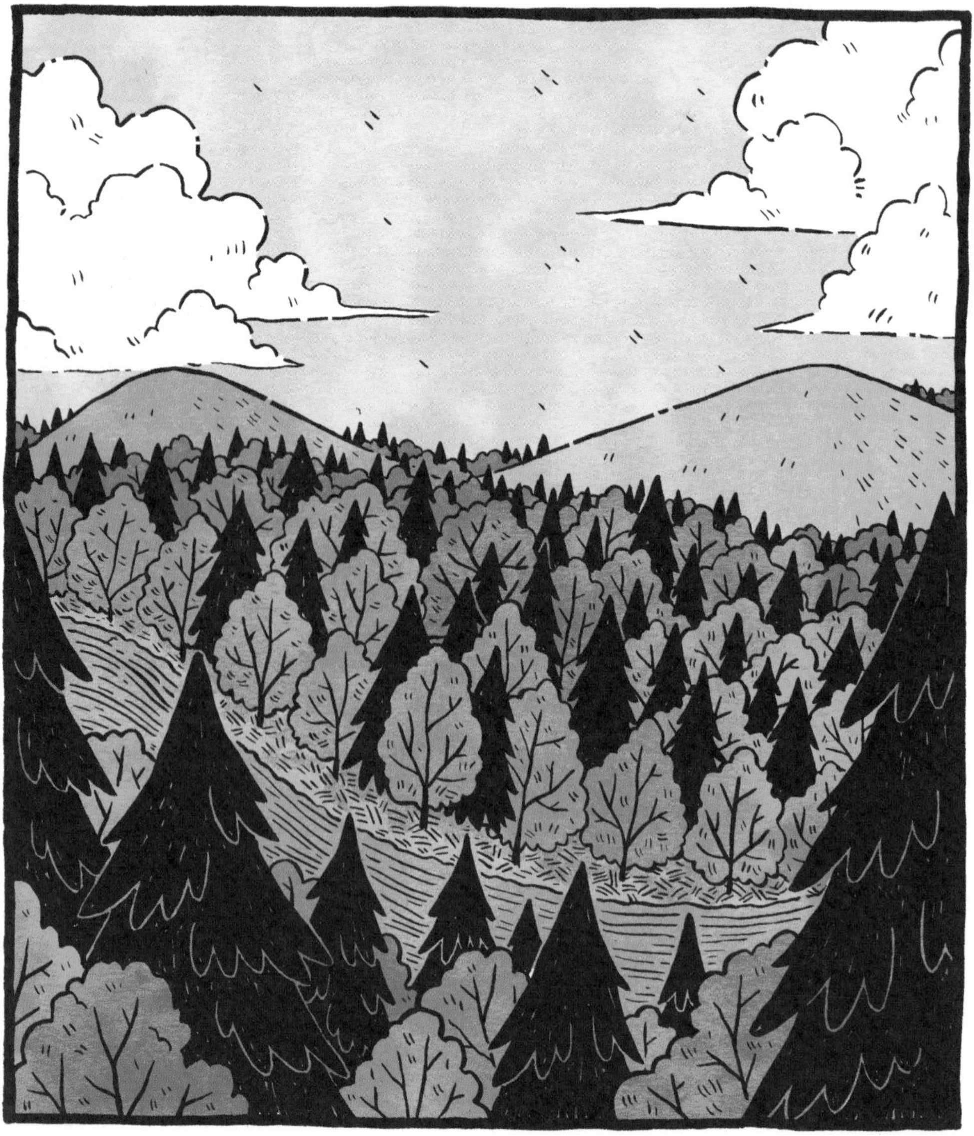

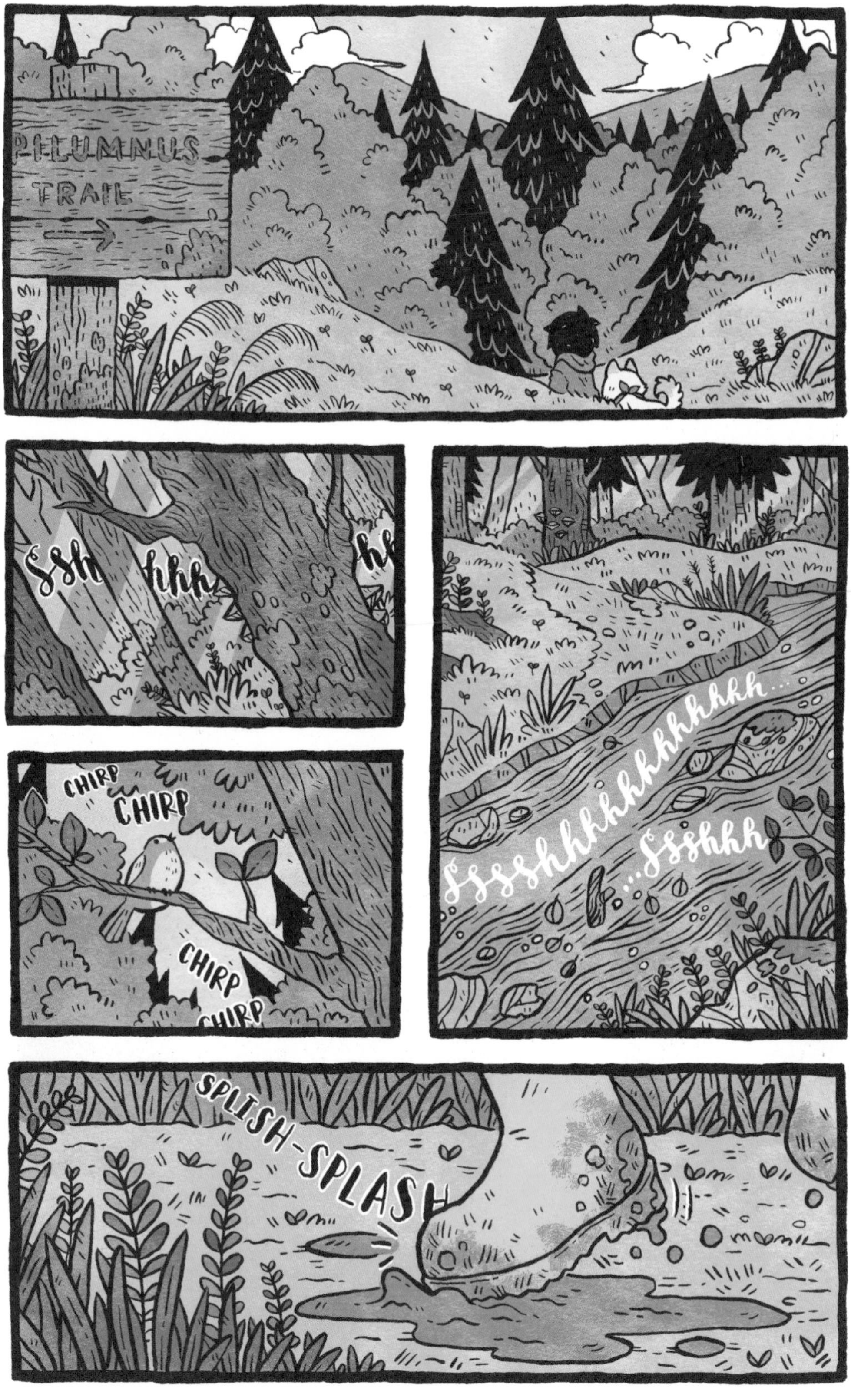
PILUMNUS
TRAIL
SShhhhh
CHIRP
CHIRP
CHIRP
CHIRP
hhhhhhhhhh...
SSShhhhhhhhhhhh
...SSShhh
SPLISH-SPLASH

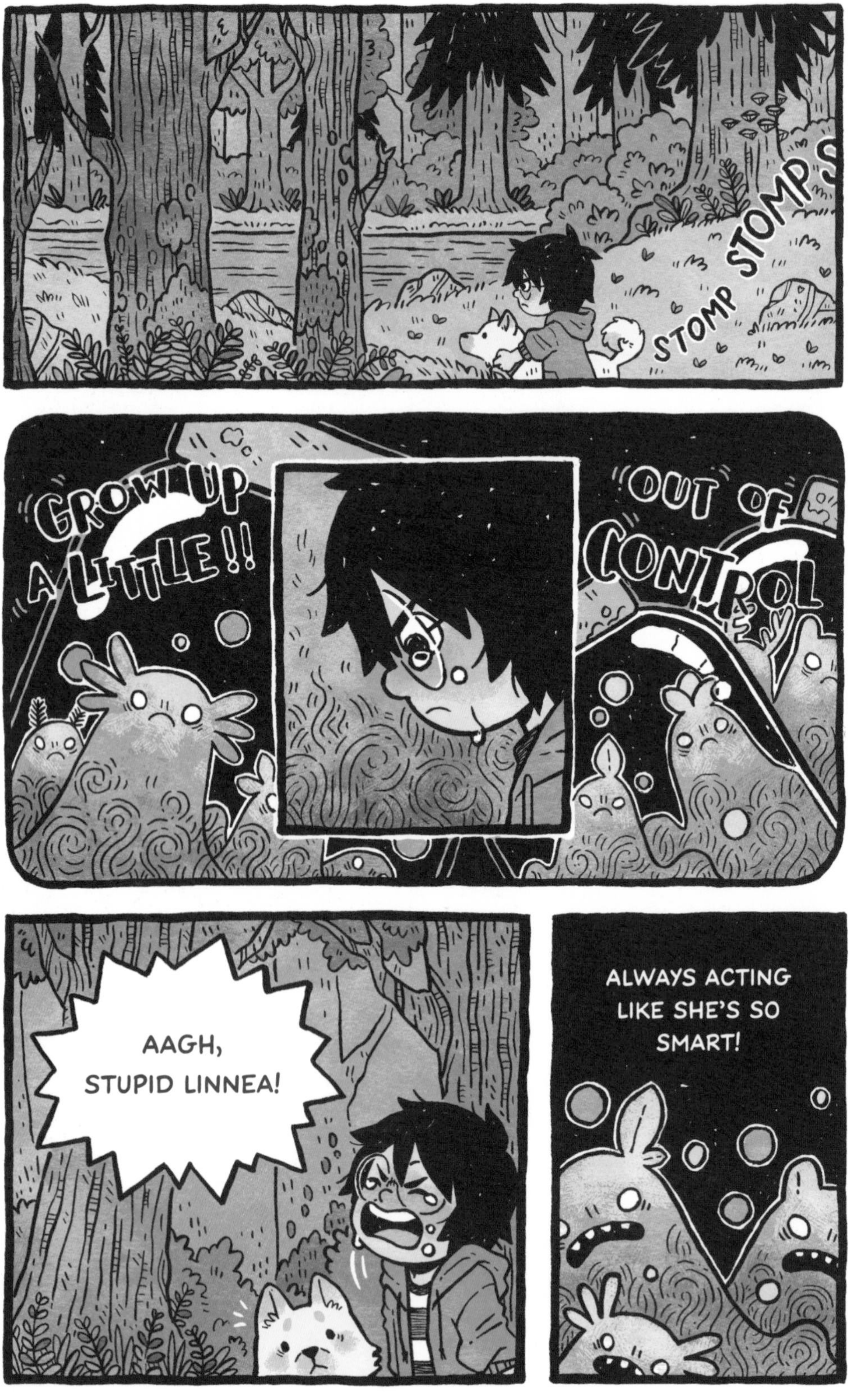
STOMP STOMP S
GROW UP A LITTLE!!
OUT OF CONTROL
AAGH, STUPID LINNEA!
ALWAYS ACTING LIKE SHE'S SO SMART!

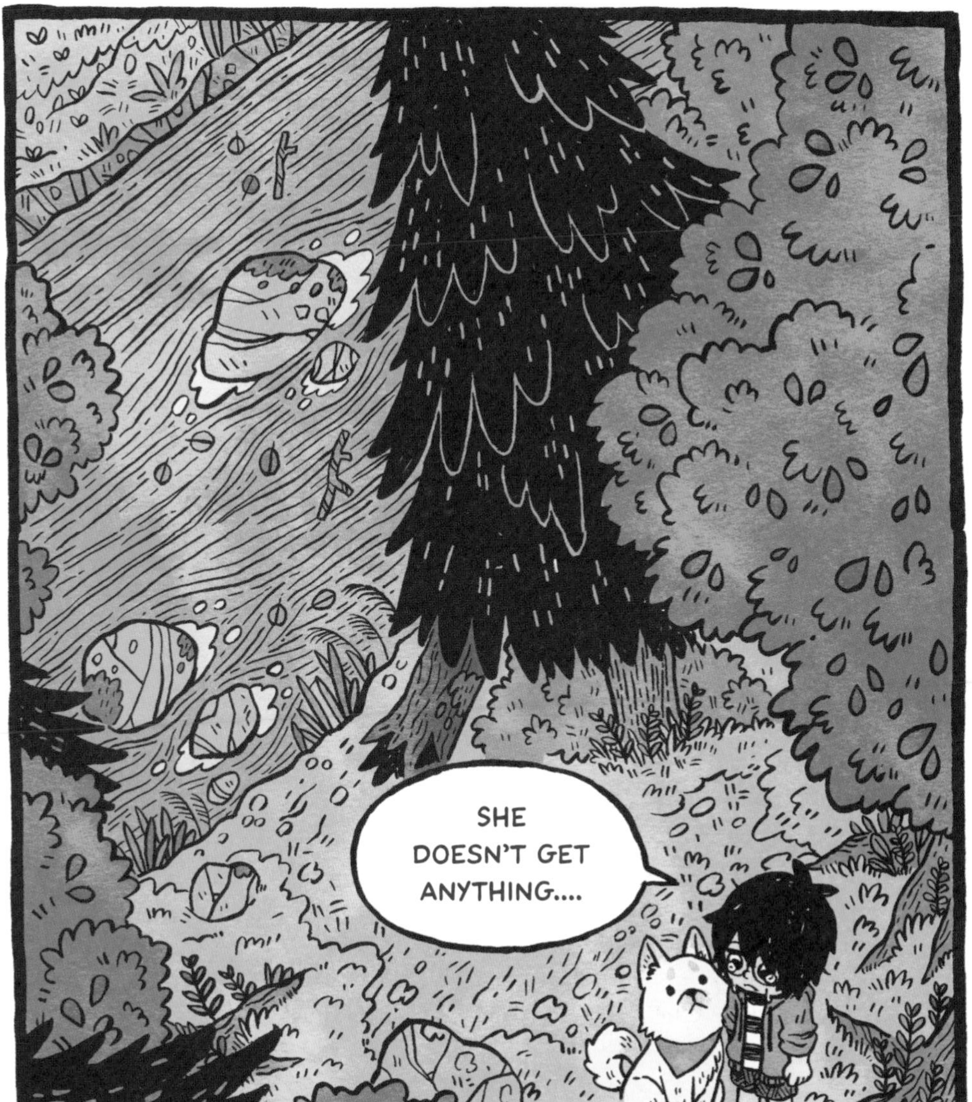
SHE DOESN'T GET ANYTHING....

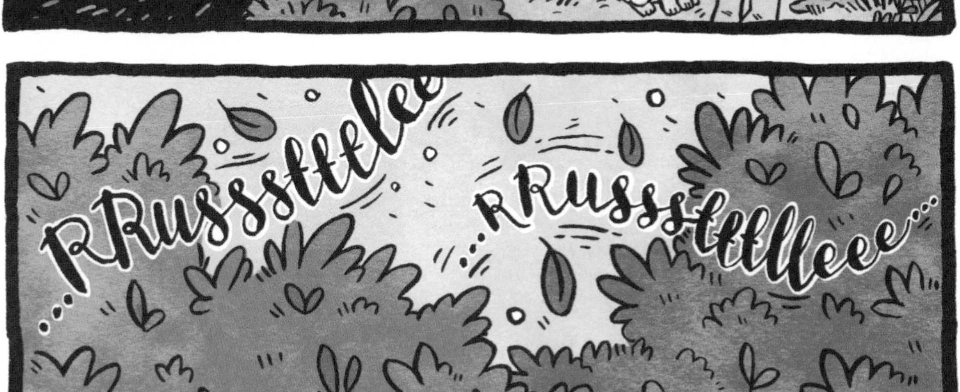
...RRUSSSTTTLEE
...RRUSSSTTTLLEEE...

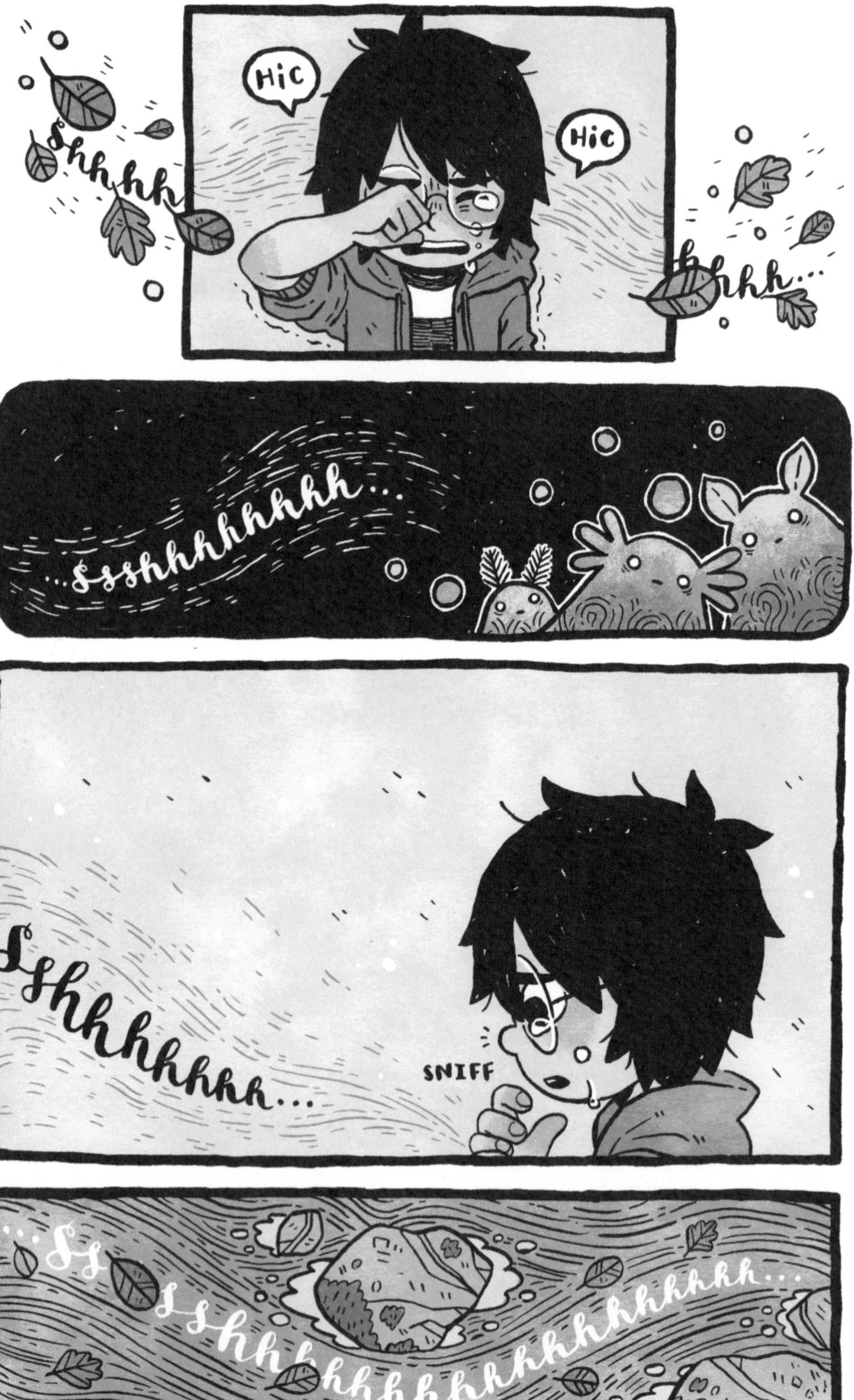
Hic
Hic
Shhhhh
hhhh...
...Ssshhhhhhhh...
Sshhhhhhh...
SNIFF
...SsSshhhhhhhhhhhhhhhhhhh...

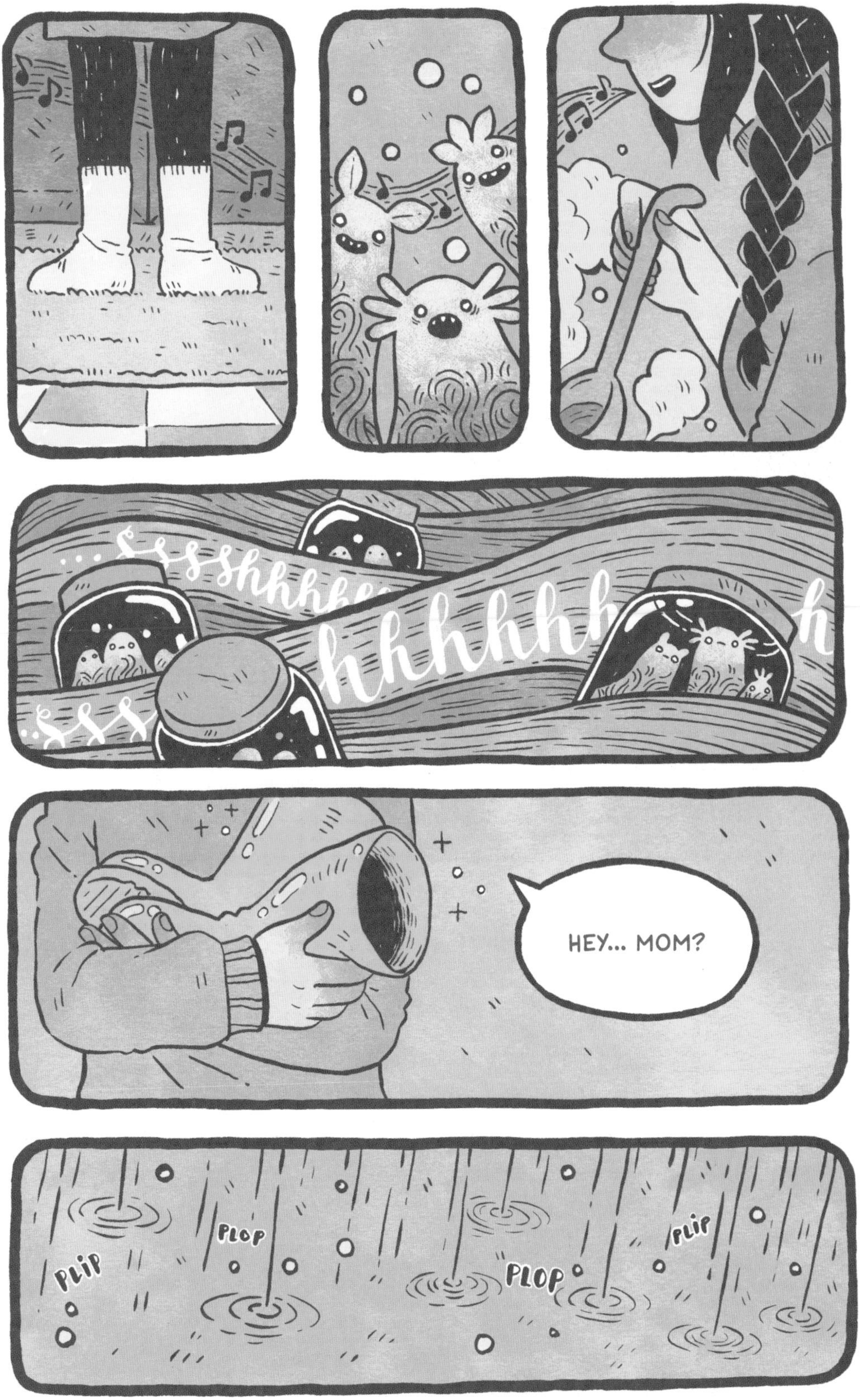
...sssshhhhh
hhhhhhh
sss
HEY... MOM?
PLIP
PLOP
PLOP
PLIP

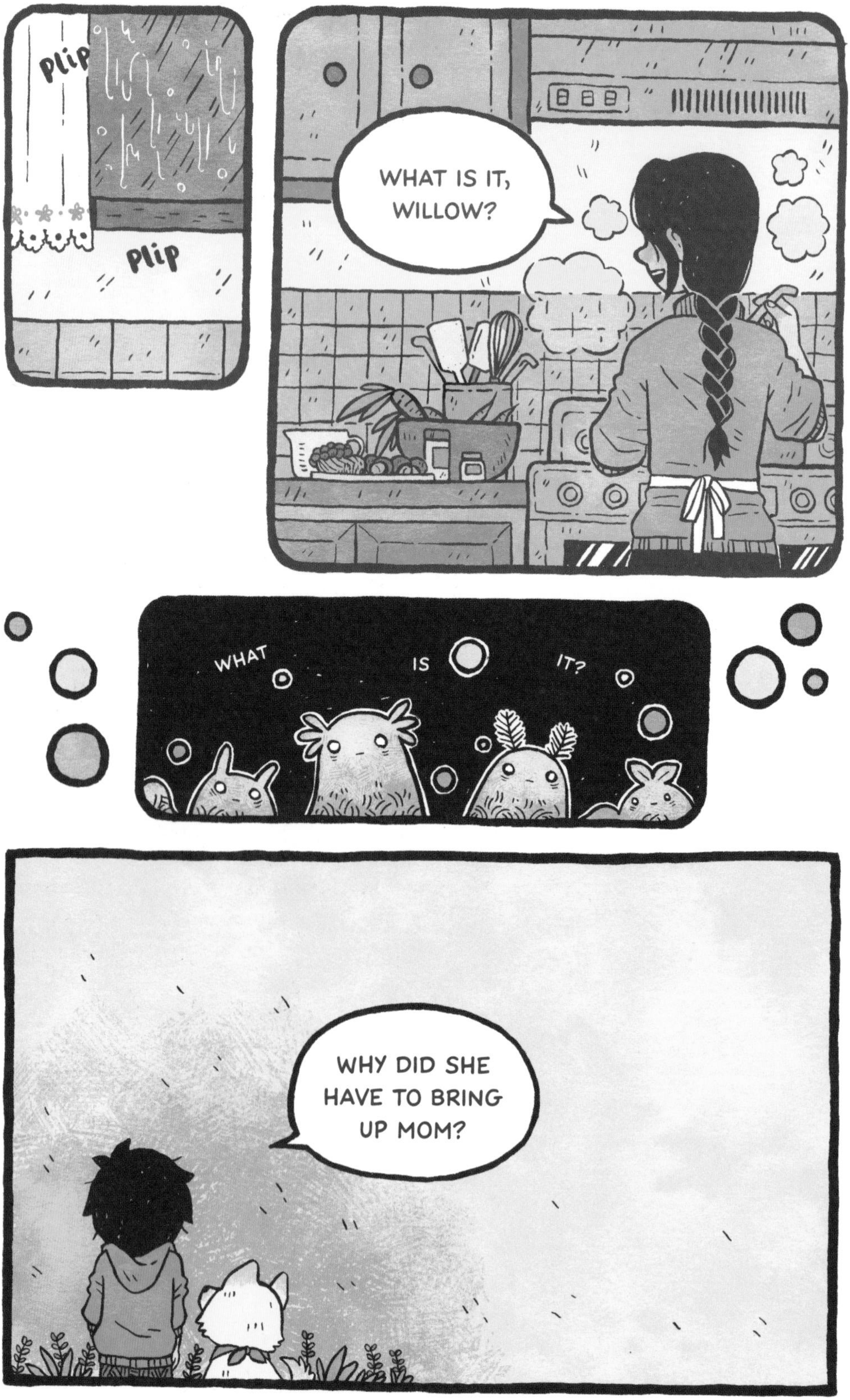
PLIP
PLIP
WHAT IS IT, WILLOW?
WHAT IS IT?
WHY DID SHE HAVE TO BRING UP MOM?

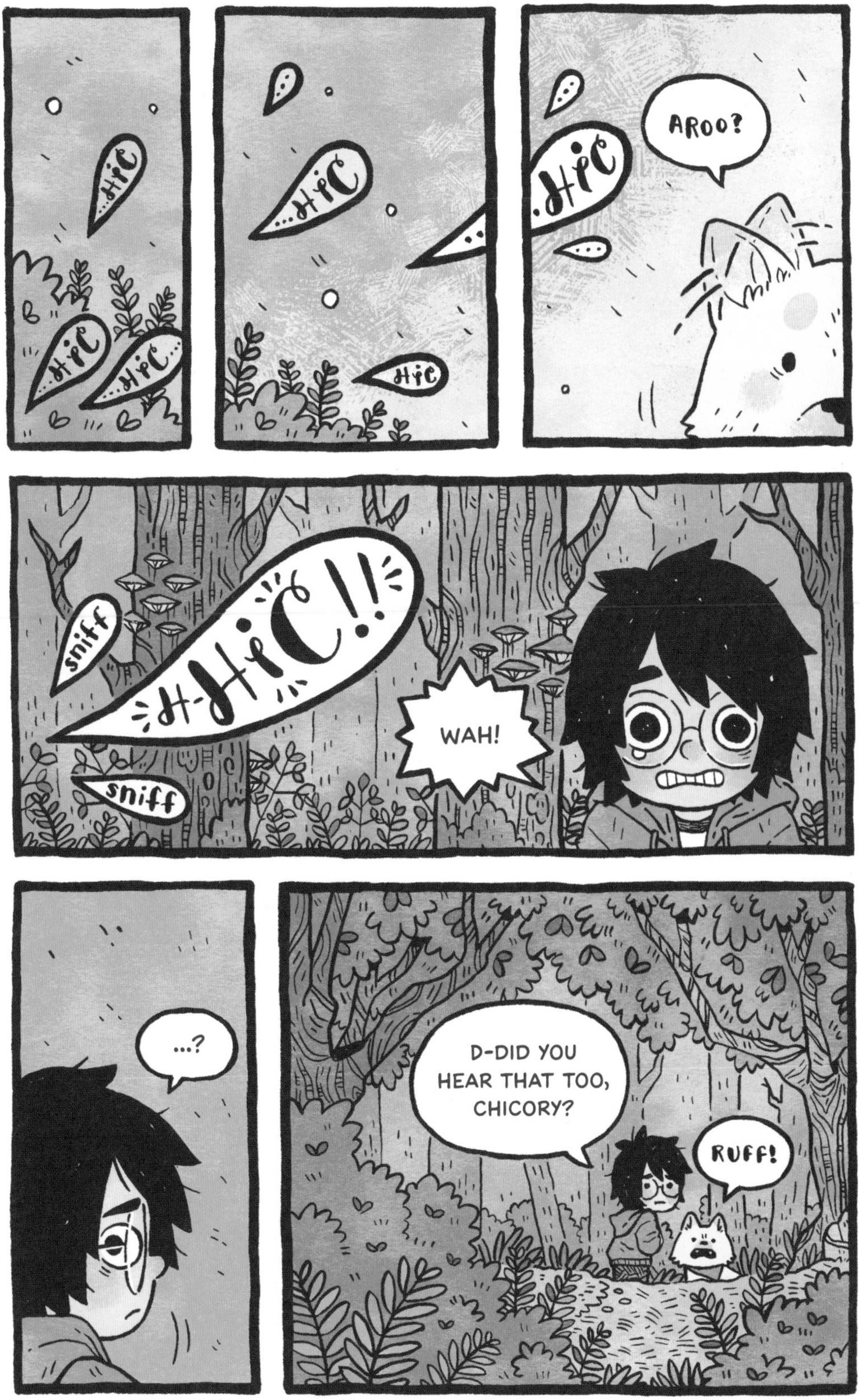

...Hic
Hic
Hic
...Hic
Hic
...Hic
AROO?
sniff
H-Hic!!
sniff
WAH!
...?
D-DID YOU HEAR THAT TOO, CHICORY?
RUFF!

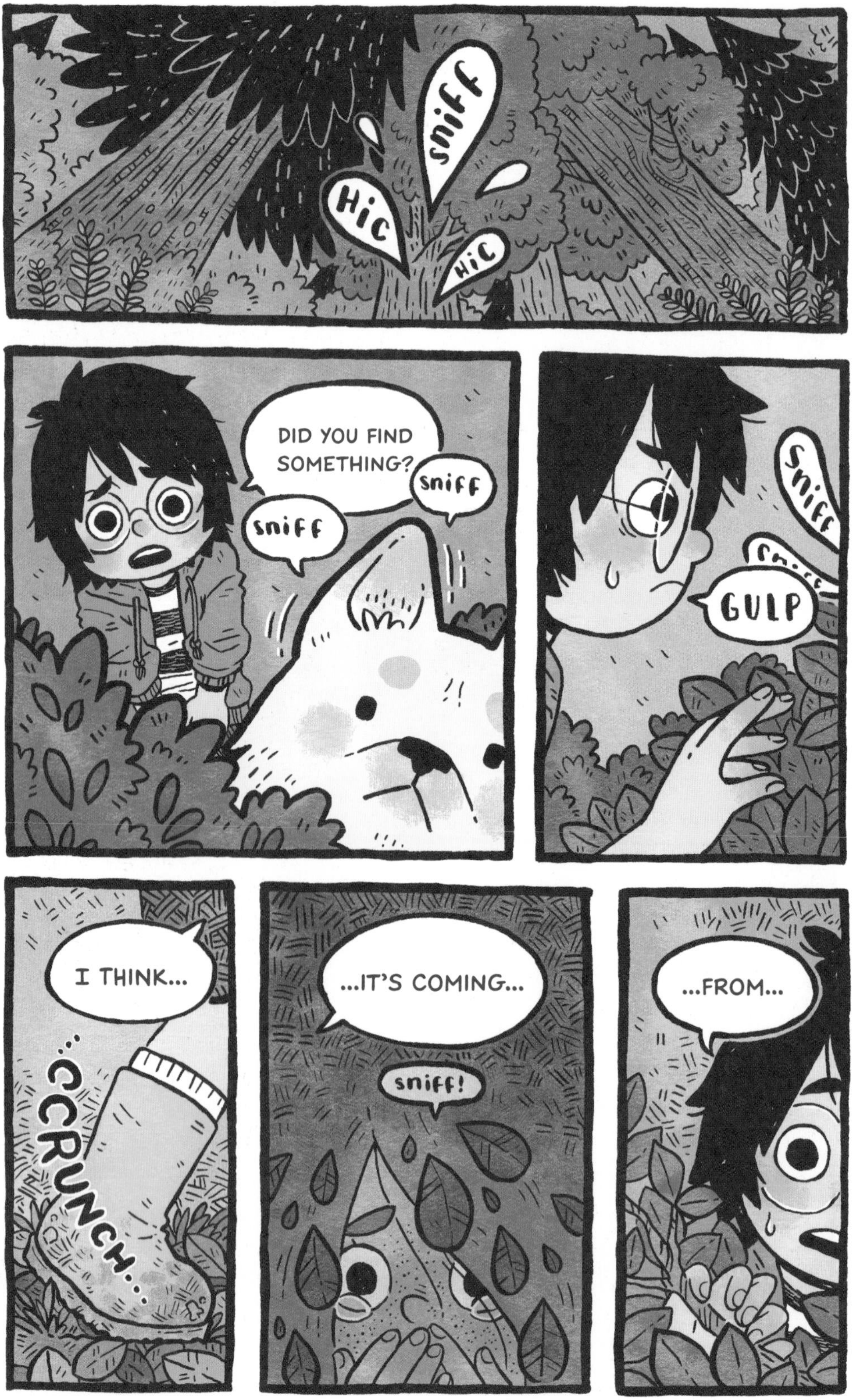
Hic
sniff
Hic
DID YOU FIND SOMETHING?
sniff
sniff
Sniff
GULP
I THINK...
...CCRUNCH...
...IT'S COMING...
sniff!
...FROM...

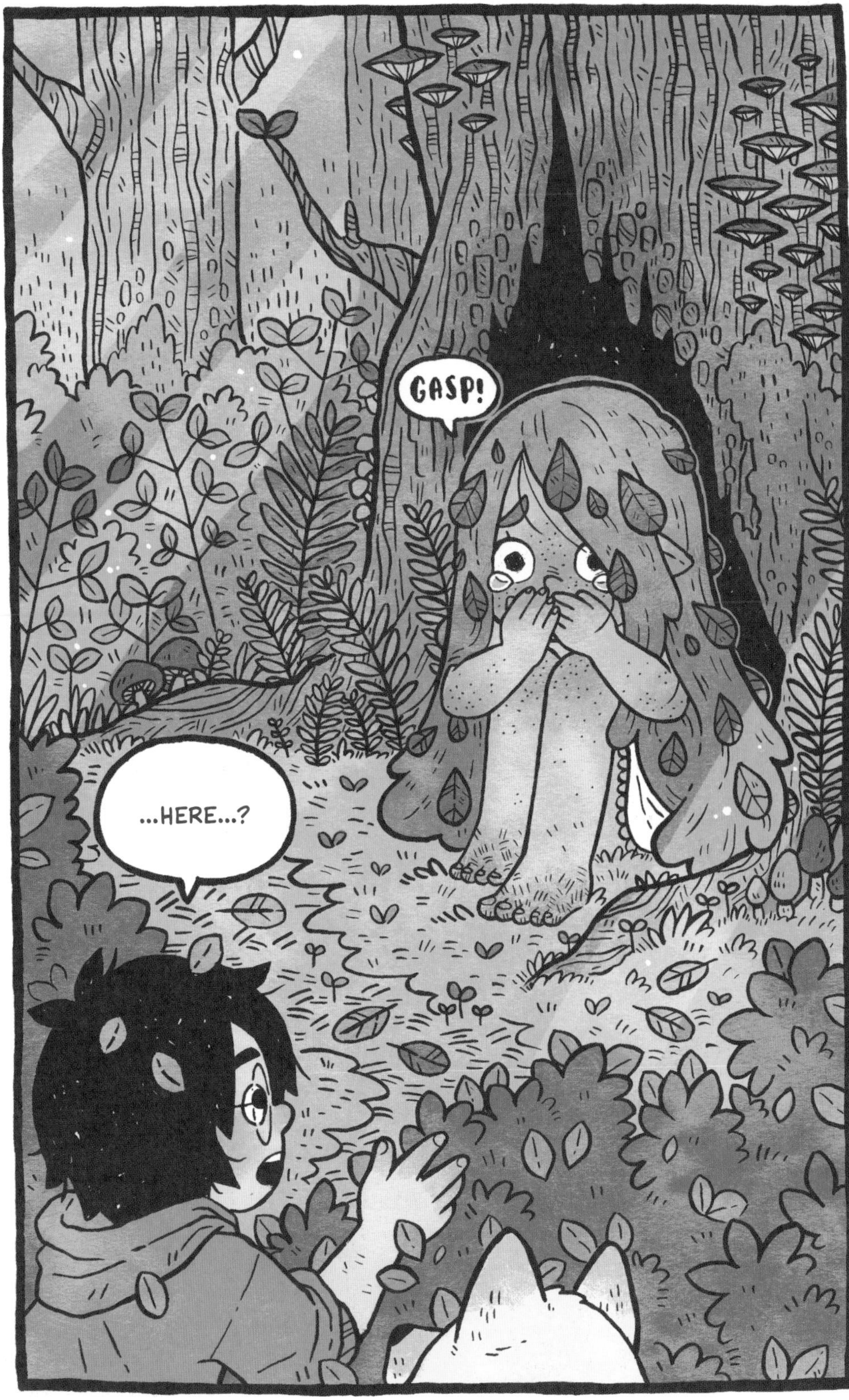
GASP!
...HERE...?

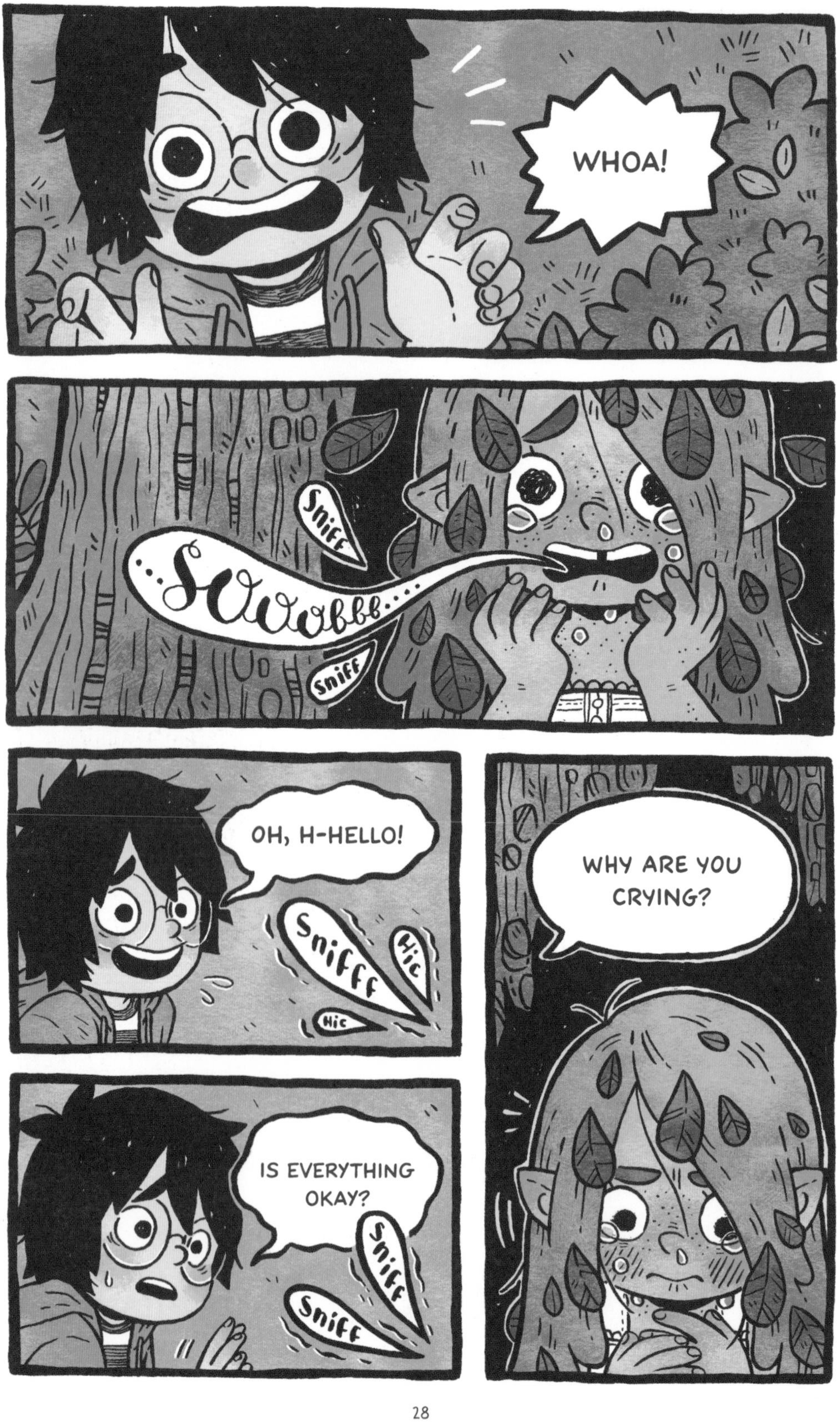
WHOA!
Sniff
...SOBBB...
sniff
OH, H-HELLO!
Snifff
Hic
Hic
WHY ARE YOU CRYING?
IS EVERYTHING OKAY?
Sniff
Sniff

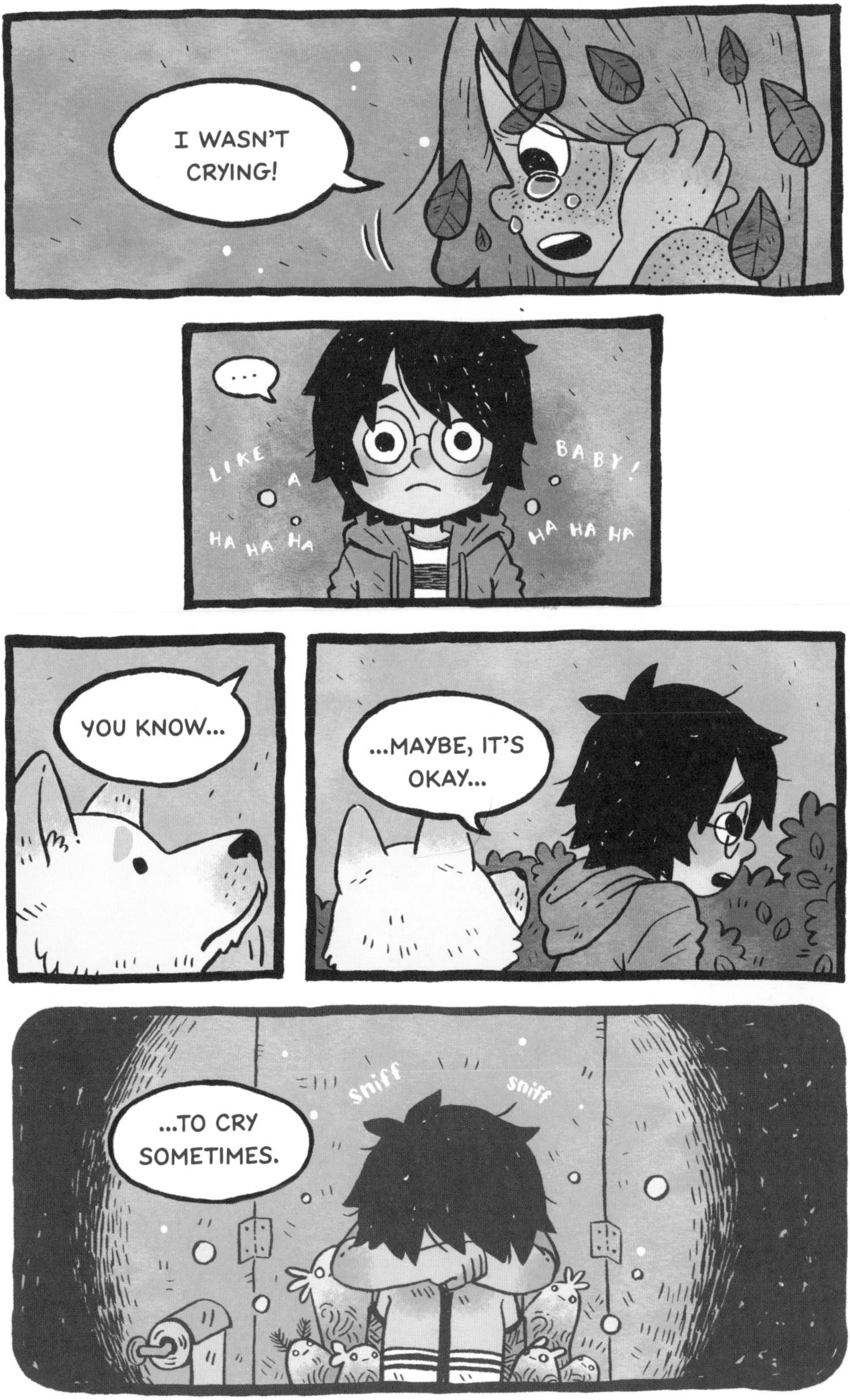
I WASN'T CRYING!
...
LIKE A BABY!
HA HA HA
HA HA HA
YOU KNOW...
...MAYBE, IT'S OKAY...
...TO CRY SOMETIMES.
sniff
sniff

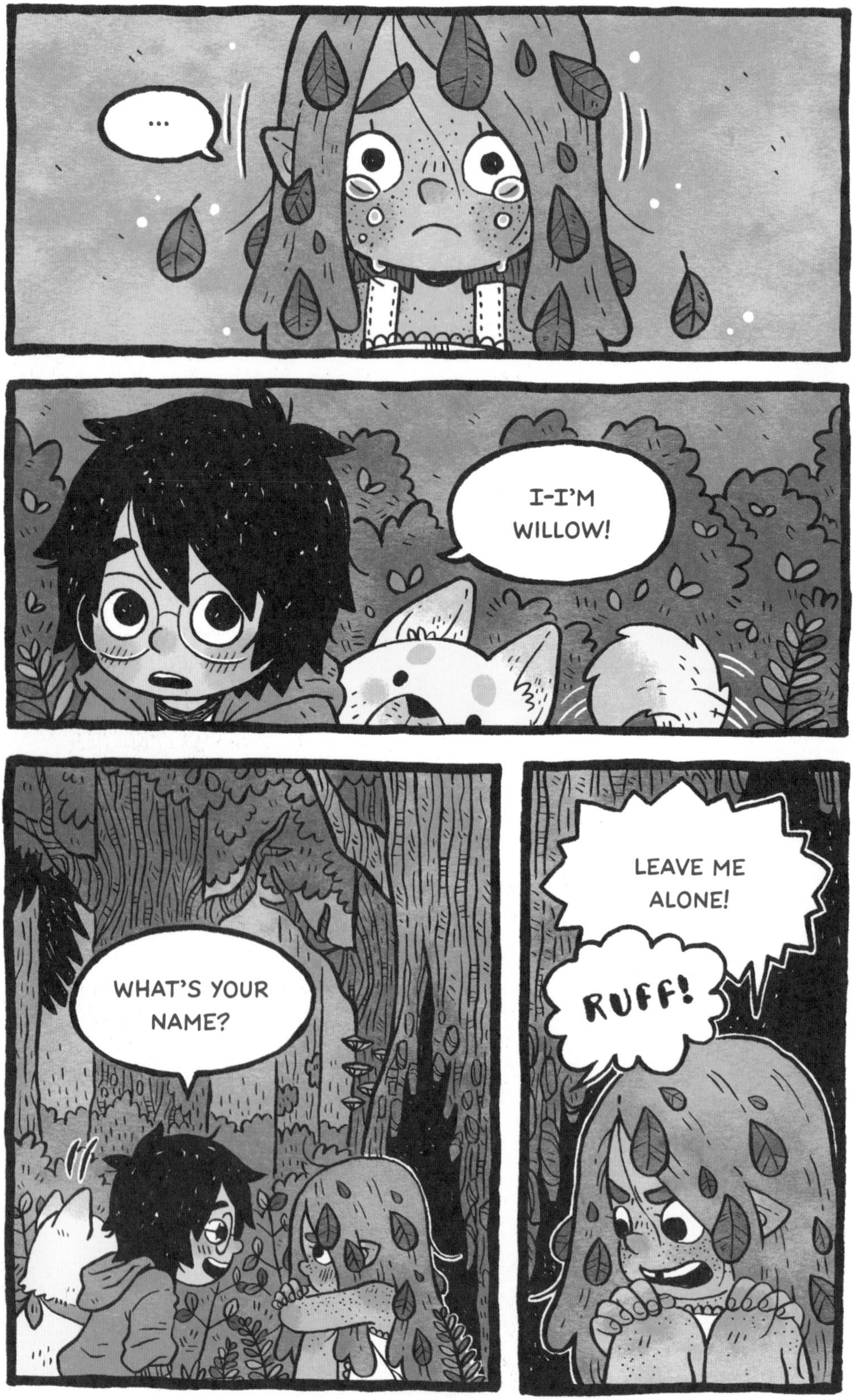
...
I-I'M WILLOW!
WHAT'S YOUR NAME?
LEAVE ME ALONE!
RUFF!

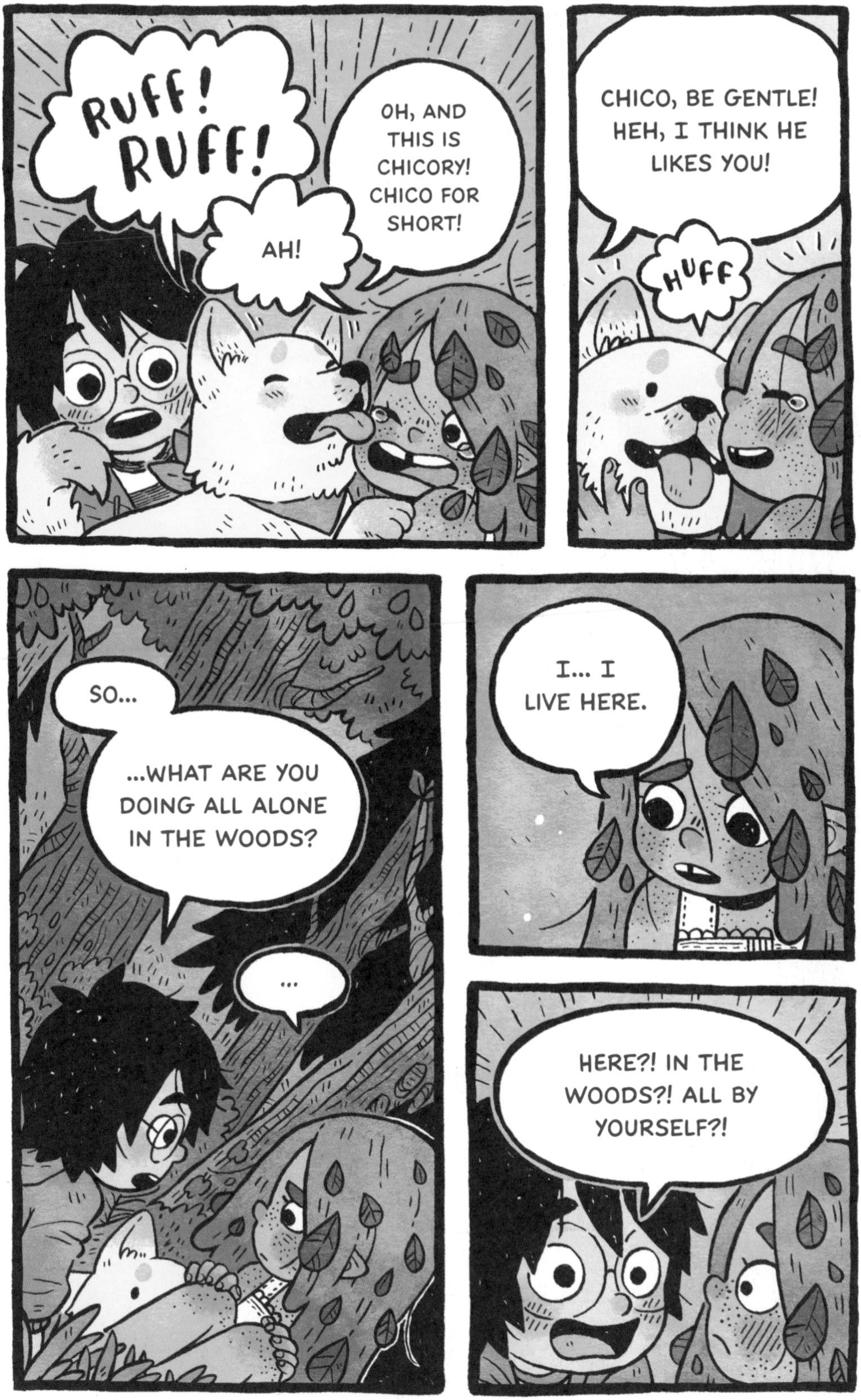
RUFF! RUFF!
AH!
OH, AND THIS IS CHICORY! CHICO FOR SHORT!
CHICO, BE GENTLE! HEH, I THINK HE LIKES YOU!
HUFF
SO...
...WHAT ARE YOU DOING ALL ALONE IN THE WOODS?
...
I... I LIVE HERE.
HERE?! IN THE WOODS?! ALL BY YOURSELF?!

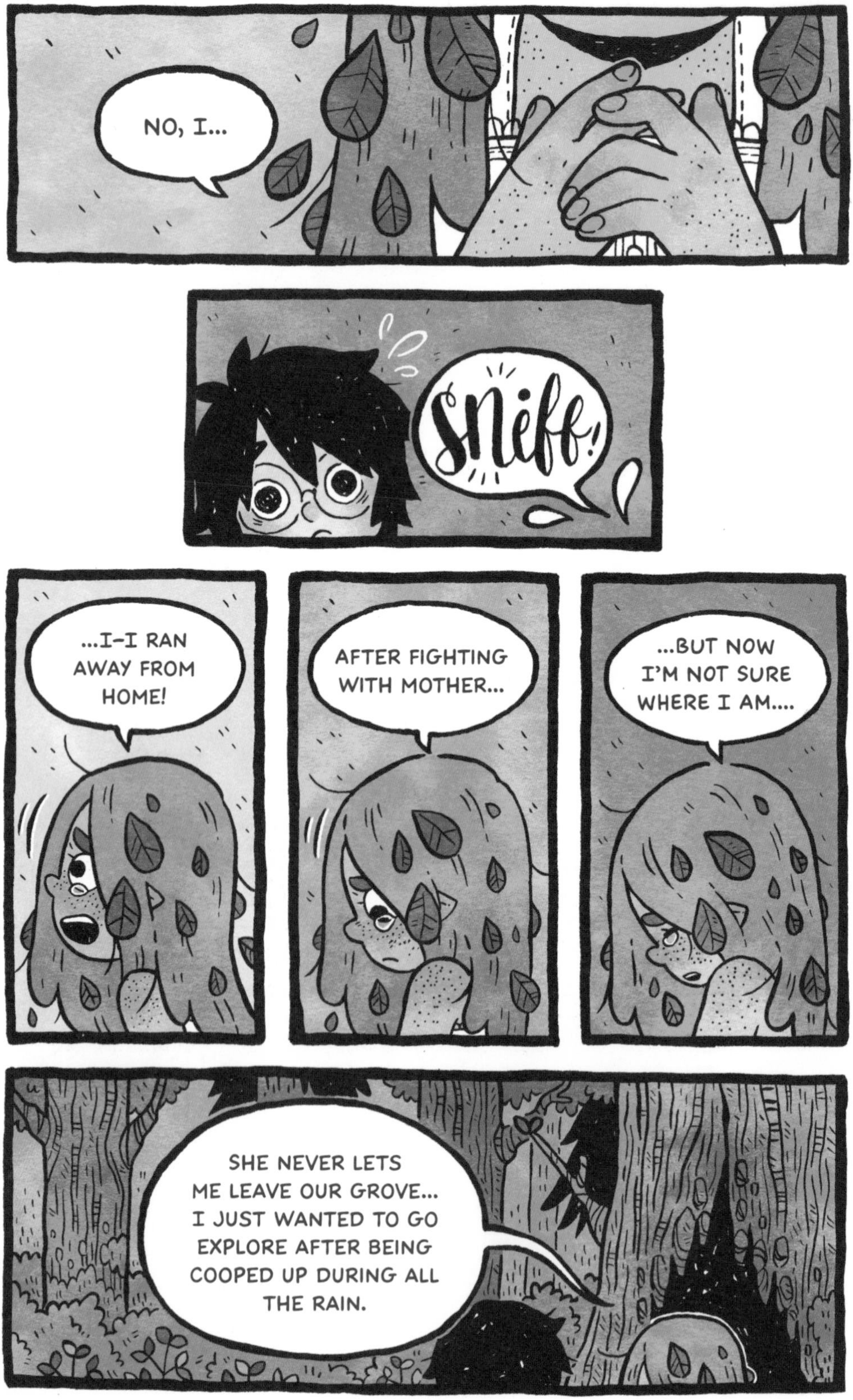
NO, I...
SNIFF!
...I-I RAN AWAY FROM HOME!
AFTER FIGHTING WITH MOTHER...
...BUT NOW I'M NOT SURE WHERE I AM....
SHE NEVER LETS ME LEAVE OUR GROVE... I JUST WANTED TO GO EXPLORE AFTER BEING COOPED UP DURING ALL THE RAIN.

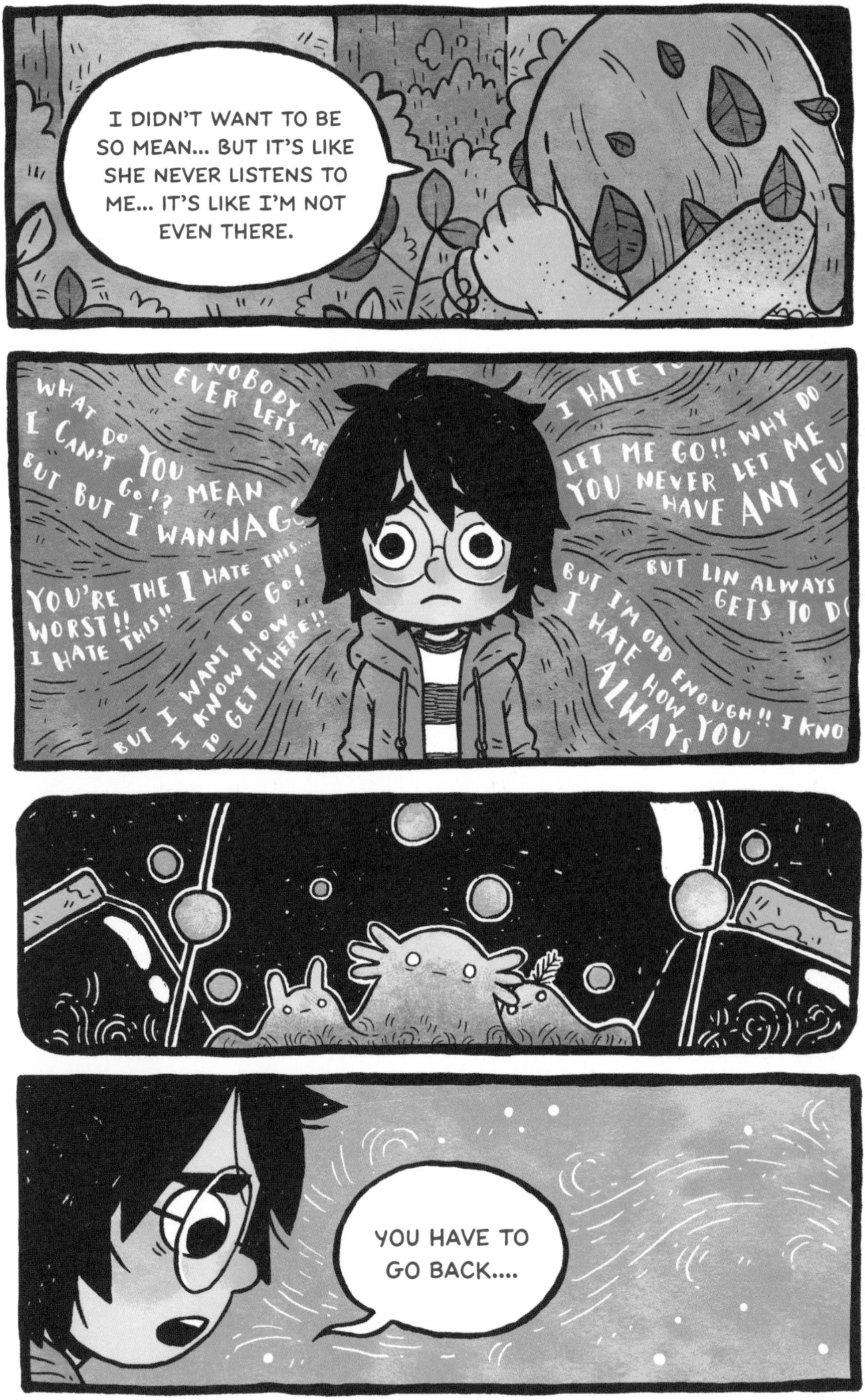
I DIDN'T WANT TO BE SO MEAN... BUT IT'S LIKE SHE NEVER LISTENS TO ME... IT'S LIKE I'M NOT EVEN THERE.
WHAT DO YOU MEAN
NOBODY EVER LETS ME
I CAN'T GO!?
BUT BUT I WANNA GO
YOU'RE THE WORST!!
I HATE THIS!!
I HATE THIS...
BUT I WANT TO GO!
I KNOW HOW TO GET THERE!!
I HATE YOU
LET ME GO!! WHY DO YOU NEVER LET ME HAVE ANY FU
BUT LIN ALWAYS GETS TO DO
BUT I'M OLD ENOUGH!! I KNO
I HATE HOW ALWAYS YOU
YOU HAVE TO GO BACK....

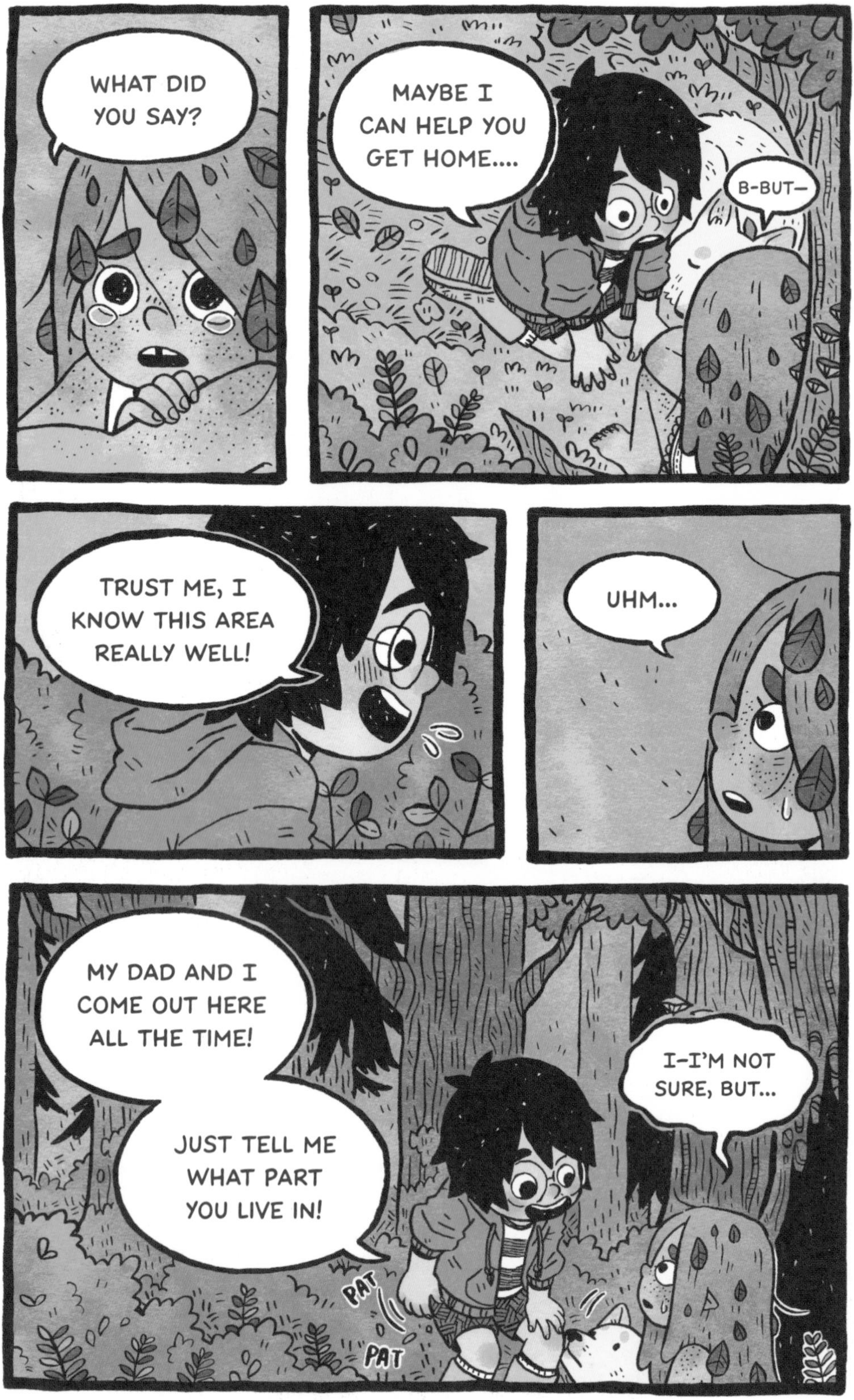
WHAT DID YOU SAY?
MAYBE I CAN HELP YOU GET HOME....
B-BUT—
TRUST ME, I KNOW THIS AREA REALLY WELL!
UHM...
MY DAD AND I COME OUT HERE ALL THE TIME!
JUST TELL ME WHAT PART YOU LIVE IN!
I-I'M NOT SURE, BUT...
PAT
PAT

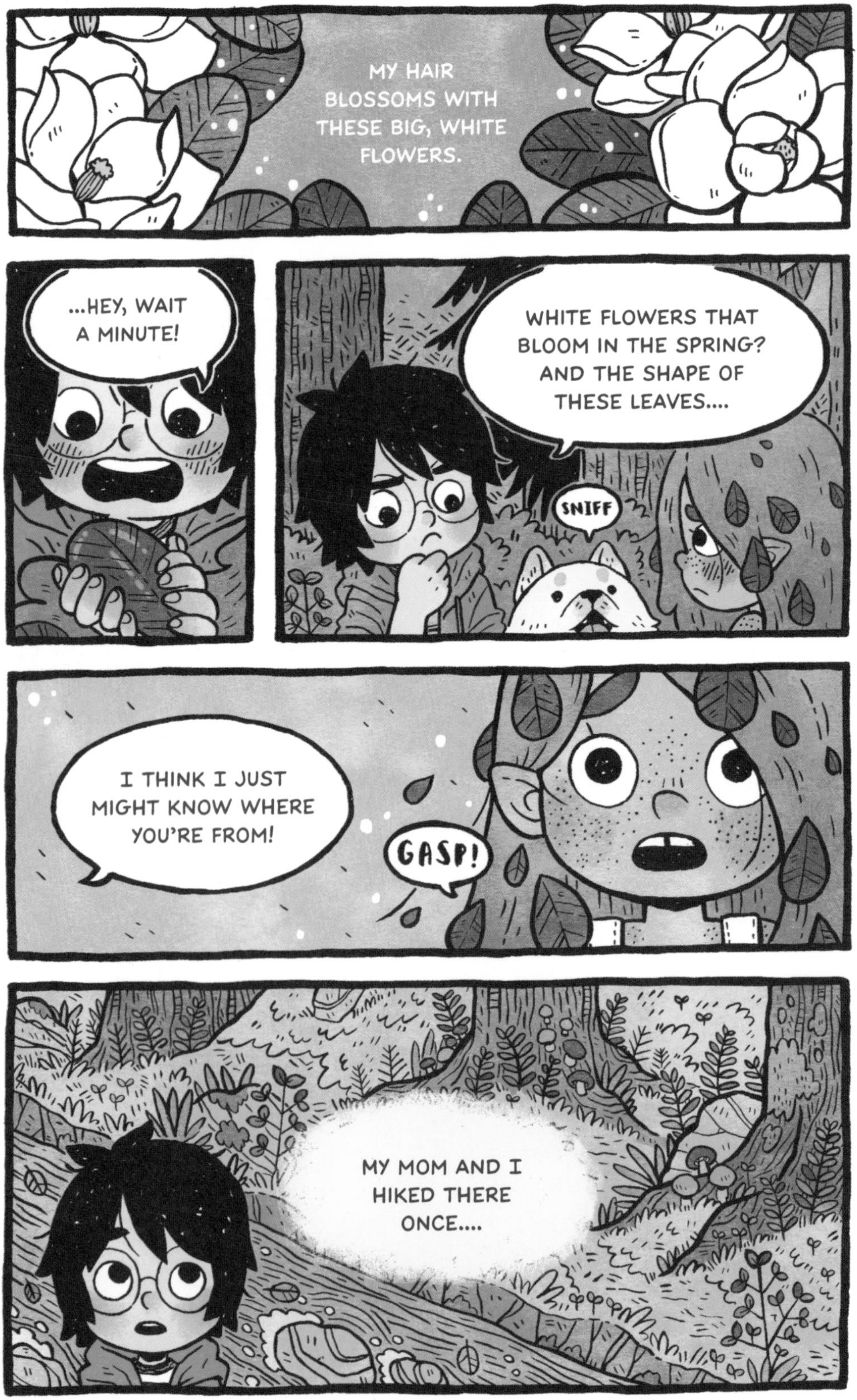
MY HAIR BLOSSOMS WITH THESE BIG, WHITE FLOWERS.
...HEY, WAIT A MINUTE!
WHITE FLOWERS THAT BLOOM IN THE SPRING? AND THE SHAPE OF THESE LEAVES....
SNIFF
I THINK I JUST MIGHT KNOW WHERE YOU'RE FROM!
GASP!
MY MOM AND I HIKED THERE ONCE....

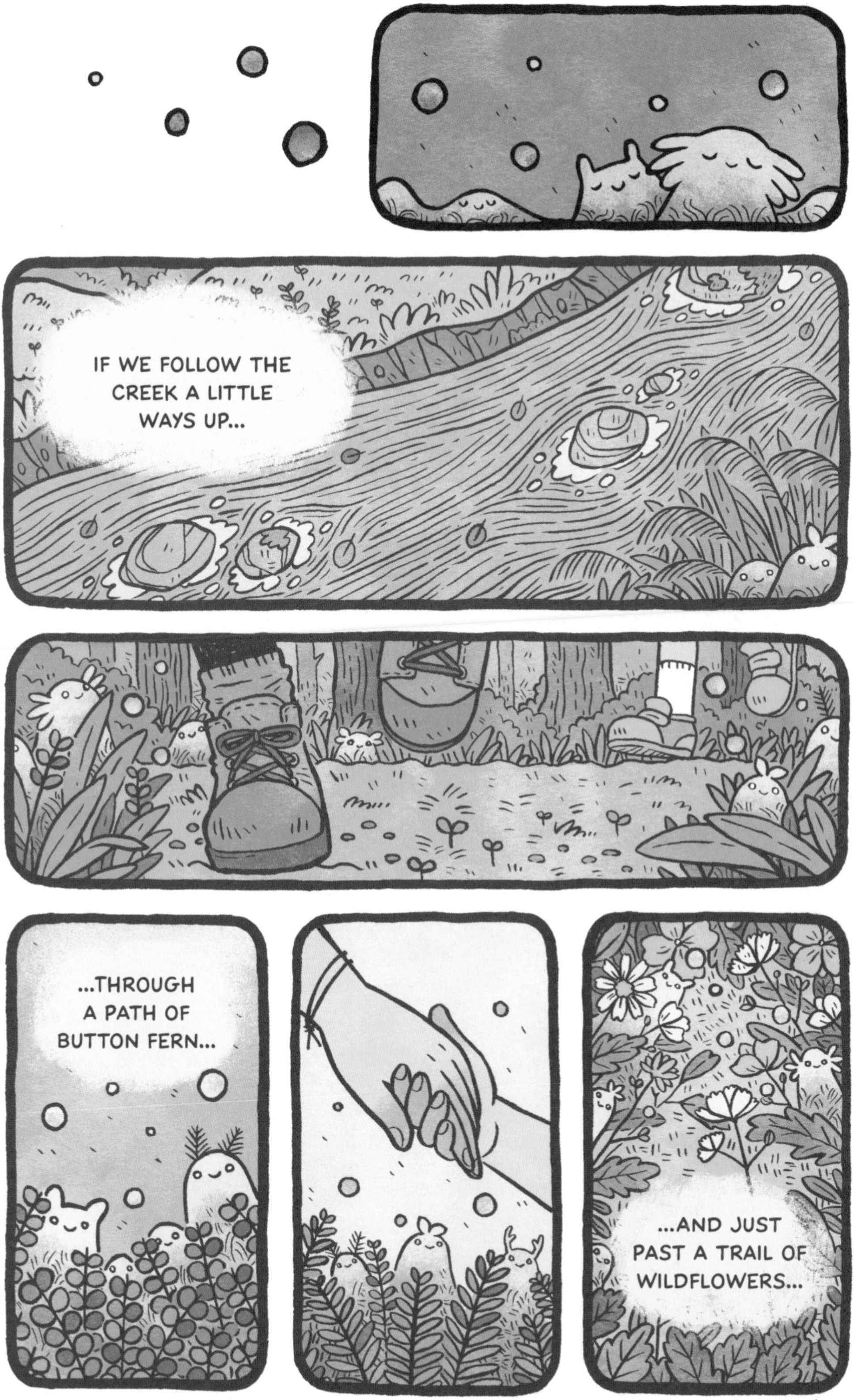
IF WE FOLLOW THE CREEK A LITTLE WAYS UP...
...THROUGH A PATH OF BUTTON FERN...
...AND JUST PAST A TRAIL OF WILDFLOWERS...

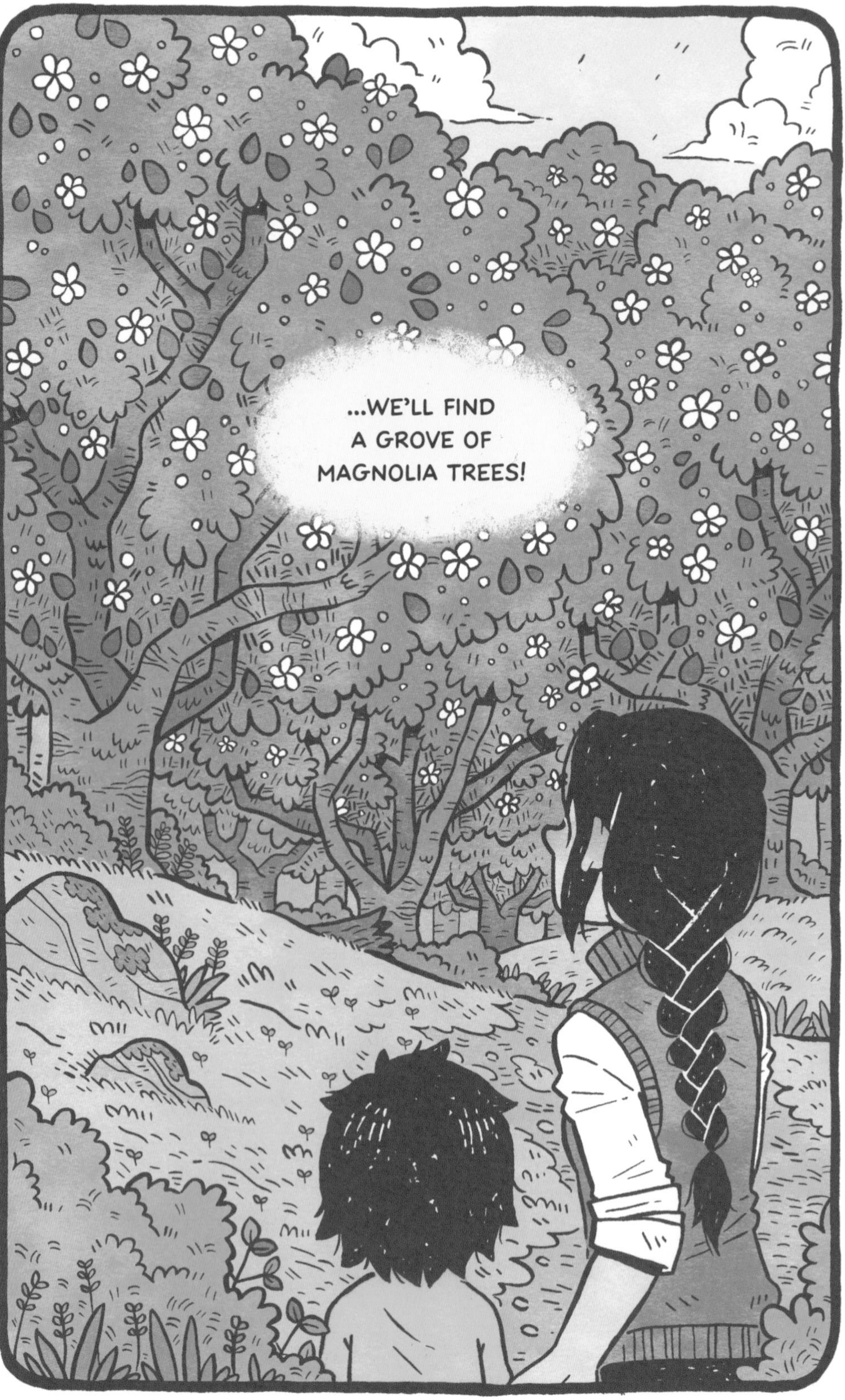
...WE'LL FIND A GROVE OF MAGNOLIA TREES!

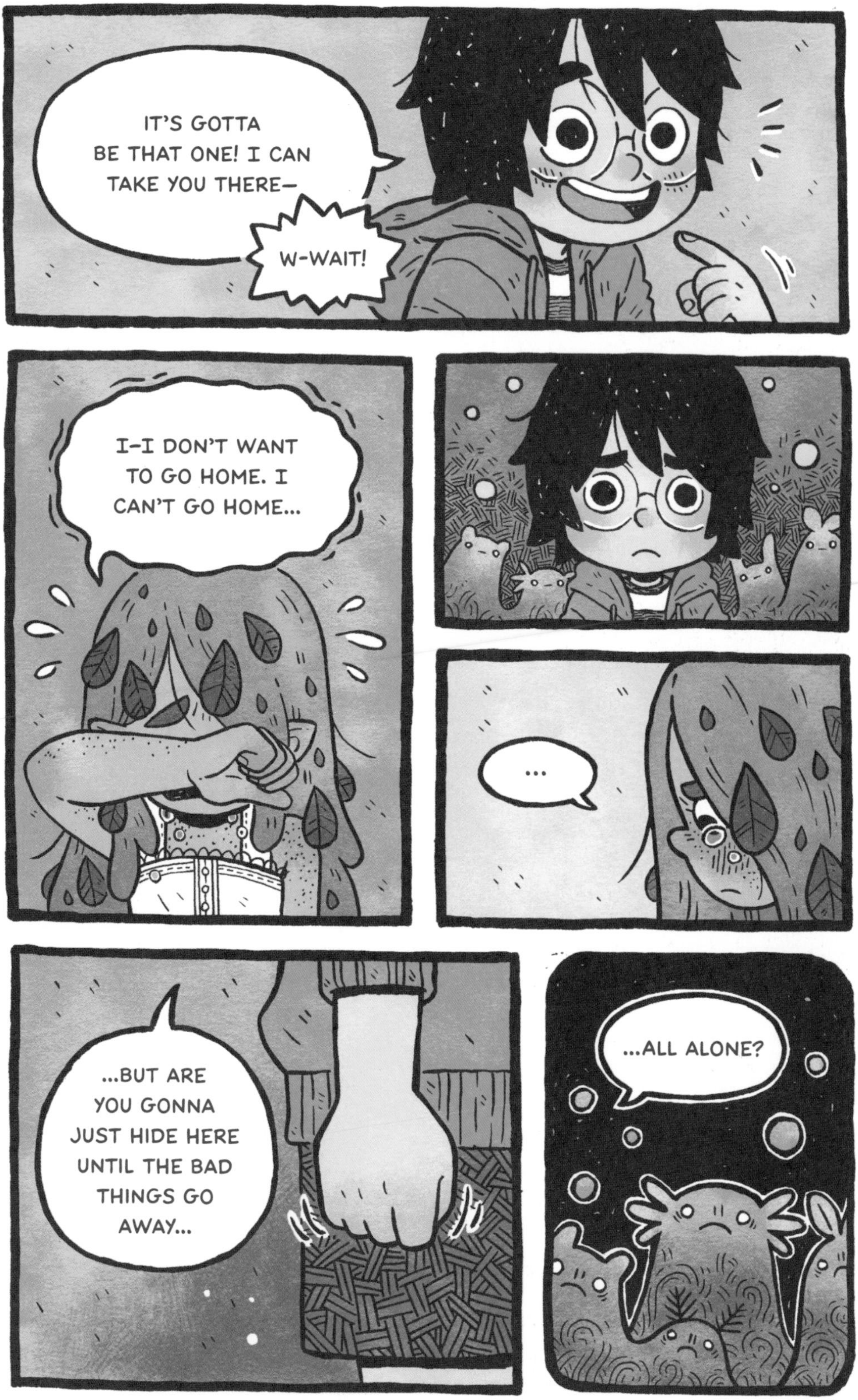
IT'S GOTTA BE THAT ONE! I CAN TAKE YOU THERE—
W-WAIT!
I-I DON'T WANT TO GO HOME. I CAN'T GO HOME...
...
...BUT ARE YOU GONNA JUST HIDE HERE UNTIL THE BAD THINGS GO AWAY...
...ALL ALONE?

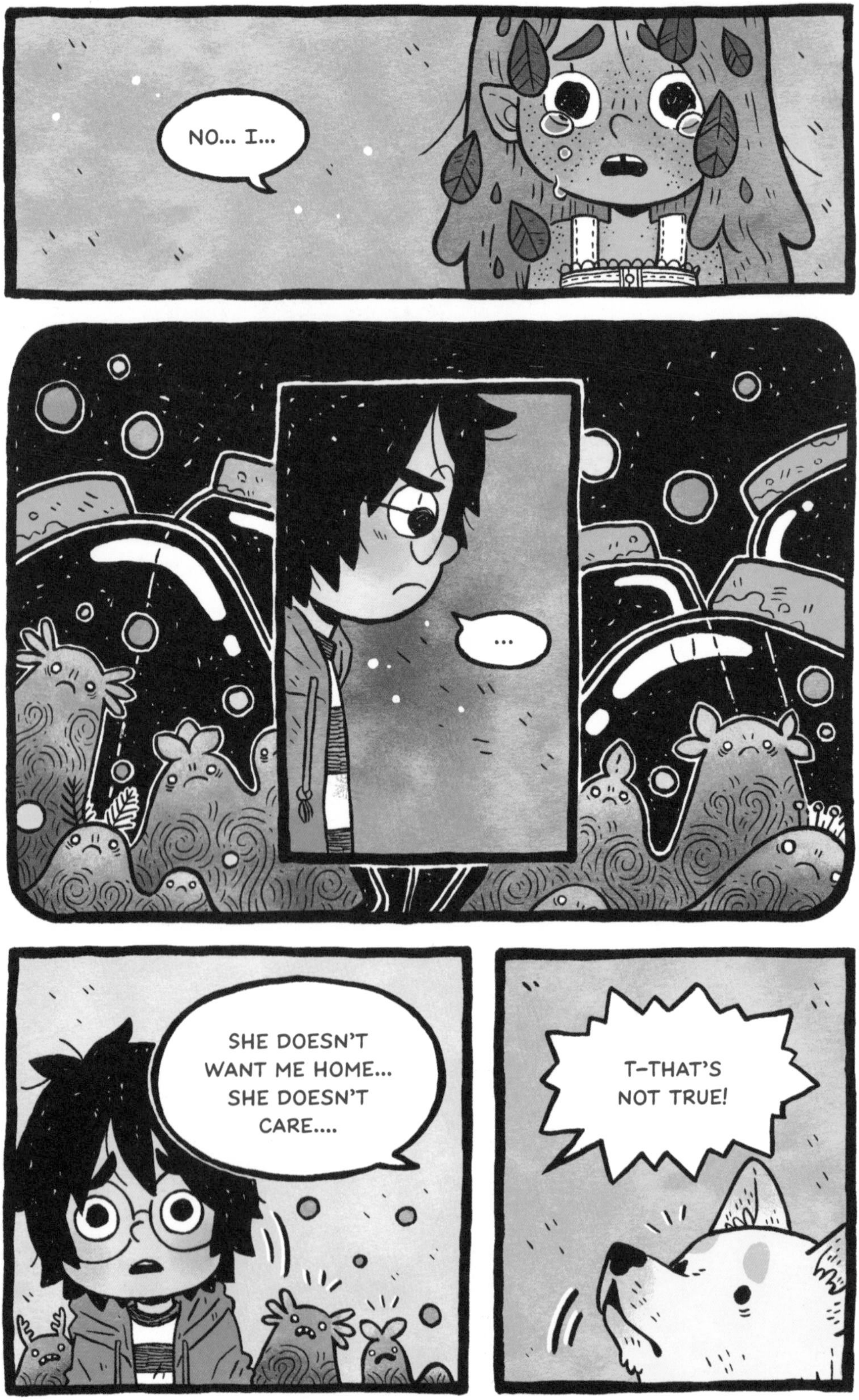
NO... I...
...
SHE DOESN'T WANT ME HOME... SHE DOESN'T CARE....
T-THAT'S NOT TRUE!

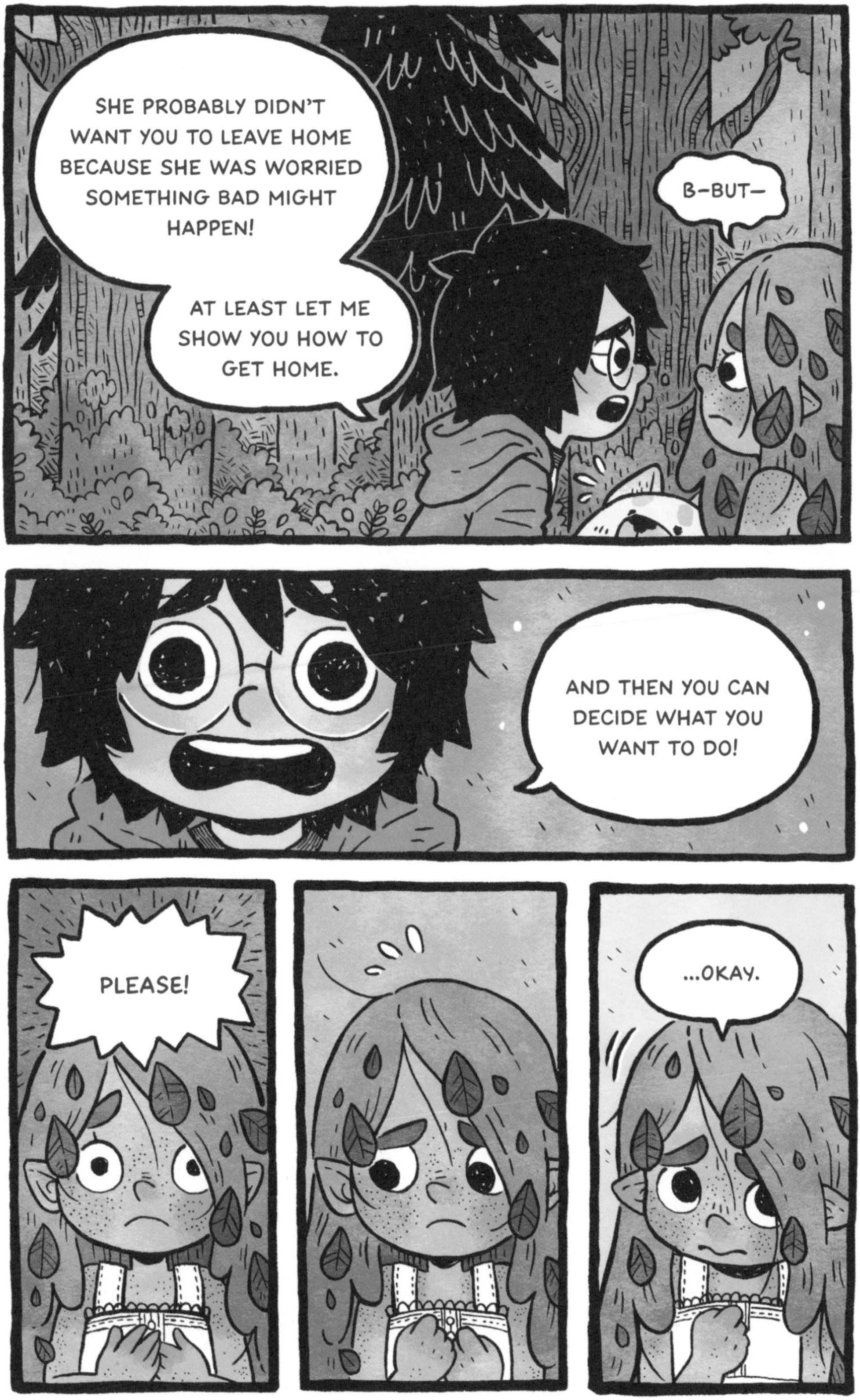
SHE PROBABLY DIDN'T WANT YOU TO LEAVE HOME BECAUSE SHE WAS WORRIED SOMETHING BAD MIGHT HAPPEN!
AT LEAST LET ME SHOW YOU HOW TO GET HOME.
B-BUT—
AND THEN YOU CAN DECIDE WHAT YOU WANT TO DO!
PLEASE!
...OKAY.

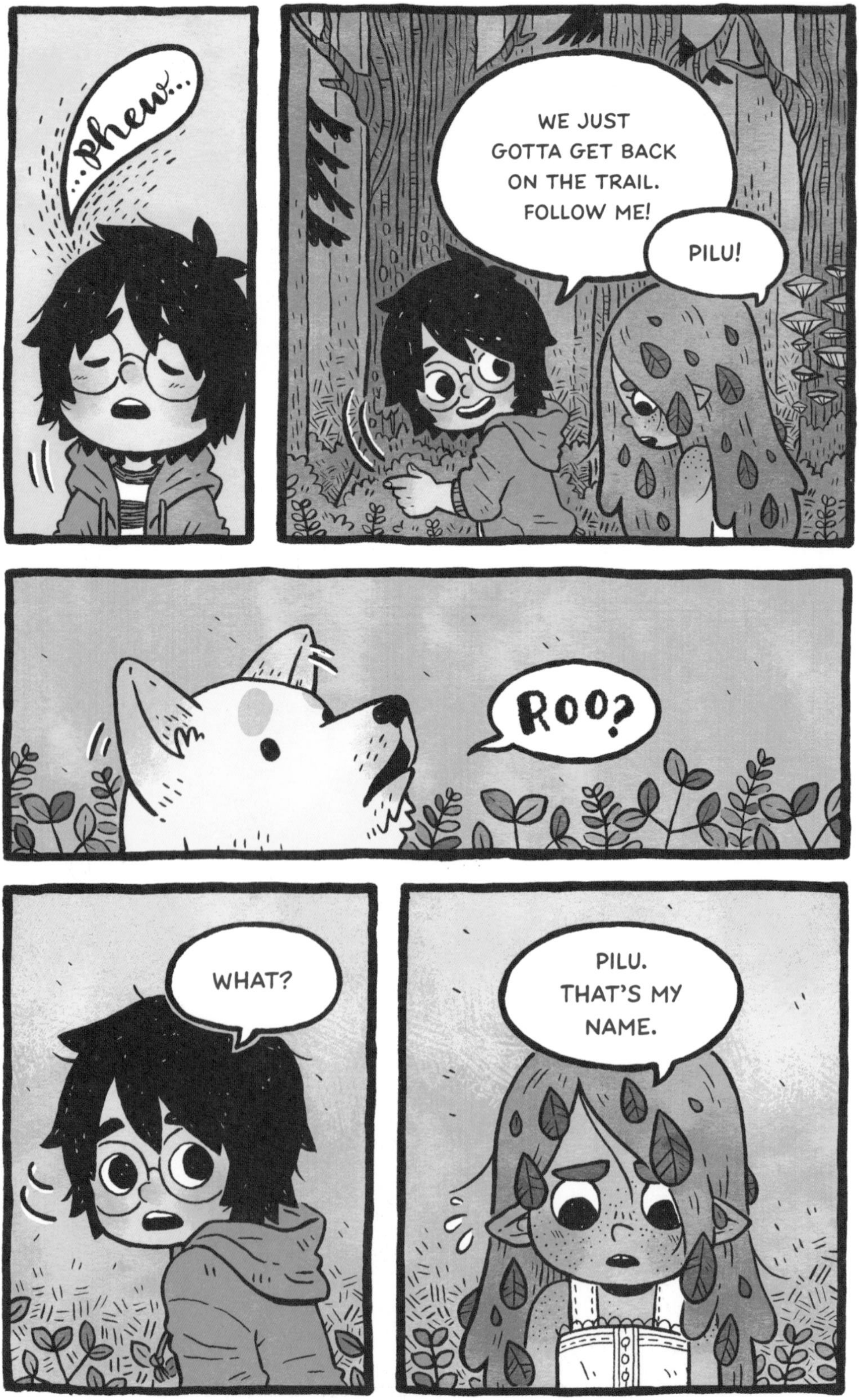
...phew...
WE JUST GOTTA GET BACK ON THE TRAIL. FOLLOW ME!
PILU!
ROO?
WHAT?
PILU. THAT'S MY NAME.

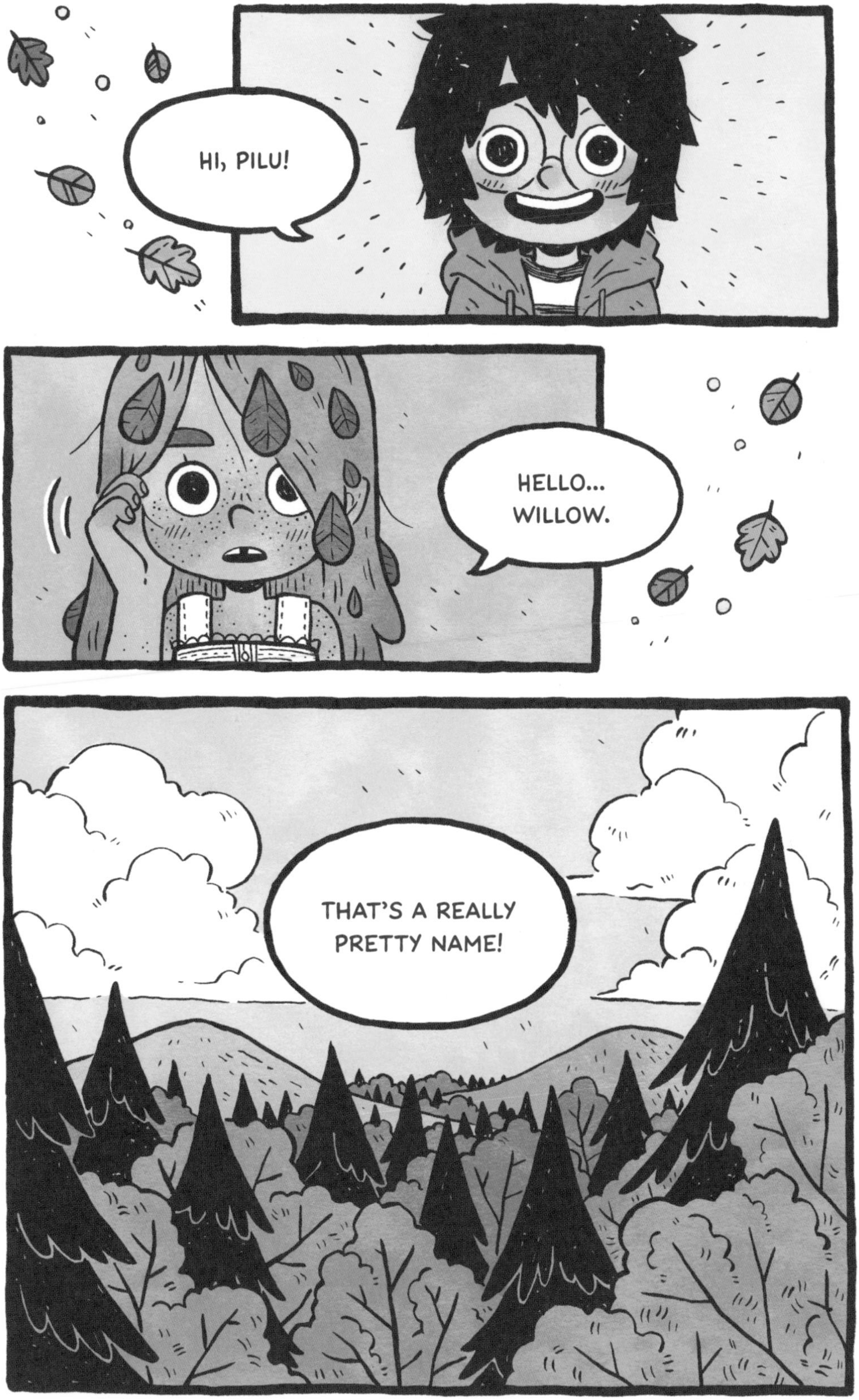
HI, PILU!
HELLO... WILLOW.
THAT'S A REALLY PRETTY NAME!

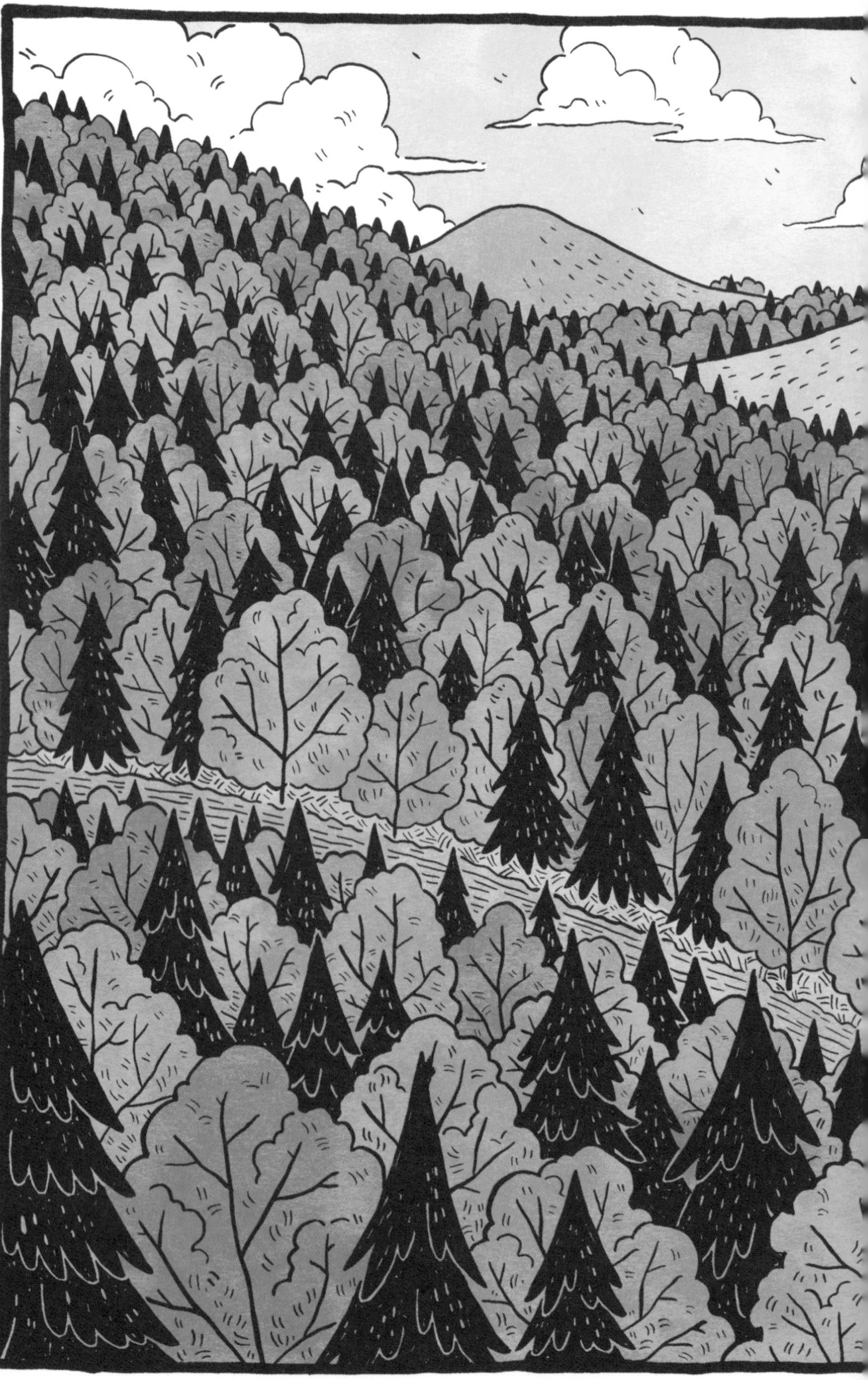

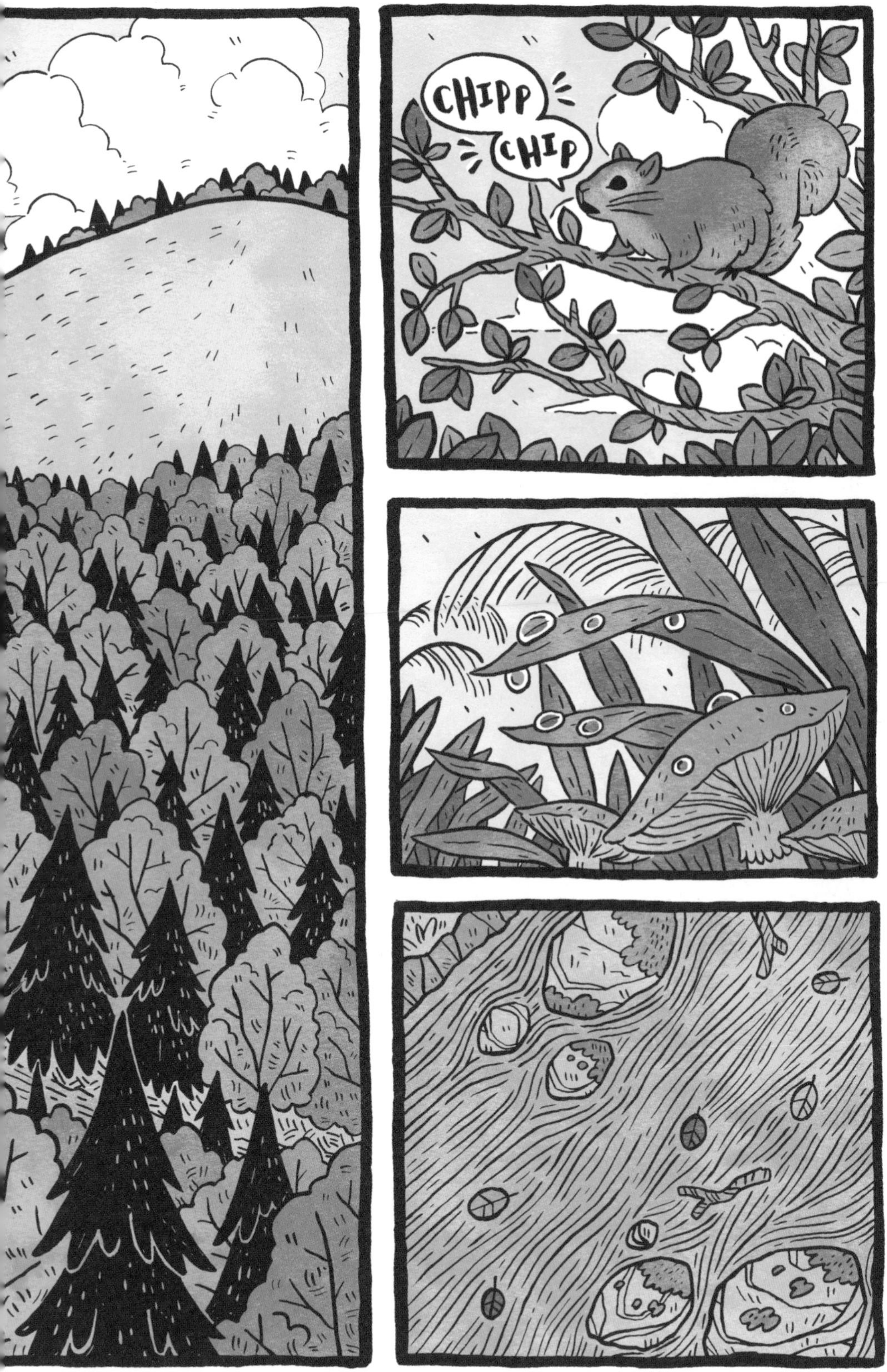
CHIPP
CHIP

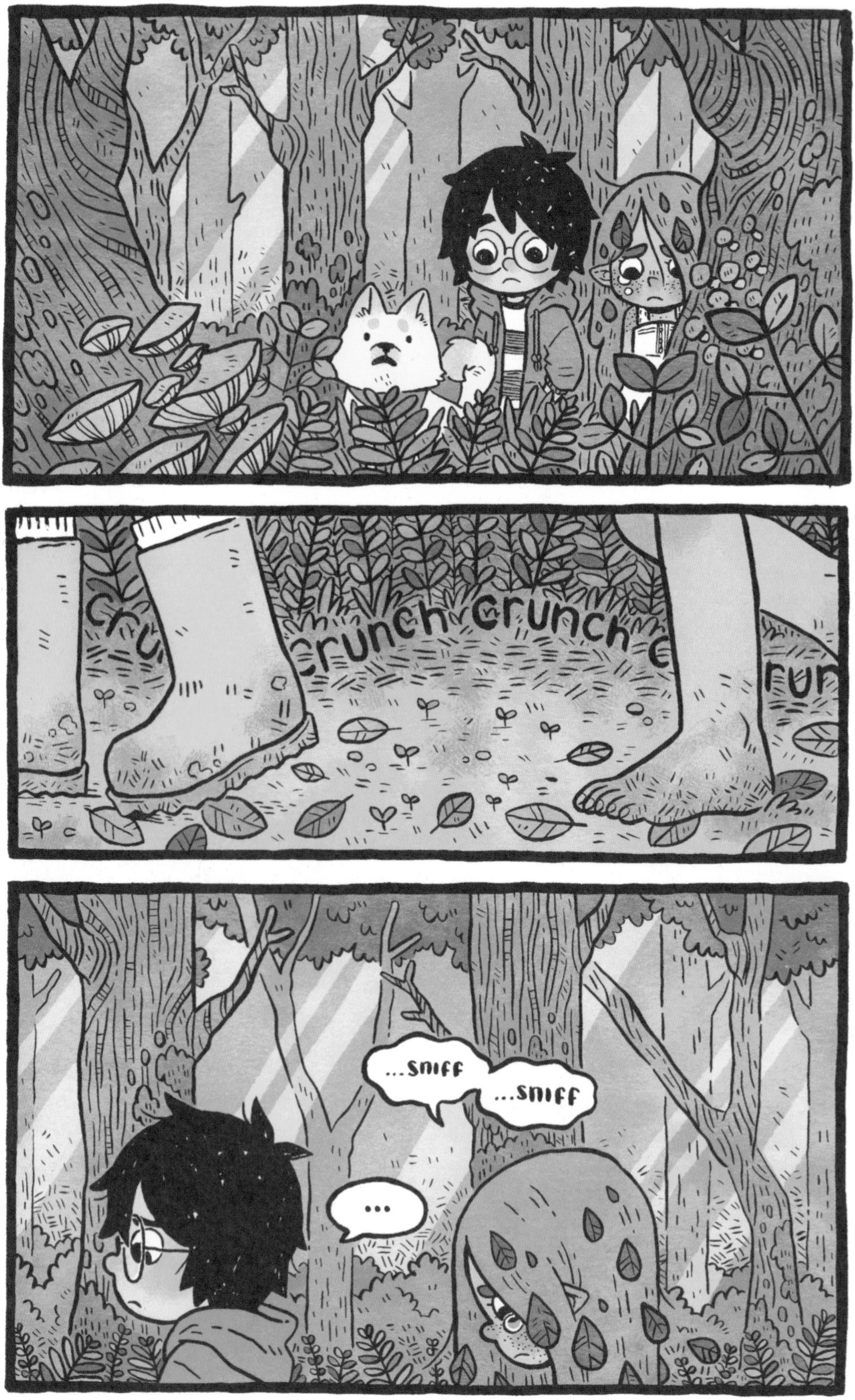
cru
crunch crunch
c
run
...sniff
...sniff
...

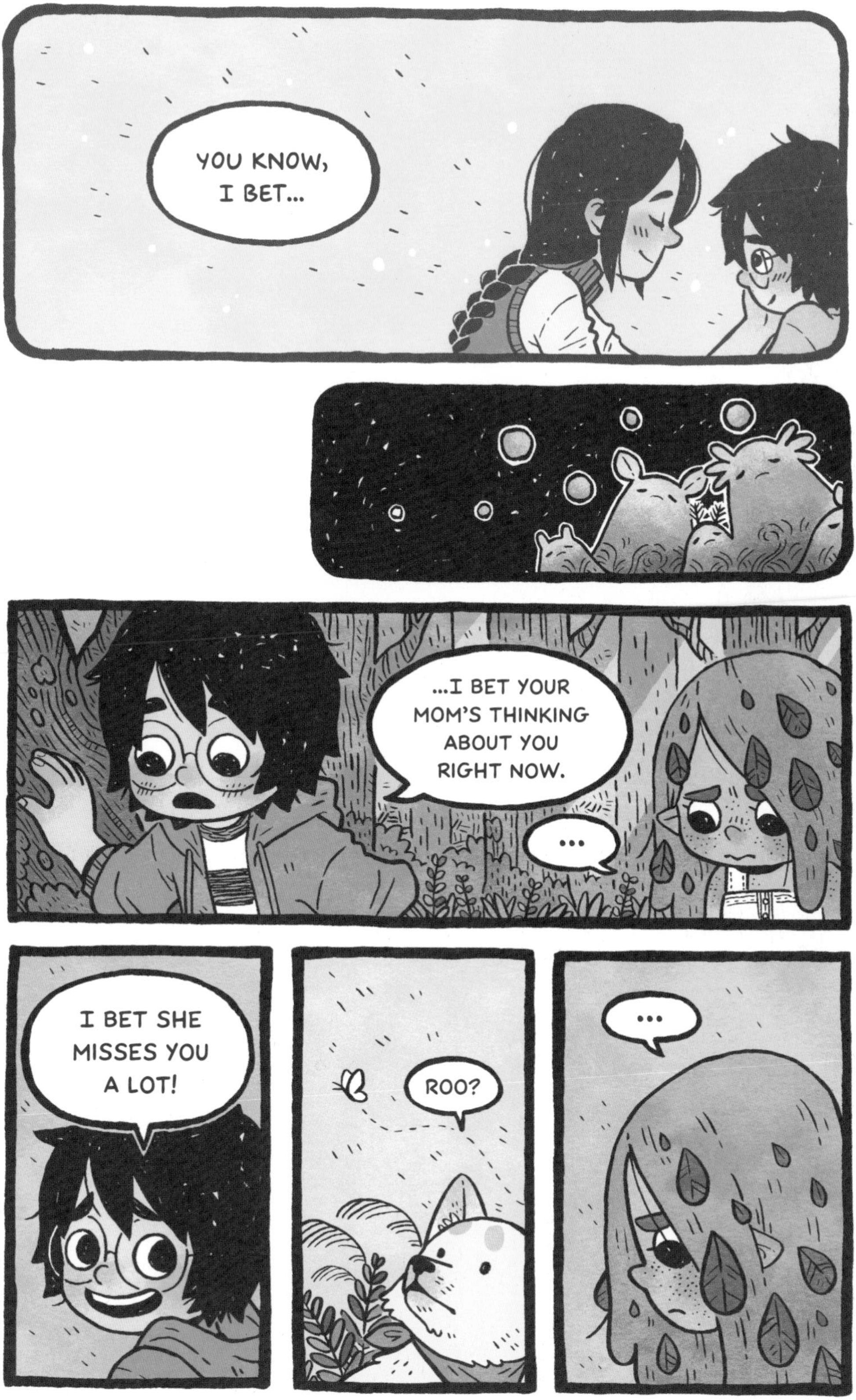
YOU KNOW, I BET...
...I BET YOUR MOM'S THINKING ABOUT YOU RIGHT NOW.
...
I BET SHE MISSES YOU A LOT!
ROO?
...

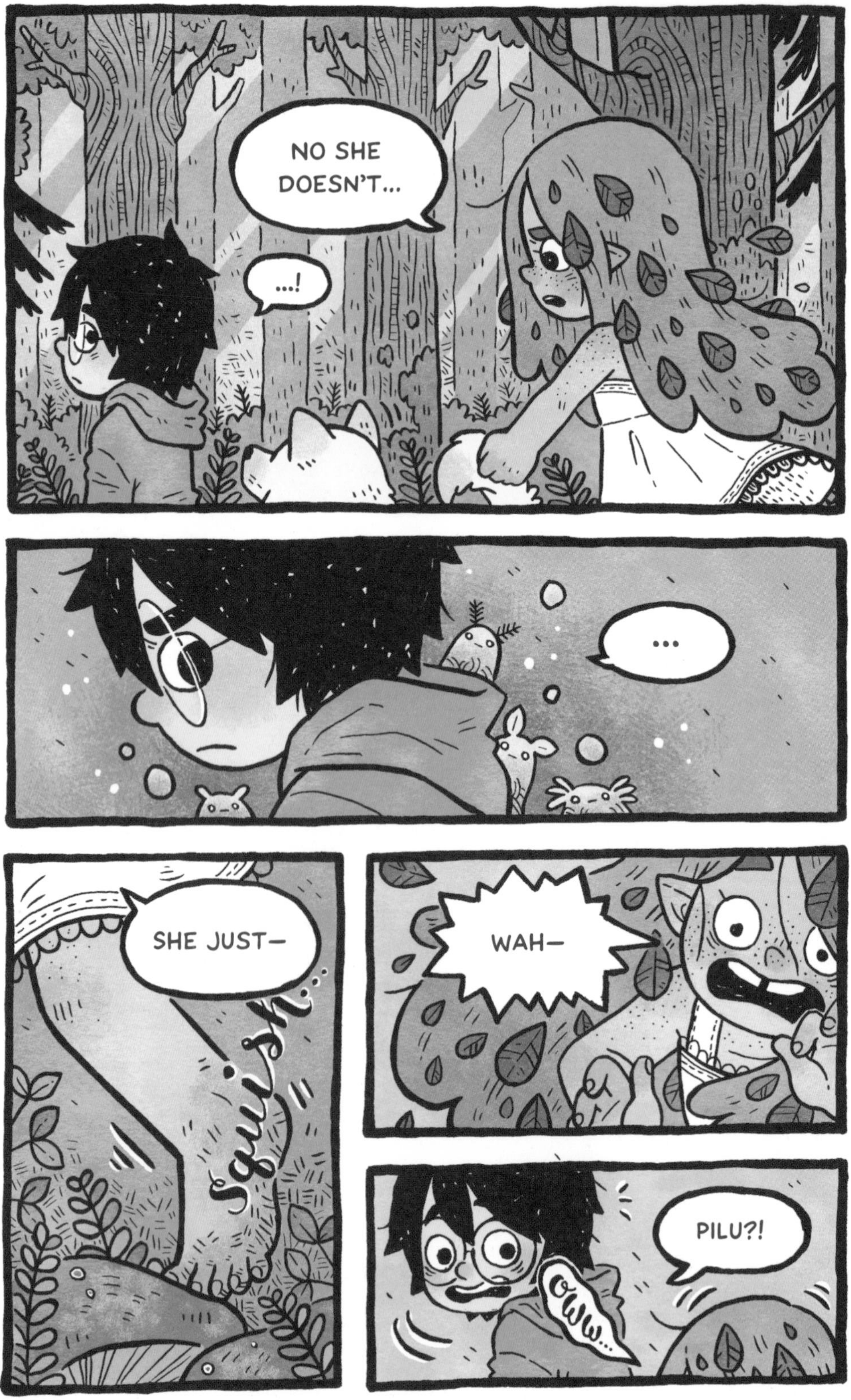
NO SHE DOESN'T...
...!
...
SHE JUST—
Squish...
WAH—
PILU?!
Oww...

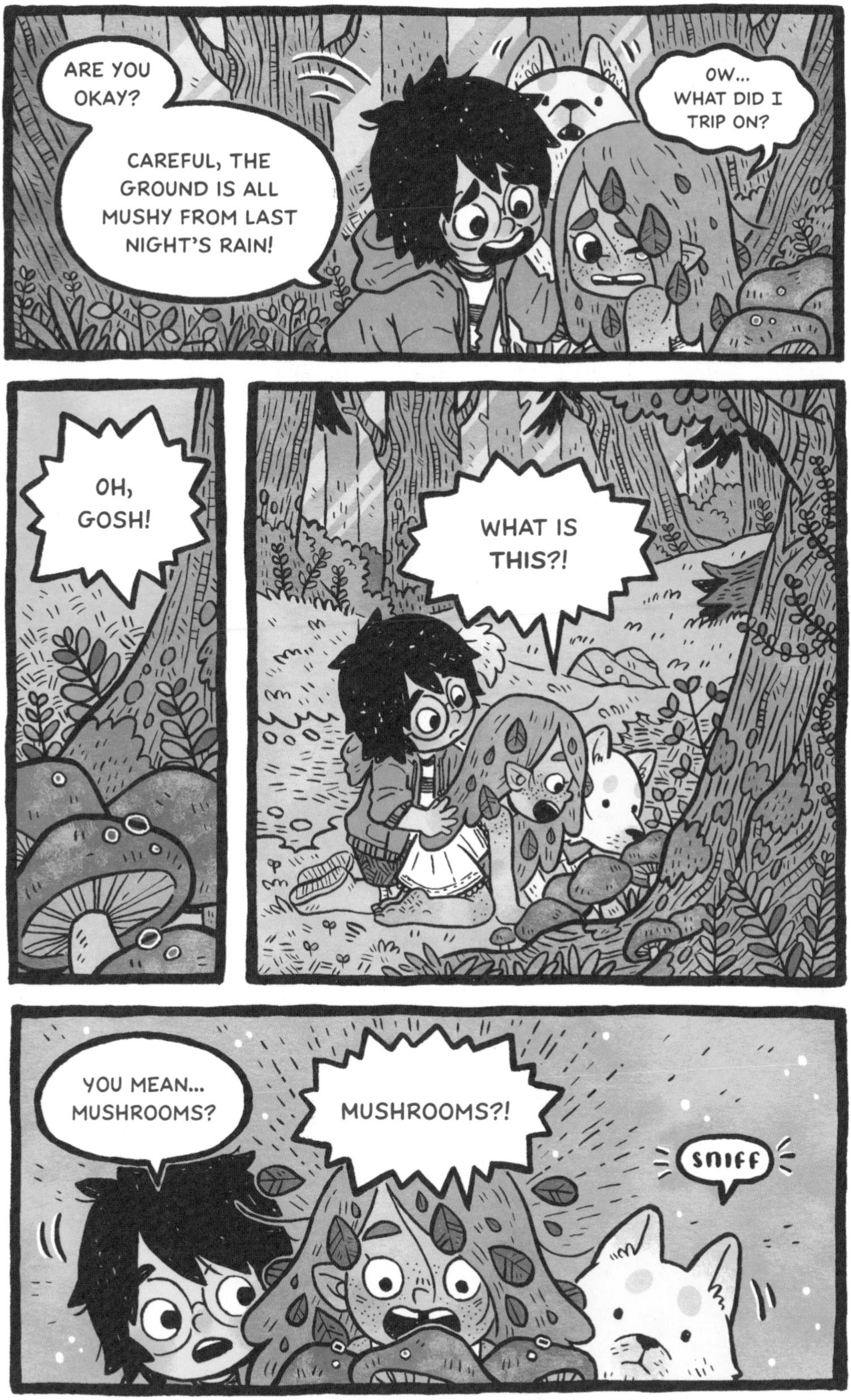
ARE YOU OKAY?
CAREFUL, THE GROUND IS ALL MUSHY FROM LAST NIGHT'S RAIN!
OW... WHAT DID I TRIP ON?
OH, GOSH!
WHAT IS THIS?!
YOU MEAN... MUSHROOMS?
MUSHROOMS?!
SNIFF

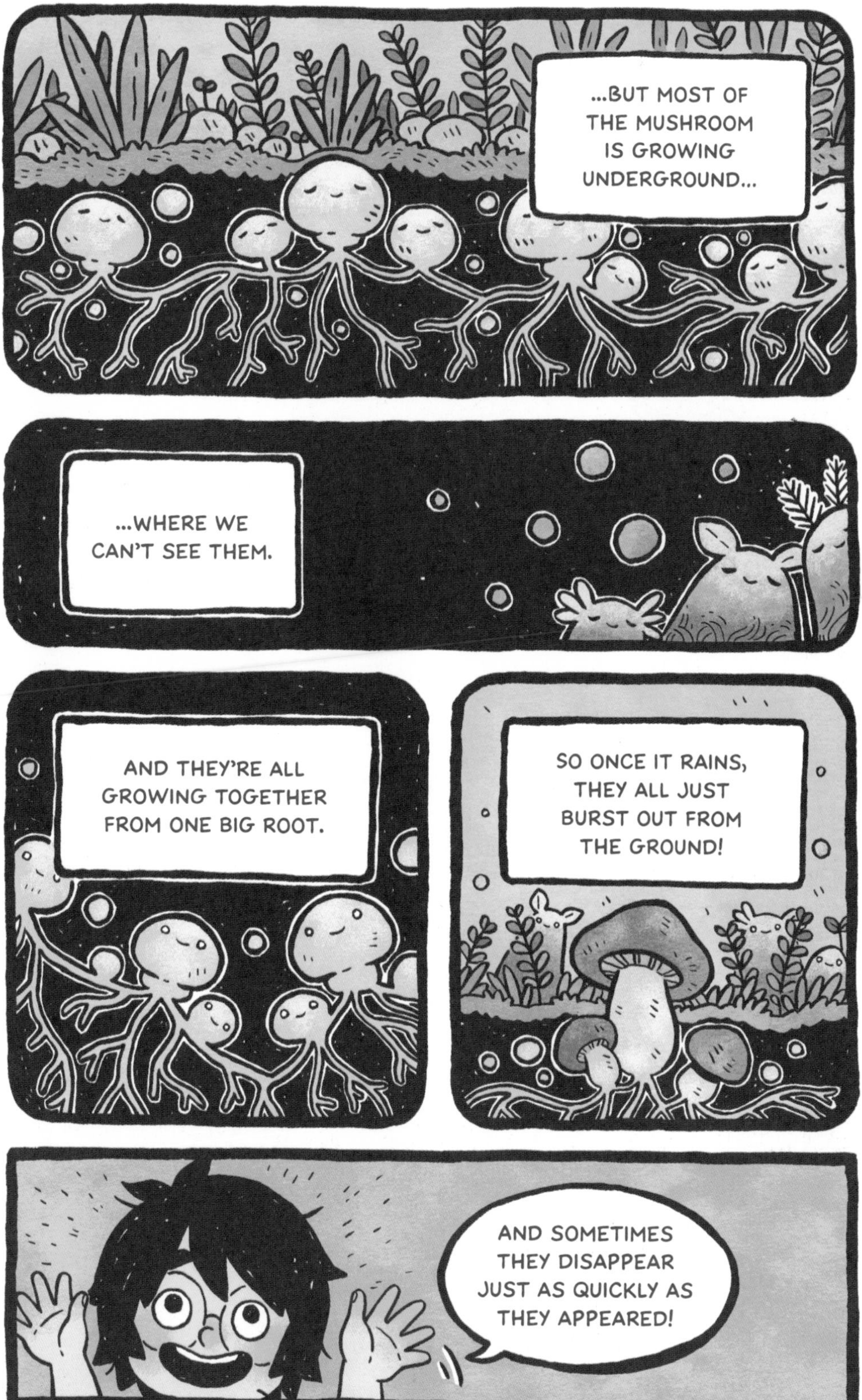
...BUT MOST OF THE MUSHROOM IS GROWING UNDERGROUND...
...WHERE WE CAN'T SEE THEM.
AND THEY'RE ALL GROWING TOGETHER FROM ONE BIG ROOT.
SO ONCE IT RAINS, THEY ALL JUST BURST OUT FROM THE GROUND!
AND SOMETIMES THEY DISAPPEAR JUST AS QUICKLY AS THEY APPEARED!

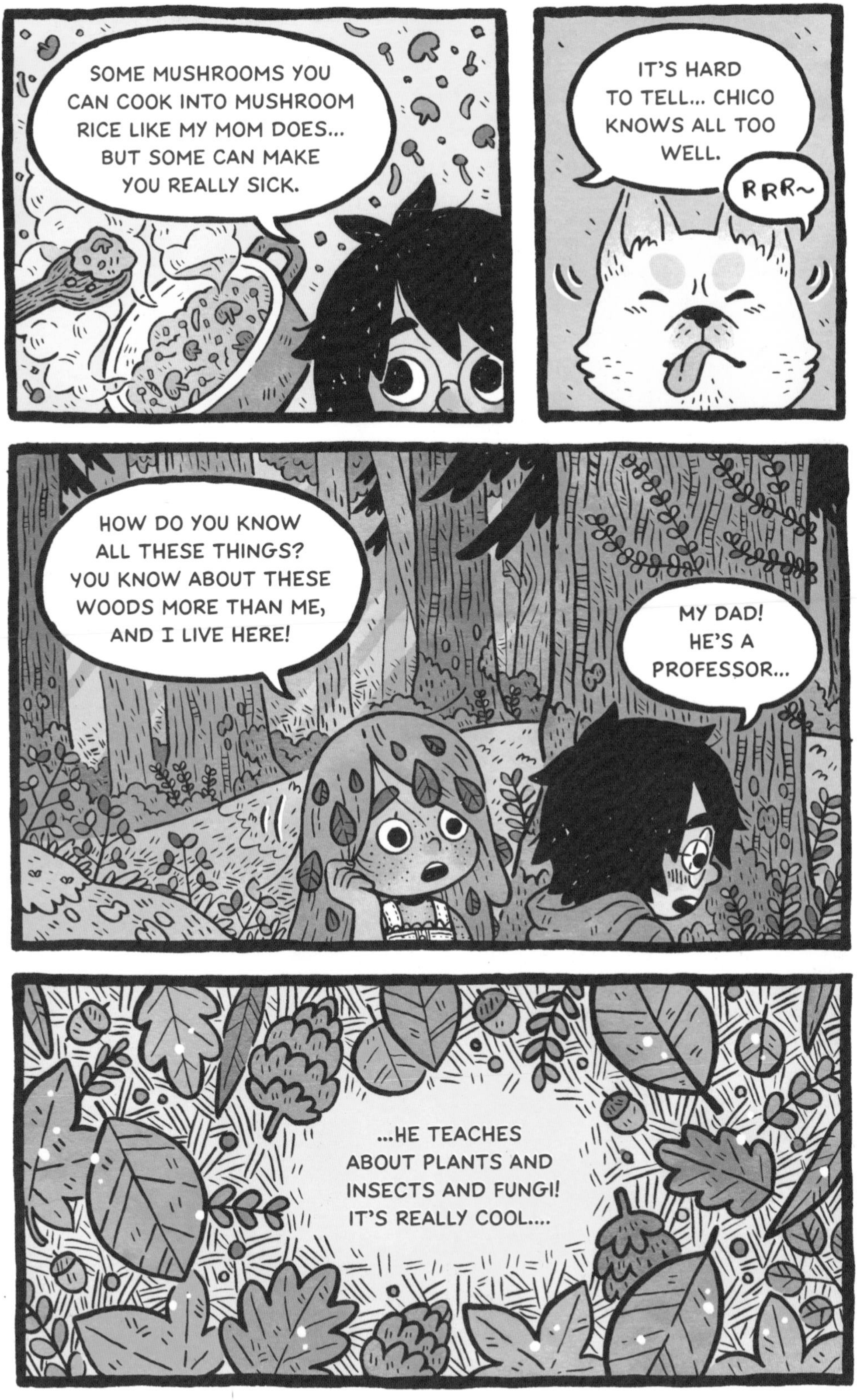
SOME MUSHROOMS YOU CAN COOK INTO MUSHROOM RICE LIKE MY MOM DOES... BUT SOME CAN MAKE YOU REALLY SICK.
IT'S HARD TO TELL... CHICO KNOWS ALL TOO WELL.
RRR~
HOW DO YOU KNOW ALL THESE THINGS? YOU KNOW ABOUT THESE WOODS MORE THAN ME, AND I LIVE HERE!
MY DAD! HE'S A PROFESSOR...
...HE TEACHES ABOUT PLANTS AND INSECTS AND FUNGI! IT'S REALLY COOL....

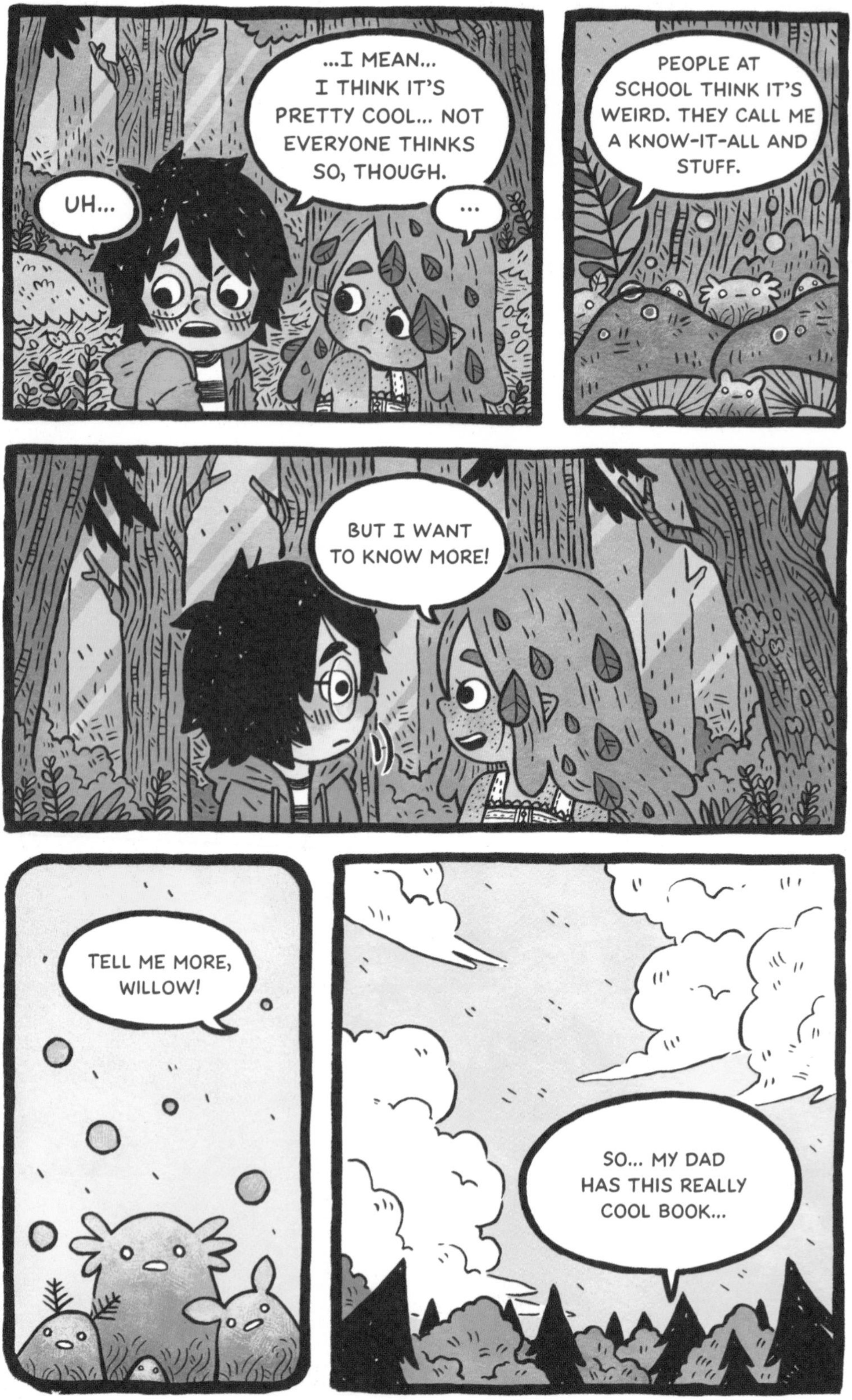

UH...
...I MEAN... I THINK IT'S PRETTY COOL... NOT EVERYONE THINKS SO, THOUGH.
...
PEOPLE AT SCHOOL THINK IT'S WEIRD. THEY CALL ME A KNOW-IT-ALL AND STUFF.
BUT I WANT TO KNOW MORE!
TELL ME MORE, WILLOW!
SO... MY DAD HAS THIS REALLY COOL BOOK...

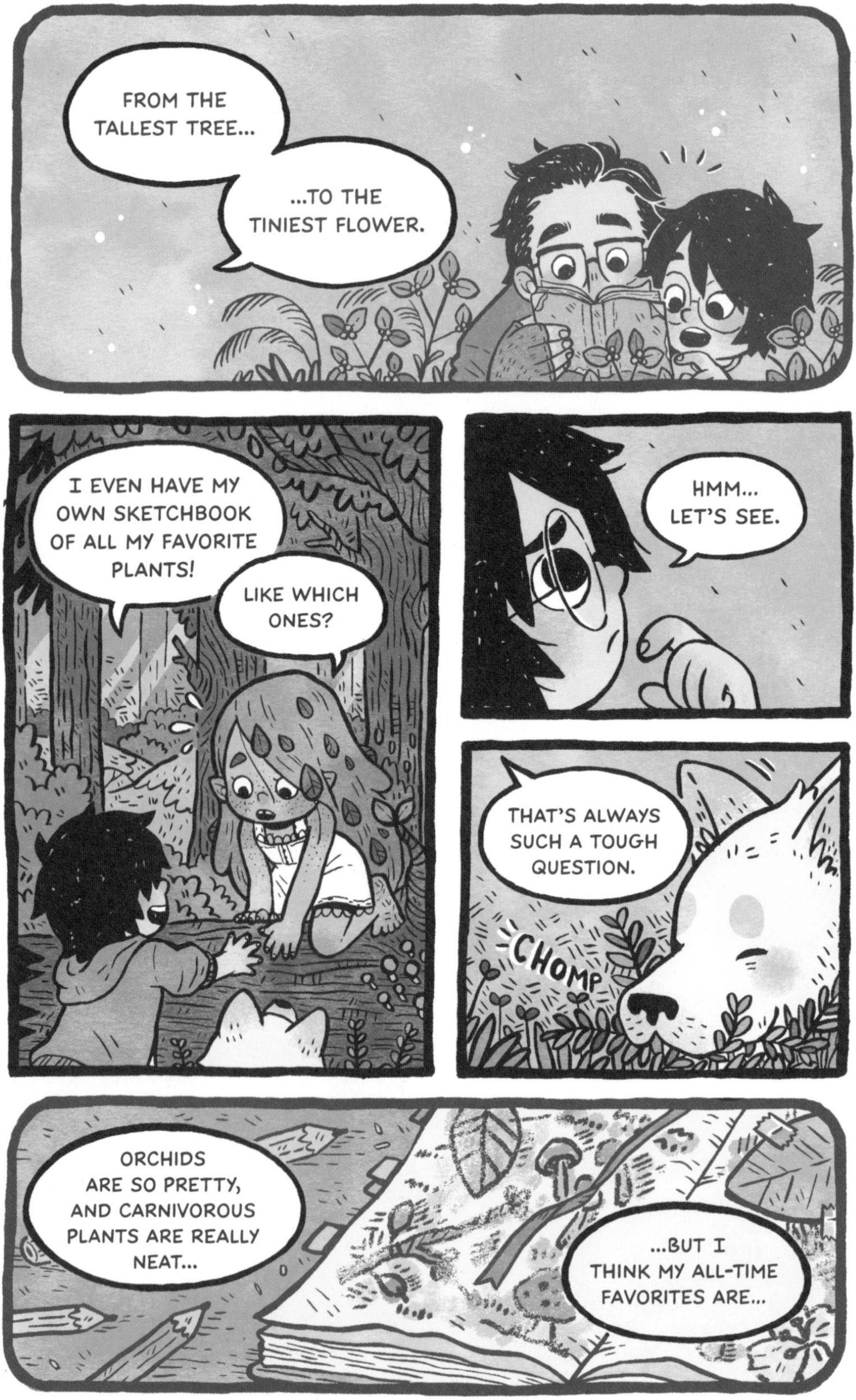
FROM THE TALLEST TREE...
...TO THE TINIEST FLOWER.
I EVEN HAVE MY OWN SKETCHBOOK OF ALL MY FAVORITE PLANTS!
LIKE WHICH ONES?
HMM... LET'S SEE.
THAT'S ALWAYS SUCH A TOUGH QUESTION.
CHOMP
ORCHIDS ARE SO PRETTY, AND CARNIVOROUS PLANTS ARE REALLY NEAT...
...BUT I THINK MY ALL-TIME FAVORITES ARE...

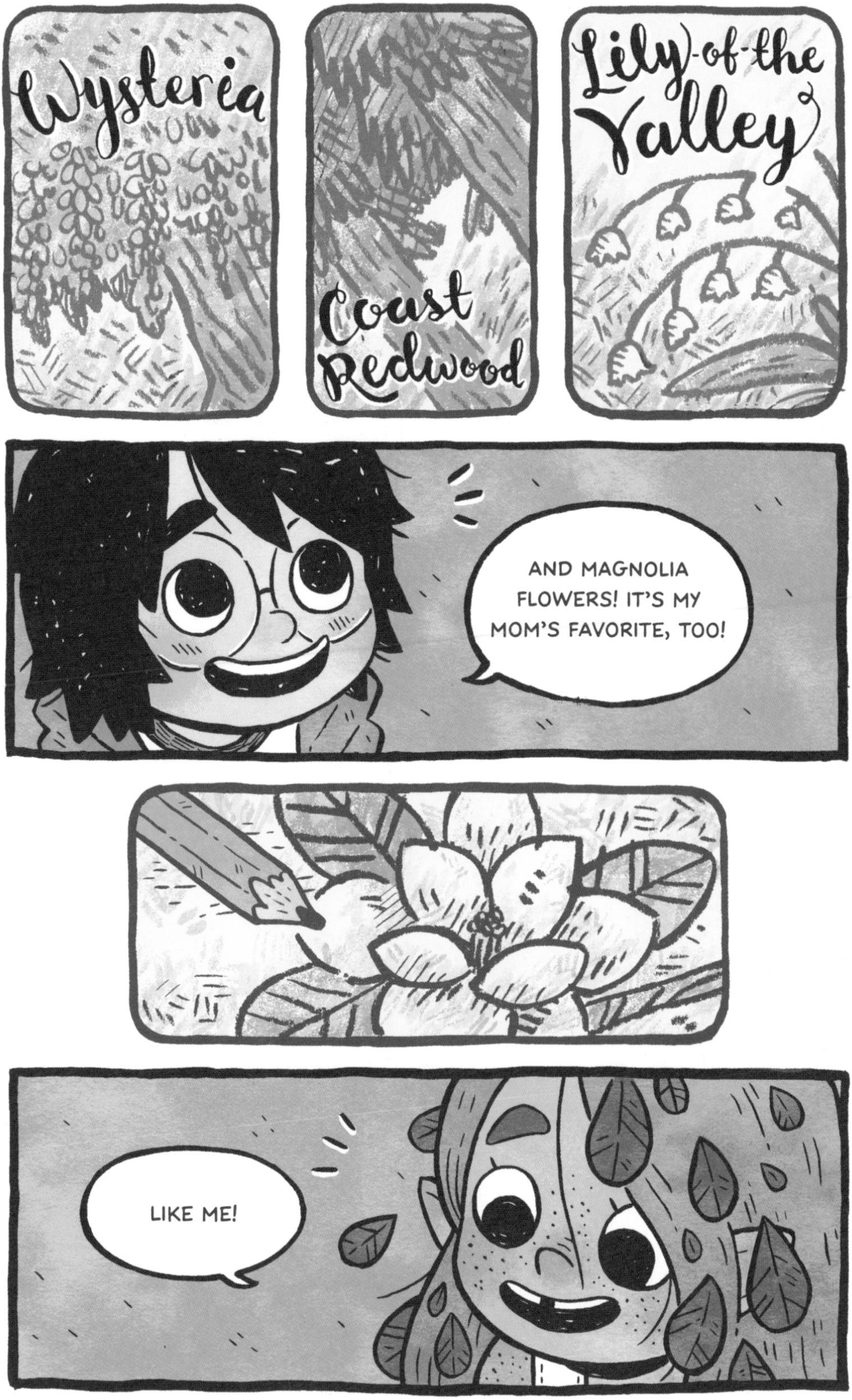
Wysteria
Coast Redwood
Lily-of-the Valley
AND MAGNOLIA FLOWERS! IT'S MY MOM'S FAVORITE, TOO!
LIKE ME!

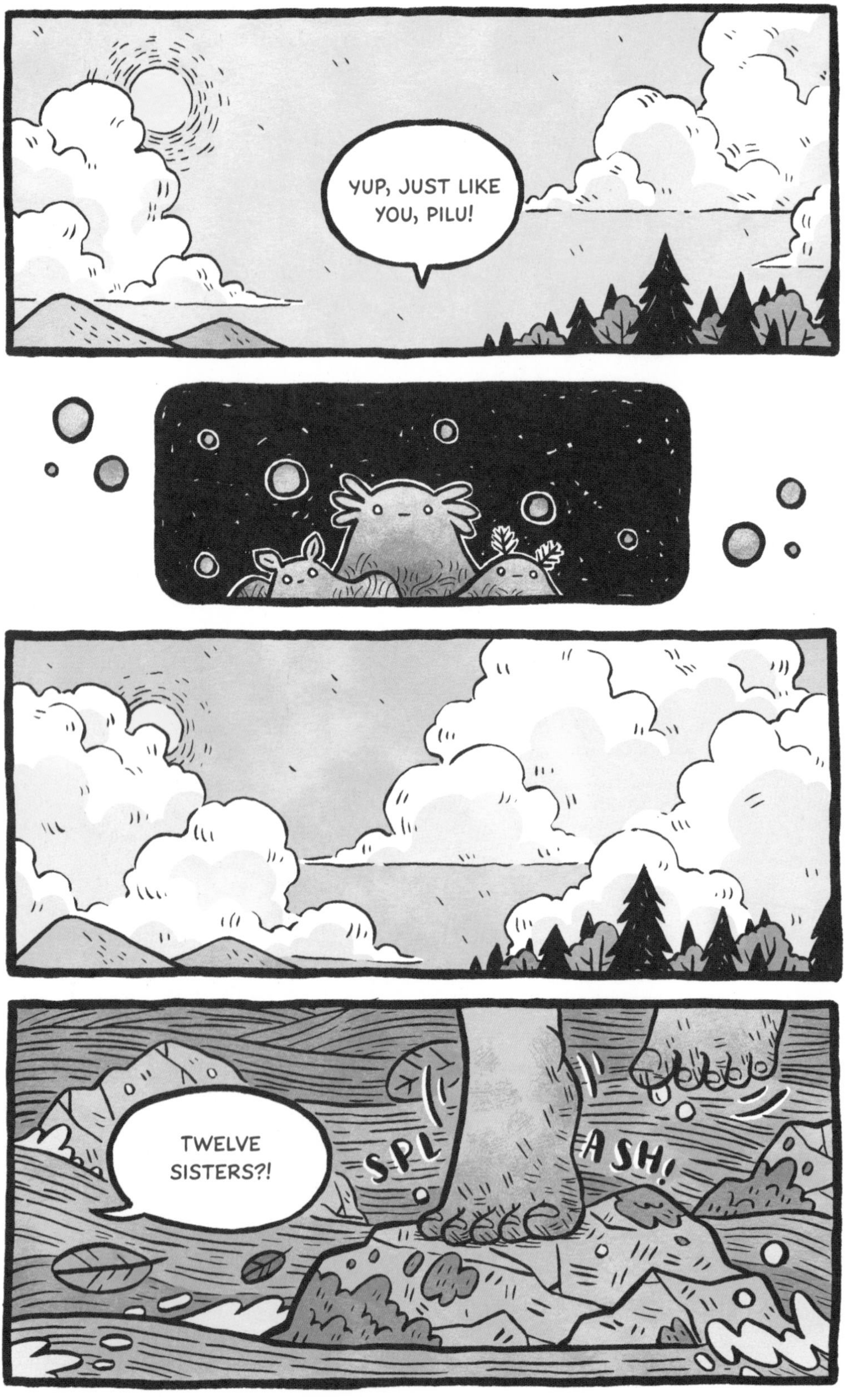
YUP, JUST LIKE YOU, PILU!
TWELVE SISTERS?!
SPLASH!

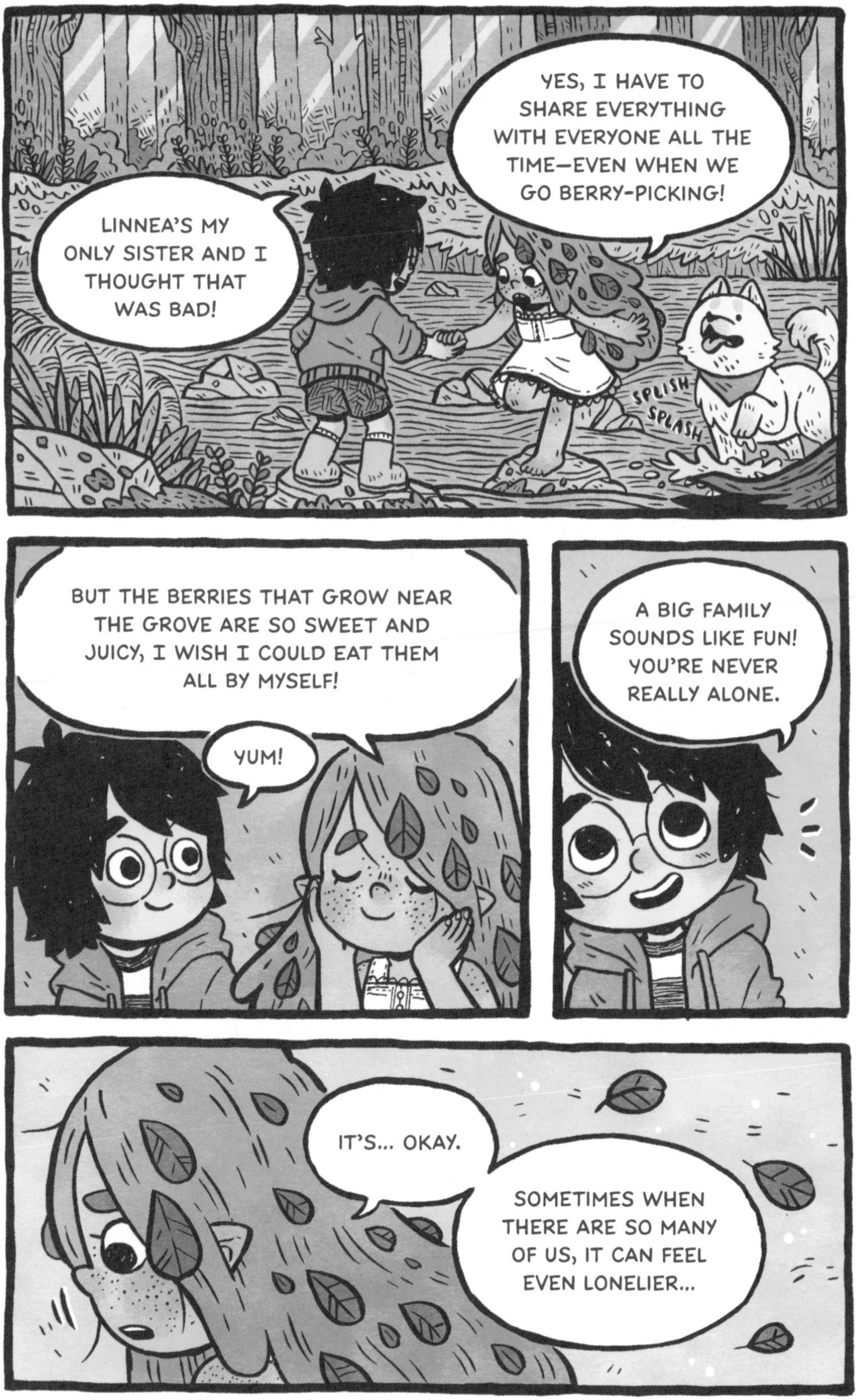
LINNEA'S MY ONLY SISTER AND I THOUGHT THAT WAS BAD!
YES, I HAVE TO SHARE EVERYTHING WITH EVERYONE ALL THE TIME—EVEN WHEN WE GO BERRY-PICKING!
SPLISH
SPLASH
BUT THE BERRIES THAT GROW NEAR THE GROVE ARE SO SWEET AND JUICY, I WISH I COULD EAT THEM ALL BY MYSELF!
YUM!
A BIG FAMILY SOUNDS LIKE FUN! YOU'RE NEVER REALLY ALONE.
IT'S... OKAY.
SOMETIMES WHEN THERE ARE SO MANY OF US, IT CAN FEEL EVEN LONELIER...

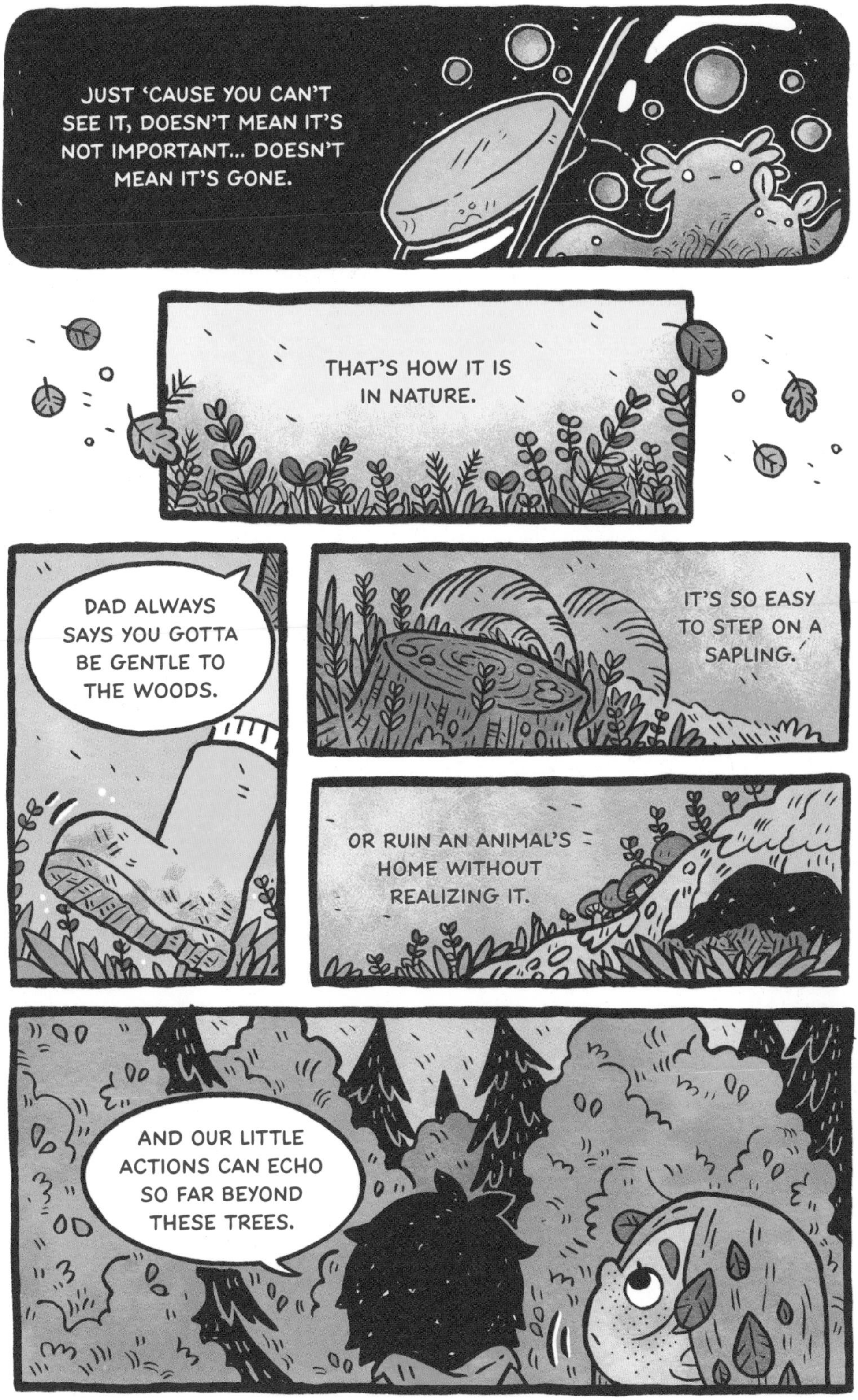
JUST 'CAUSE YOU CAN'T SEE IT, DOESN'T MEAN IT'S NOT IMPORTANT... DOESN'T MEAN IT'S GONE.
THAT'S HOW IT IS IN NATURE.
DAD ALWAYS SAYS YOU GOTTA BE GENTLE TO THE WOODS.
IT'S SO EASY TO STEP ON A SAPLING.
OR RUIN AN ANIMAL'S HOME WITHOUT REALIZING IT.
AND OUR LITTLE ACTIONS CAN ECHO SO FAR BEYOND THESE TREES.

65

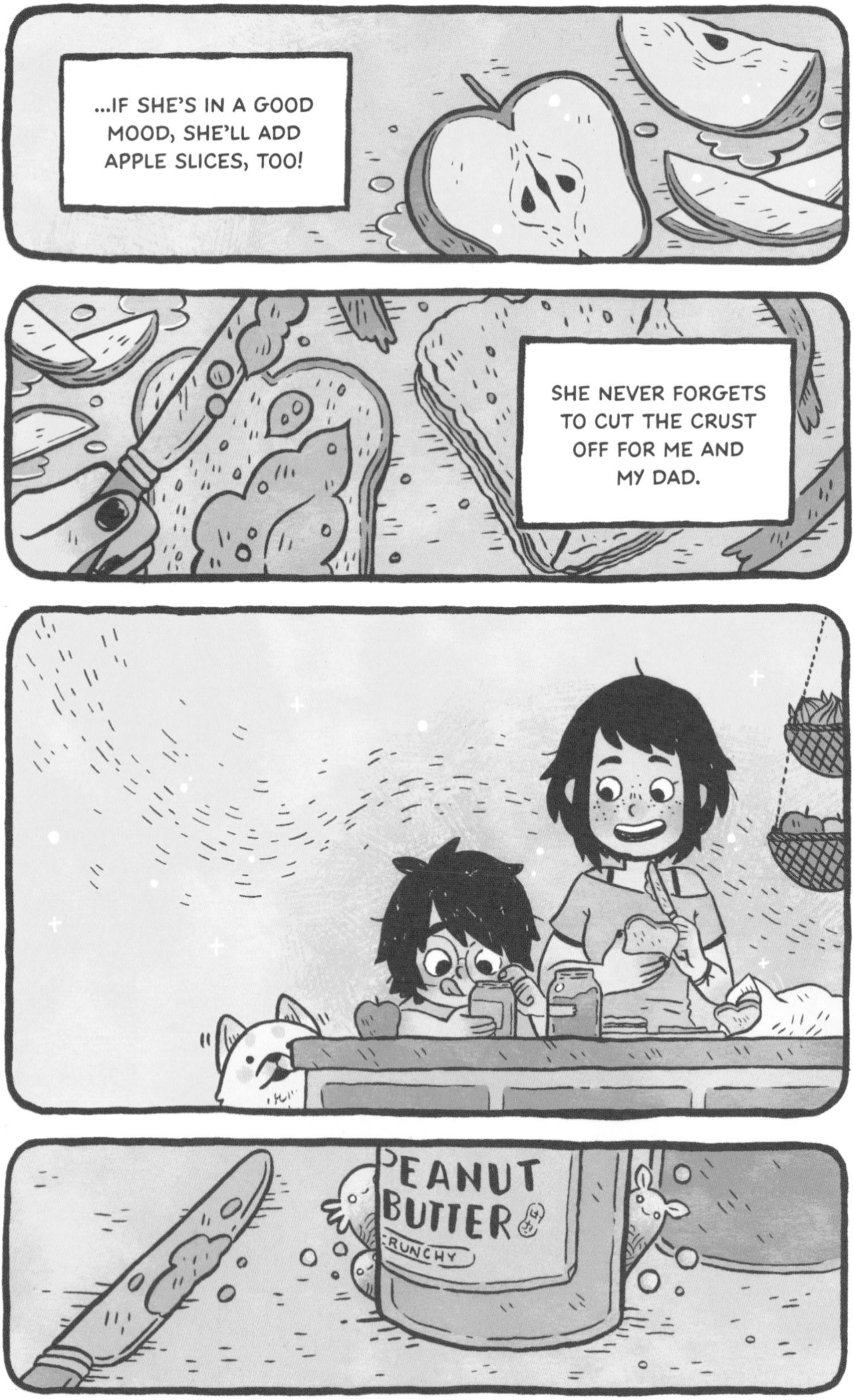
...IF SHE'S IN A GOOD MOOD, SHE'LL ADD APPLE SLICES, TOO!
SHE NEVER FORGETS TO CUT THE CRUST OFF FOR ME AND MY DAD.
PEANUT BUTTER
CRUNCHY

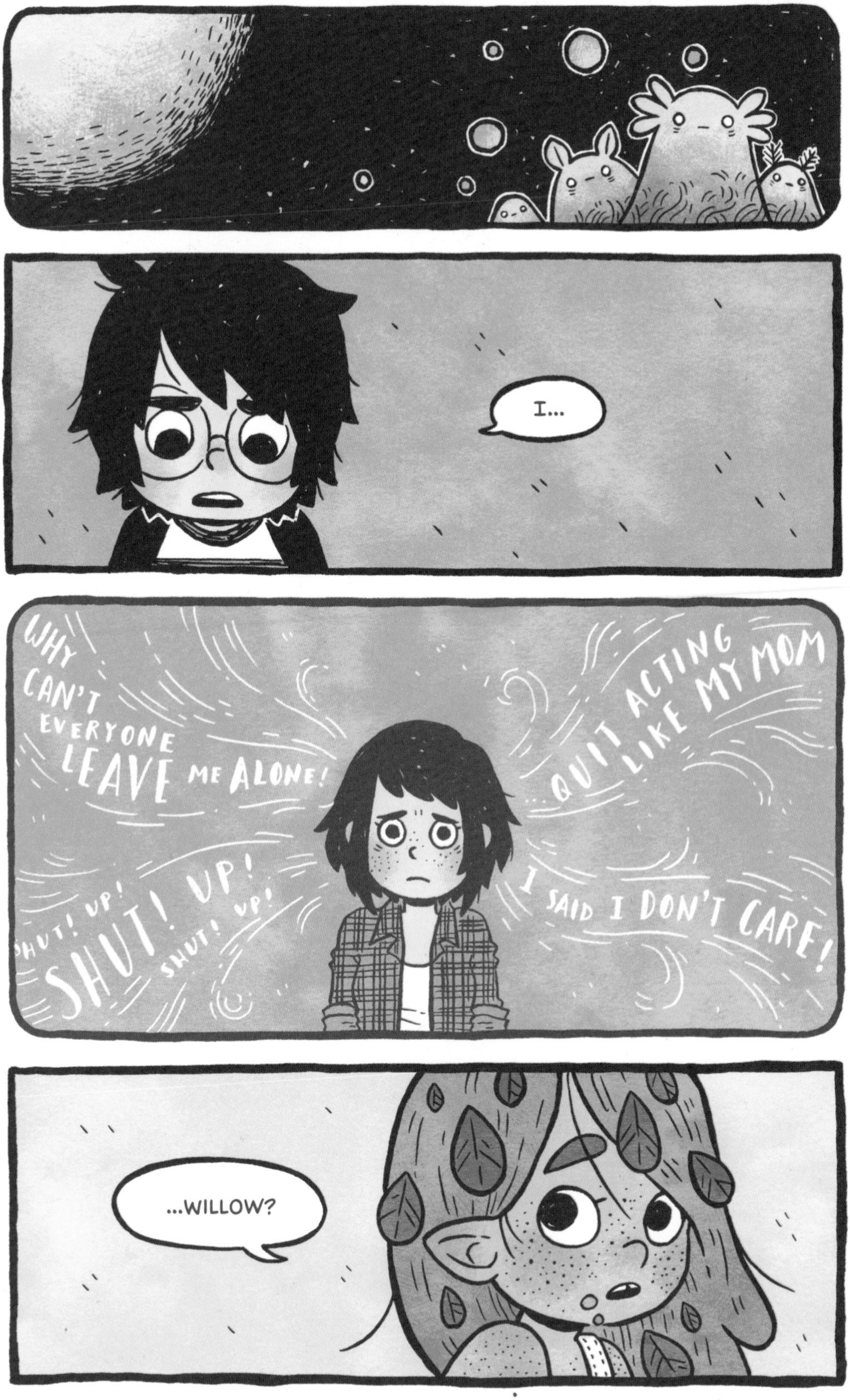
I...
WHY CAN'T EVERYONE LEAVE ME ALONE!
QUIT ACTING LIKE MY MOM
SHUT! UP! SHUT! UP! SHUT! UP!
I SAID I DON'T CARE!
...WILLOW?

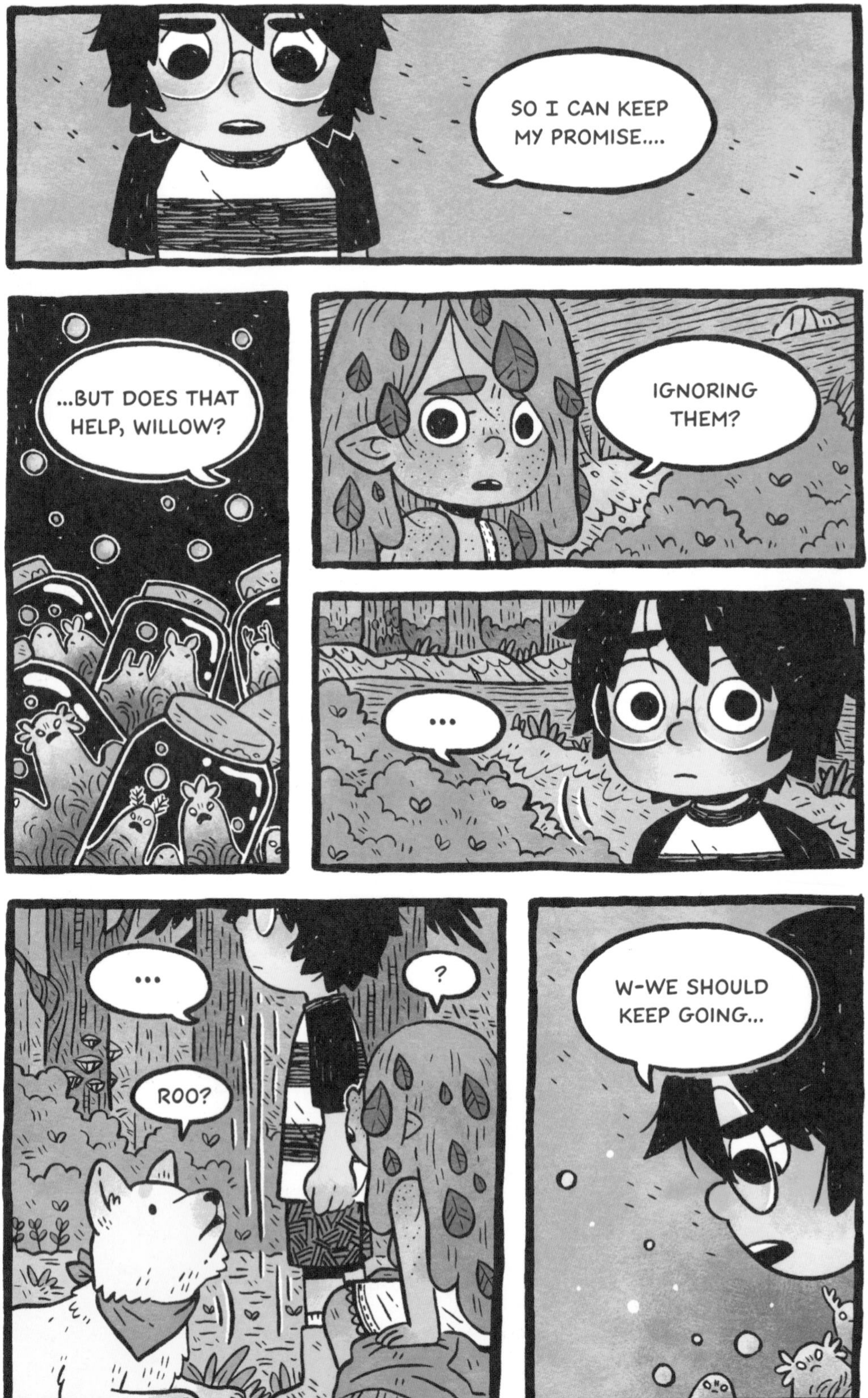
SO I CAN KEEP MY PROMISE....
...BUT DOES THAT HELP, WILLOW?
IGNORING THEM?
...
...
?
ROO?
W-WE SHOULD KEEP GOING...

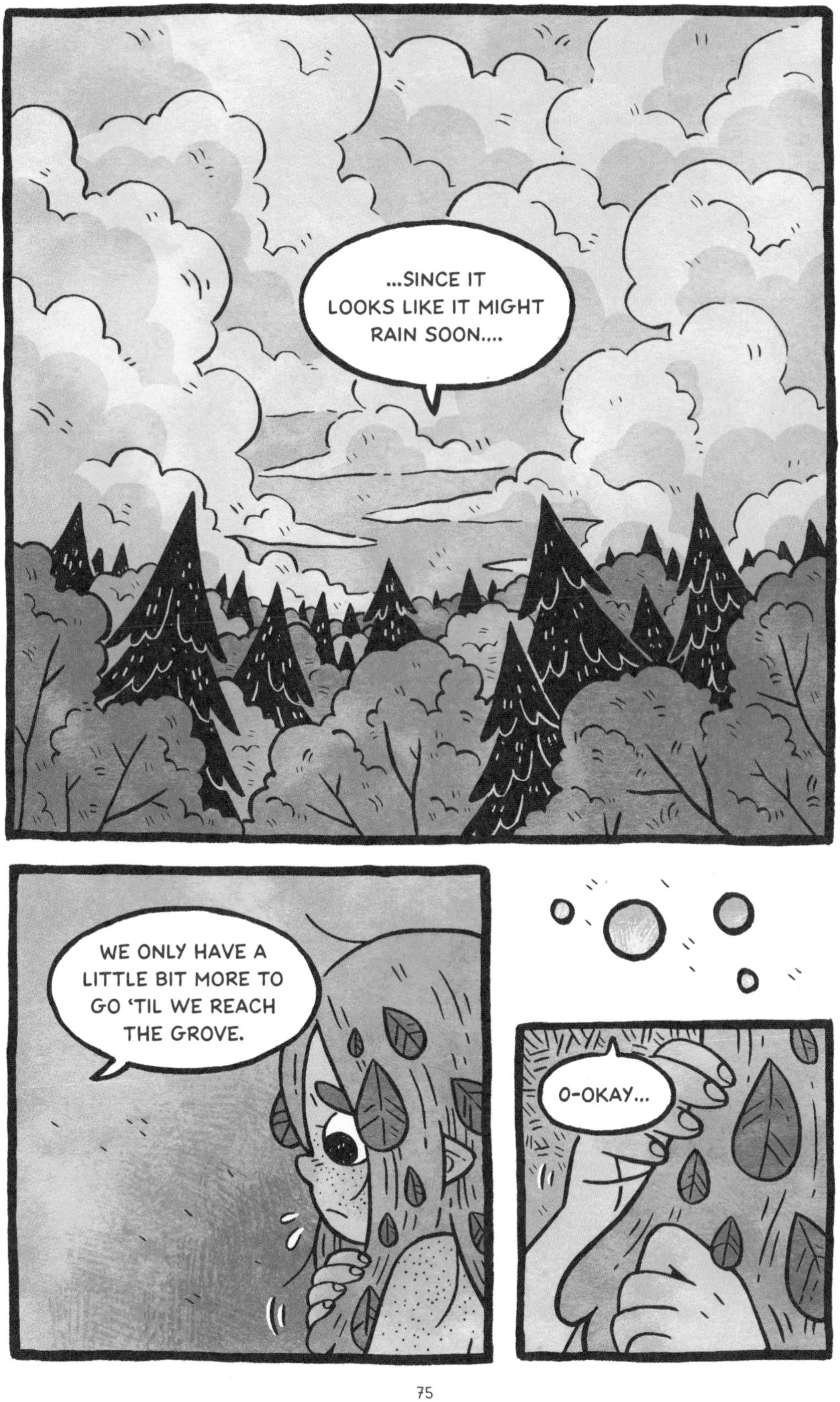
...SINCE IT LOOKS LIKE IT MIGHT RAIN SOON....
WE ONLY HAVE A LITTLE BIT MORE TO GO 'TIL WE REACH THE GROVE.
O-OKAY...

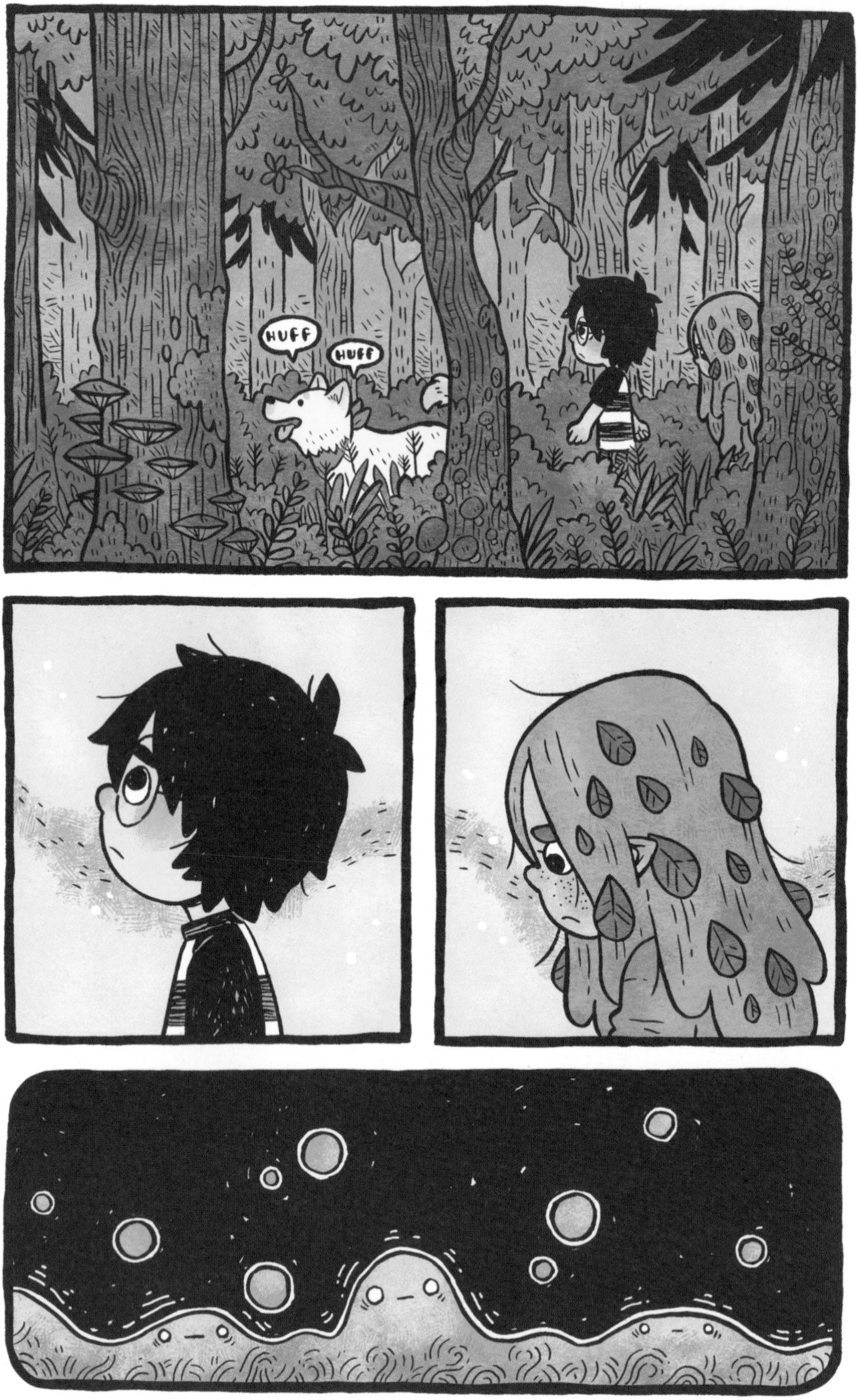
HUFF
HUFF

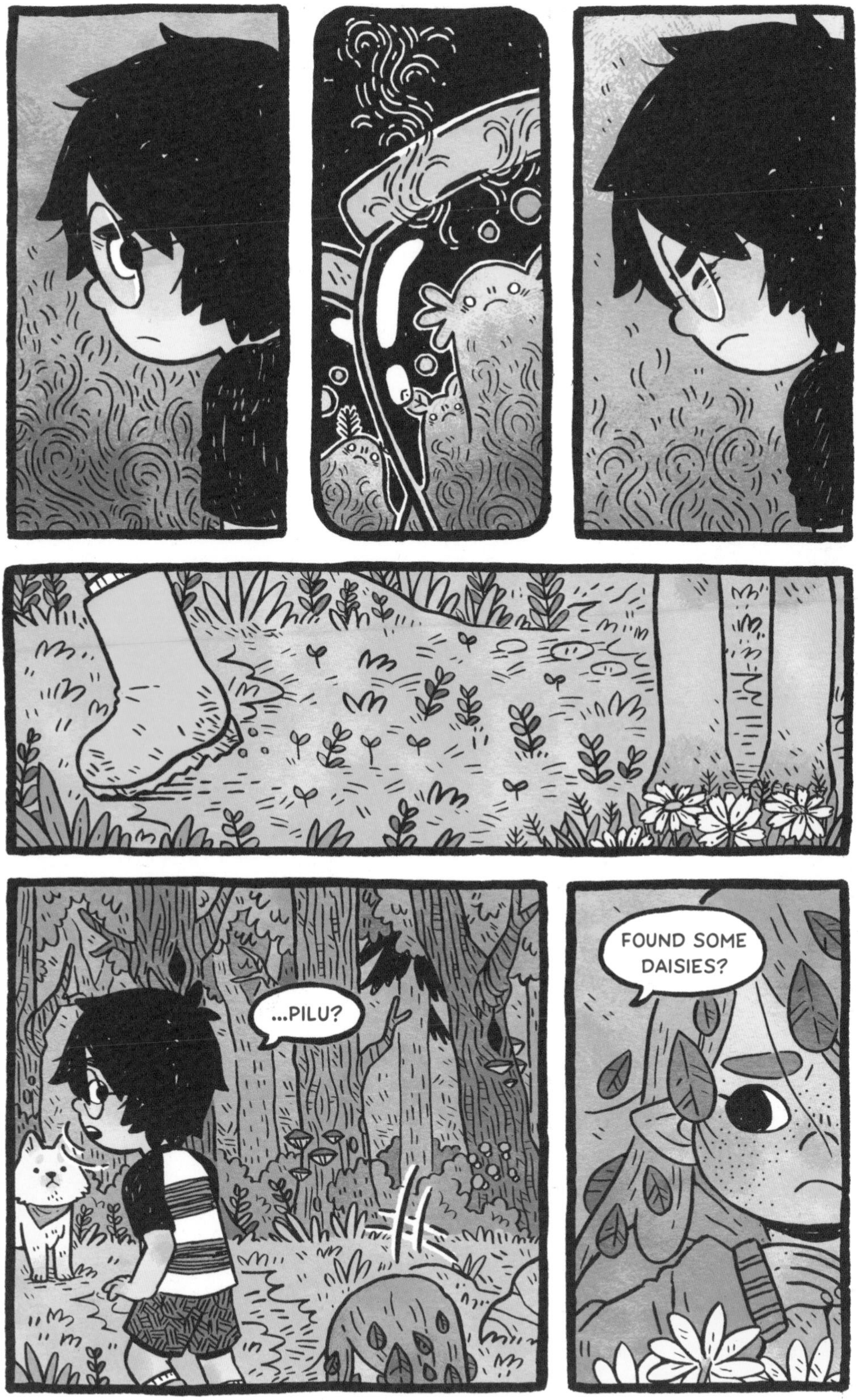
...PILU?
FOUND SOME DAISIES?

85

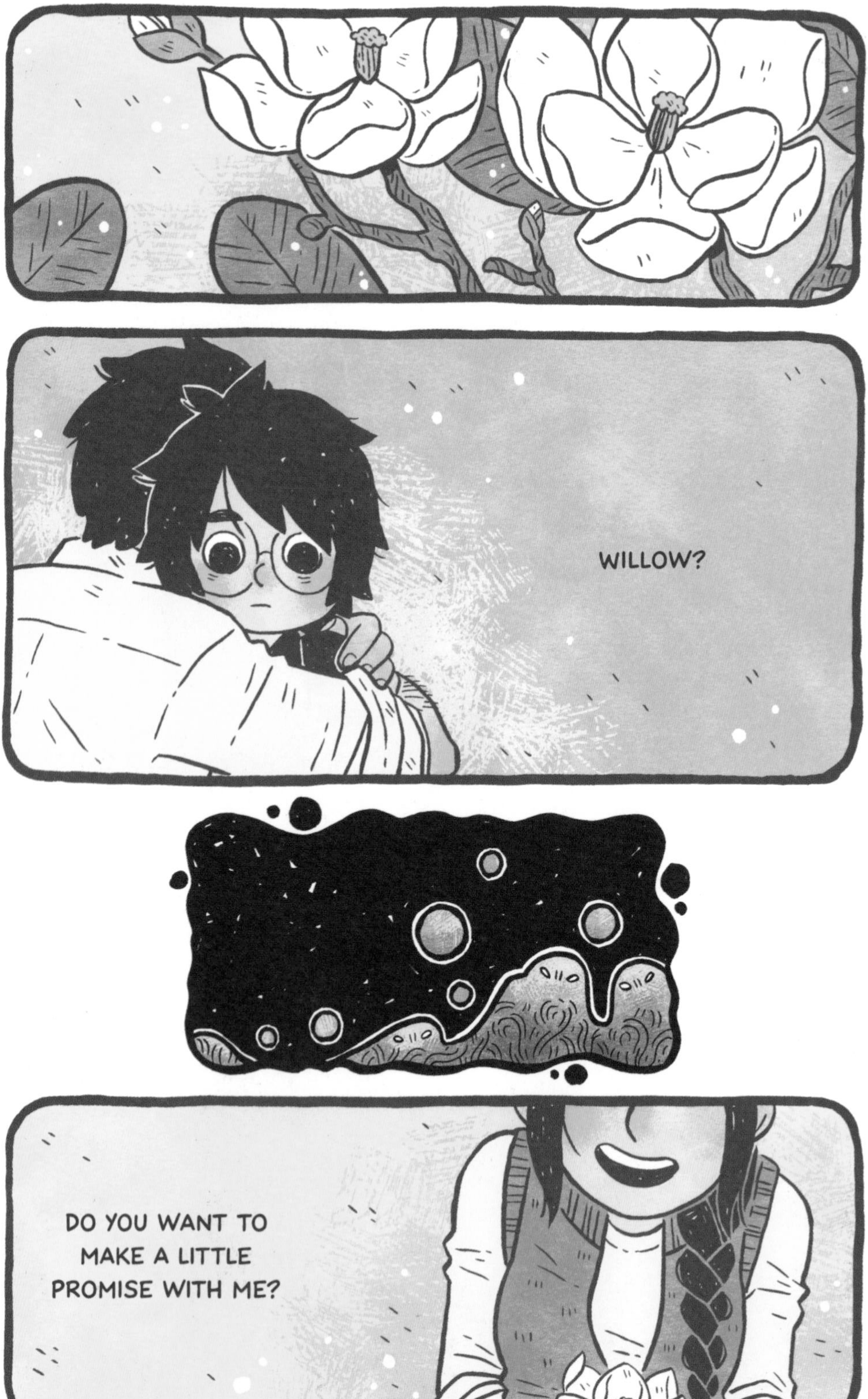
WILLOW?
DO YOU WANT TO MAKE A LITTLE PROMISE WITH ME?

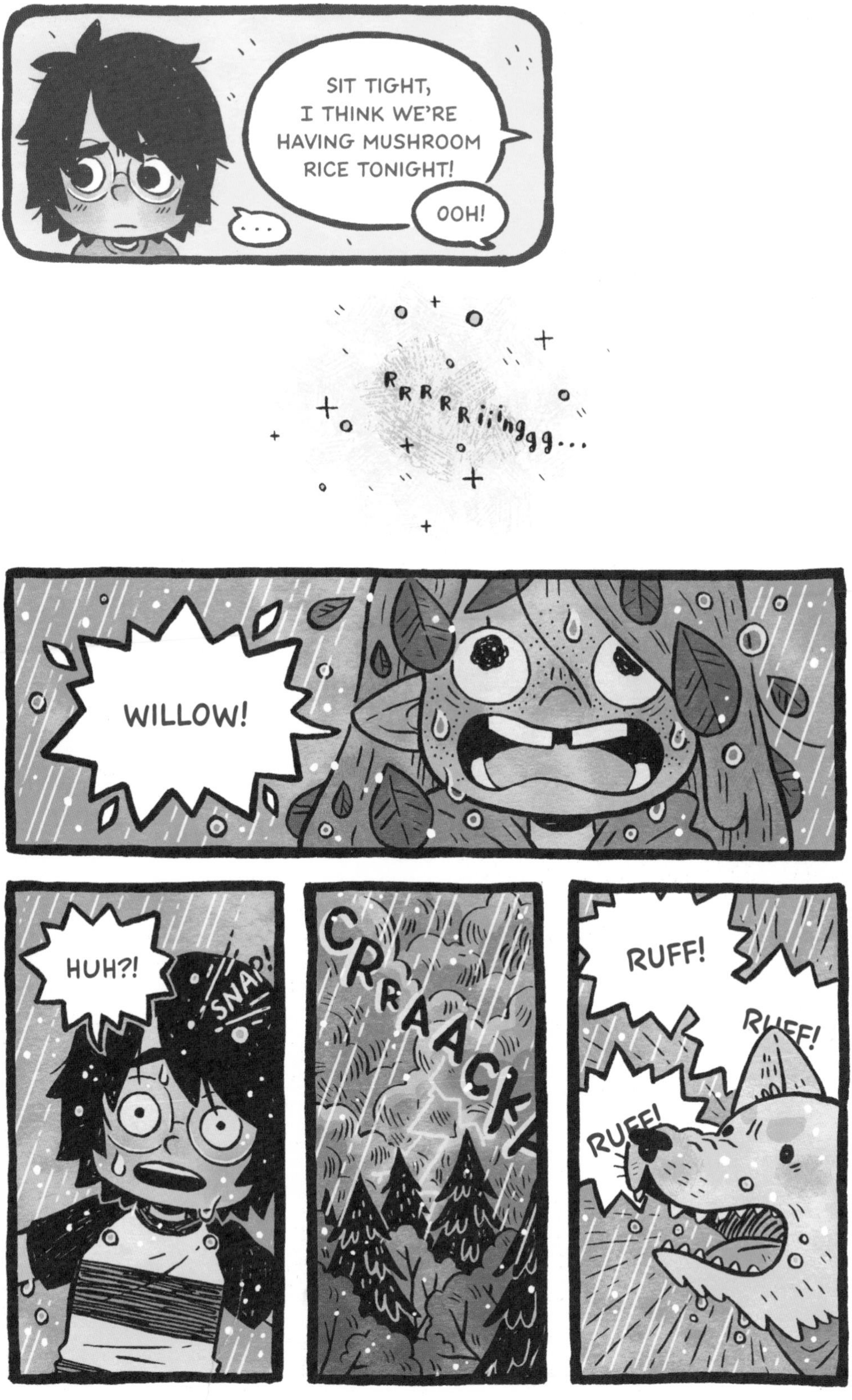
SIT TIGHT, I THINK WE'RE HAVING MUSHROOM RICE TONIGHT!
OOH!
...
RRRRRRiiinggg...
WILLOW!
HUH?!
SNAP!
CRRAAACK!
RUFF!
RUFF!
RUFF!

97

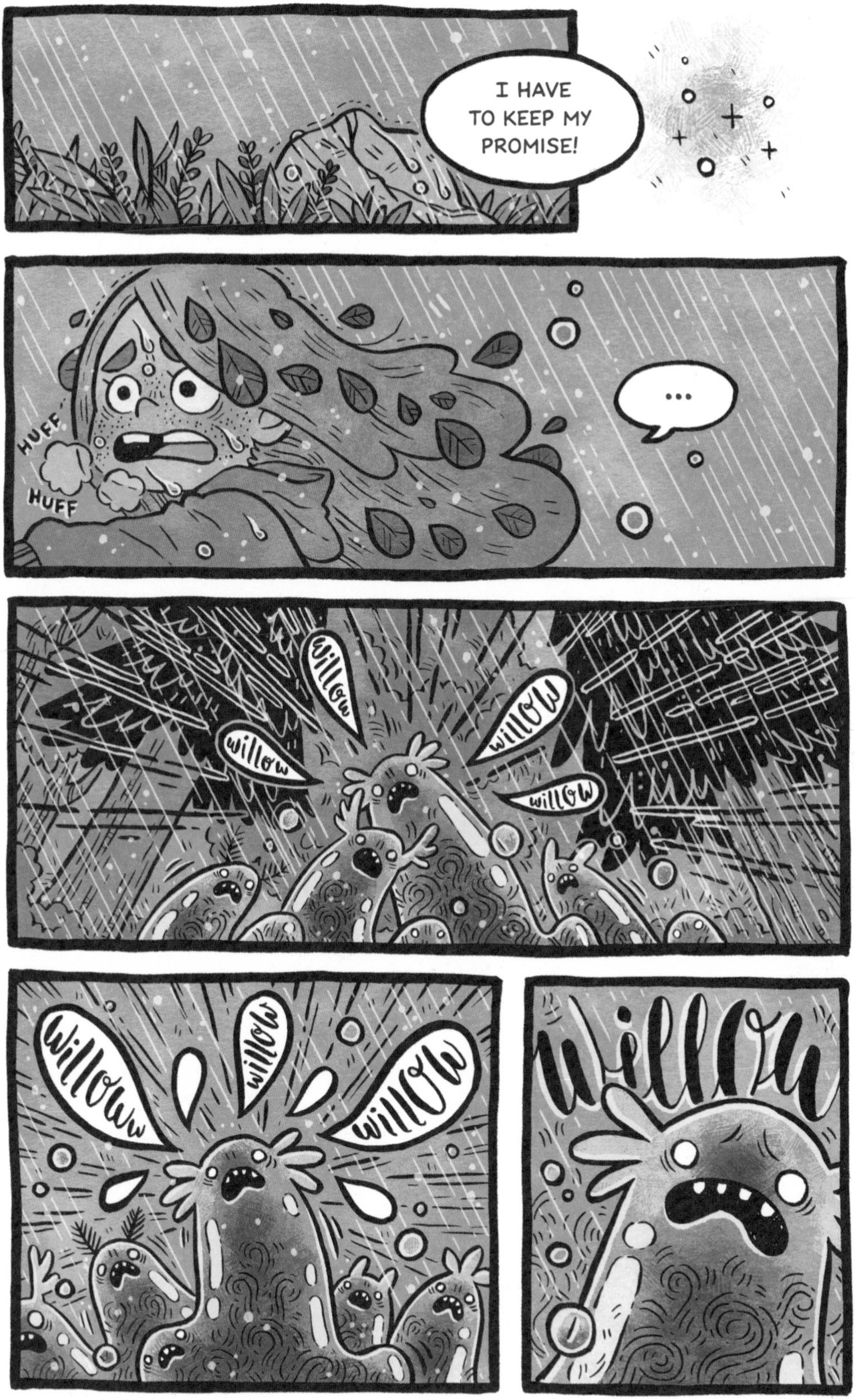
I HAVE TO KEEP MY PROMISE!
HUFF
HUFF
...
willow
willow
willow
willow
willow
willow
willow
willow
willow

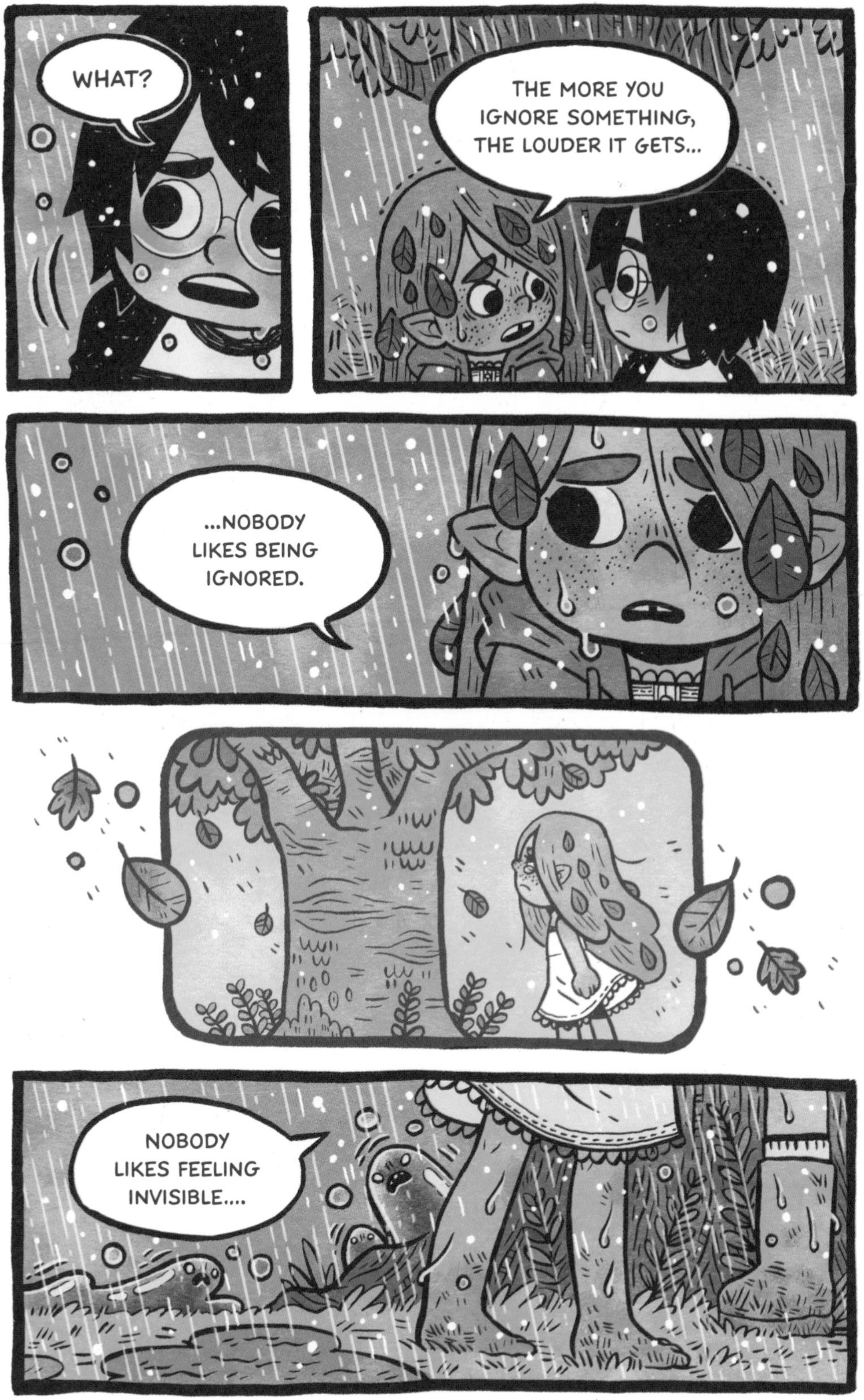
WHAT?
THE MORE YOU IGNORE SOMETHING, THE LOUDER IT GETS...
...NOBODY LIKES BEING IGNORED.
NOBODY LIKES FEELING INVISIBLE....

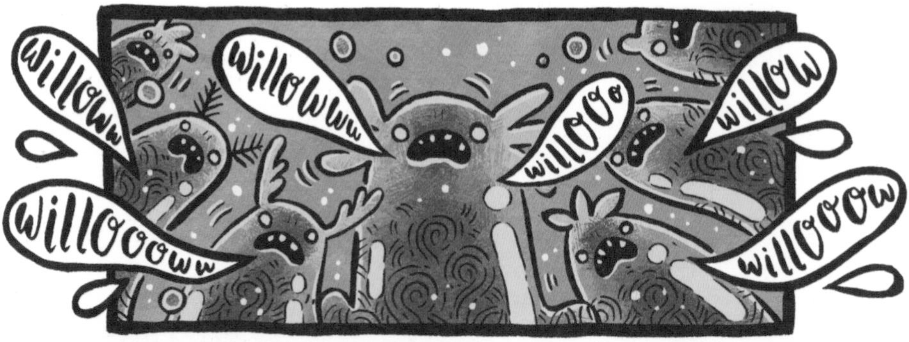
willowww
willowwww
willOOo
willow
willooooww
willOOOow

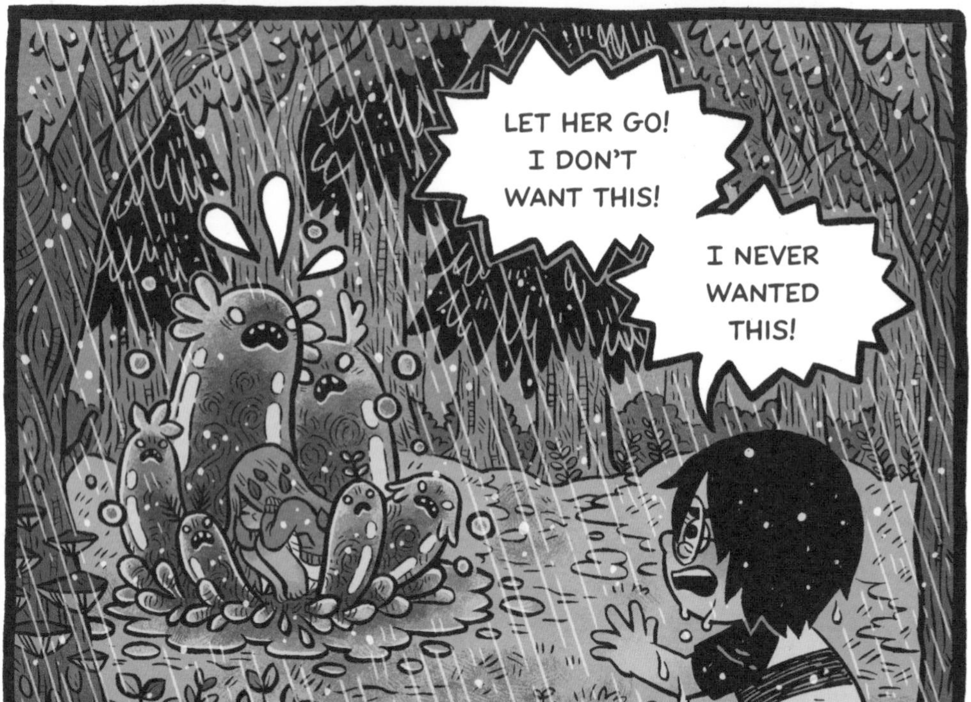
LET HER GO! I DON'T WANT THIS!
I NEVER WANTED THIS!

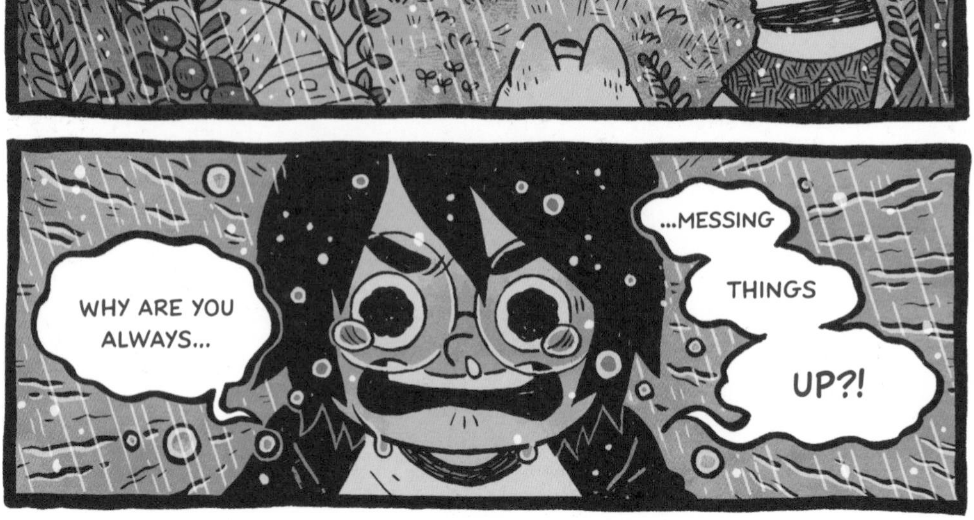
WHY ARE YOU ALWAYS...
...MESSING
THINGS
UP?!

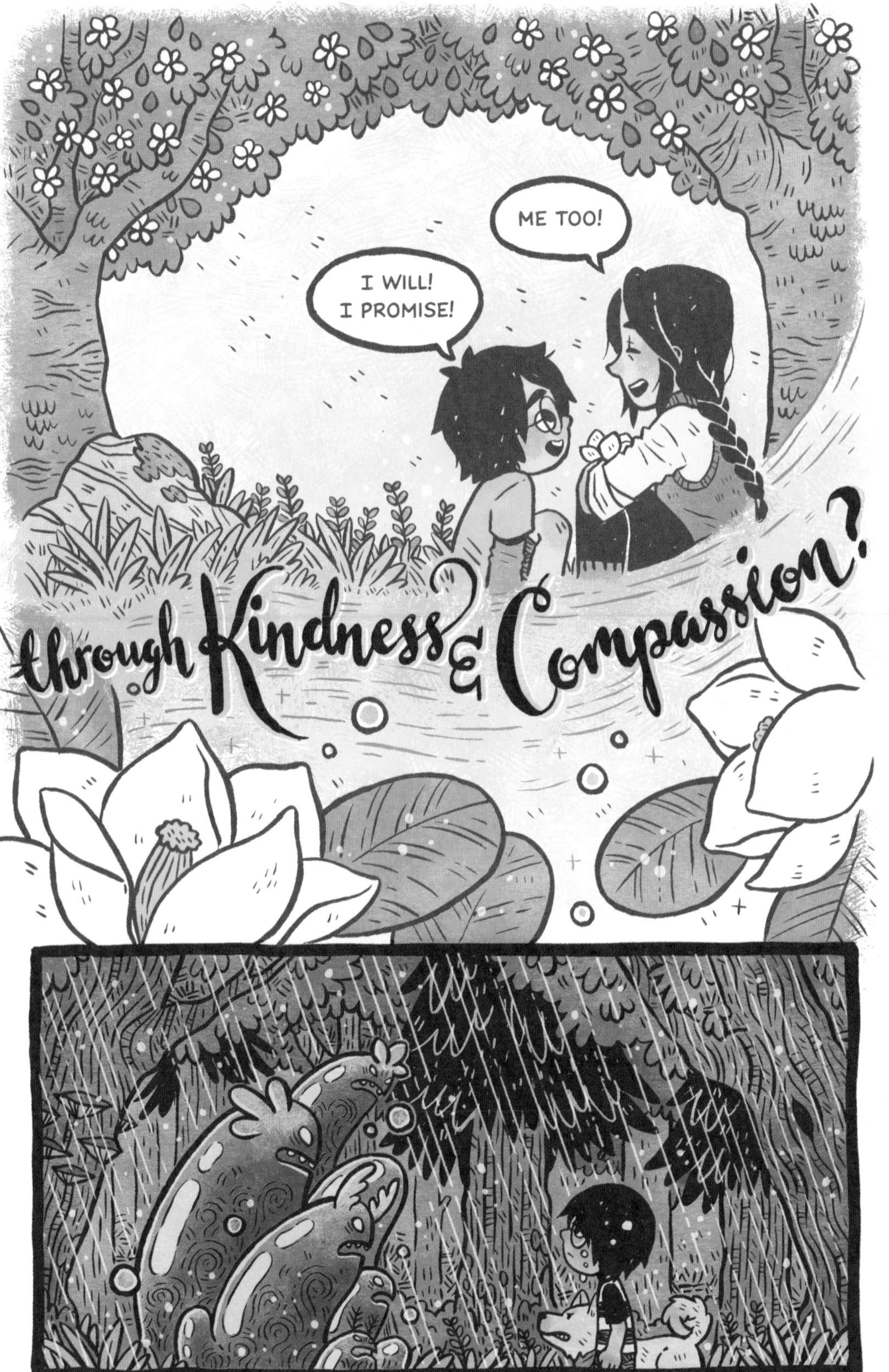
I WILL!
I PROMISE!
ME TOO!
through Kindness & Compassion?

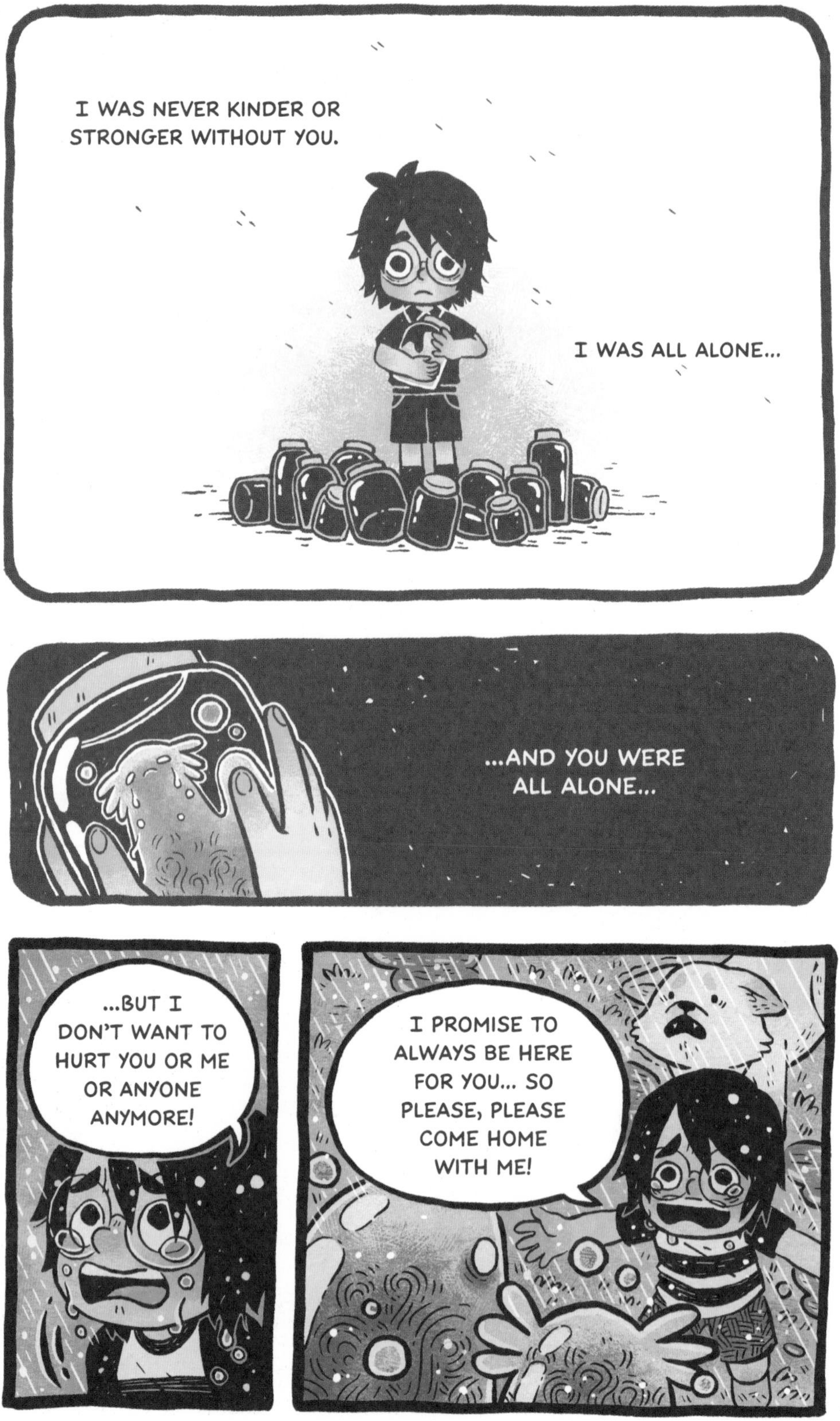
I WAS NEVER KINDER OR STRONGER WITHOUT YOU.
I WAS ALL ALONE...
...AND YOU WERE ALL ALONE...
...BUT I DON'T WANT TO HURT YOU OR ME OR ANYONE ANYMORE!
I PROMISE TO ALWAYS BE HERE FOR YOU... SO PLEASE, PLEASE COME HOME WITH ME!

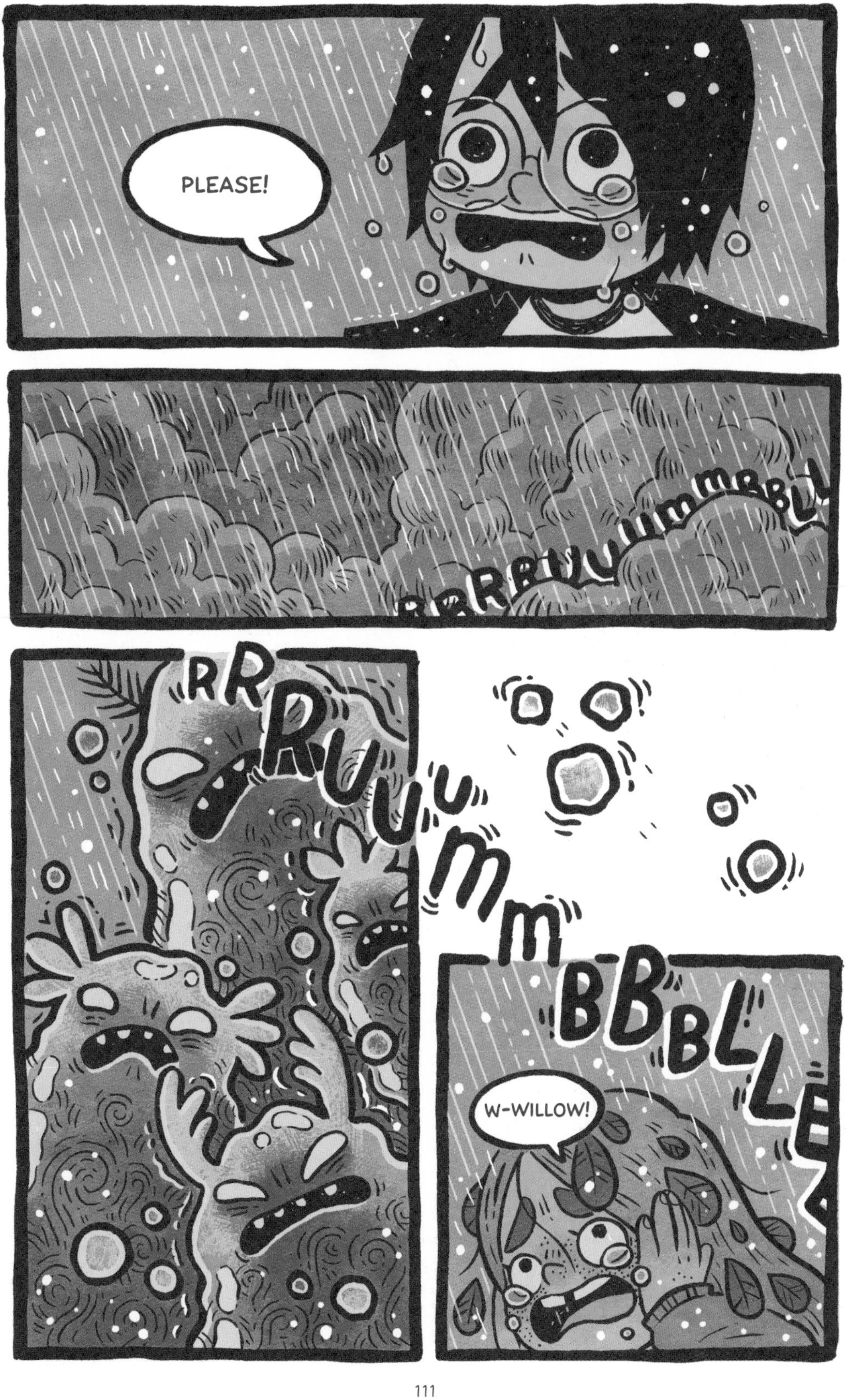
PLEASE!
RRRRUUUMMMBBLL
RRRUUUMMMBBBLLE
W-WILLOW!

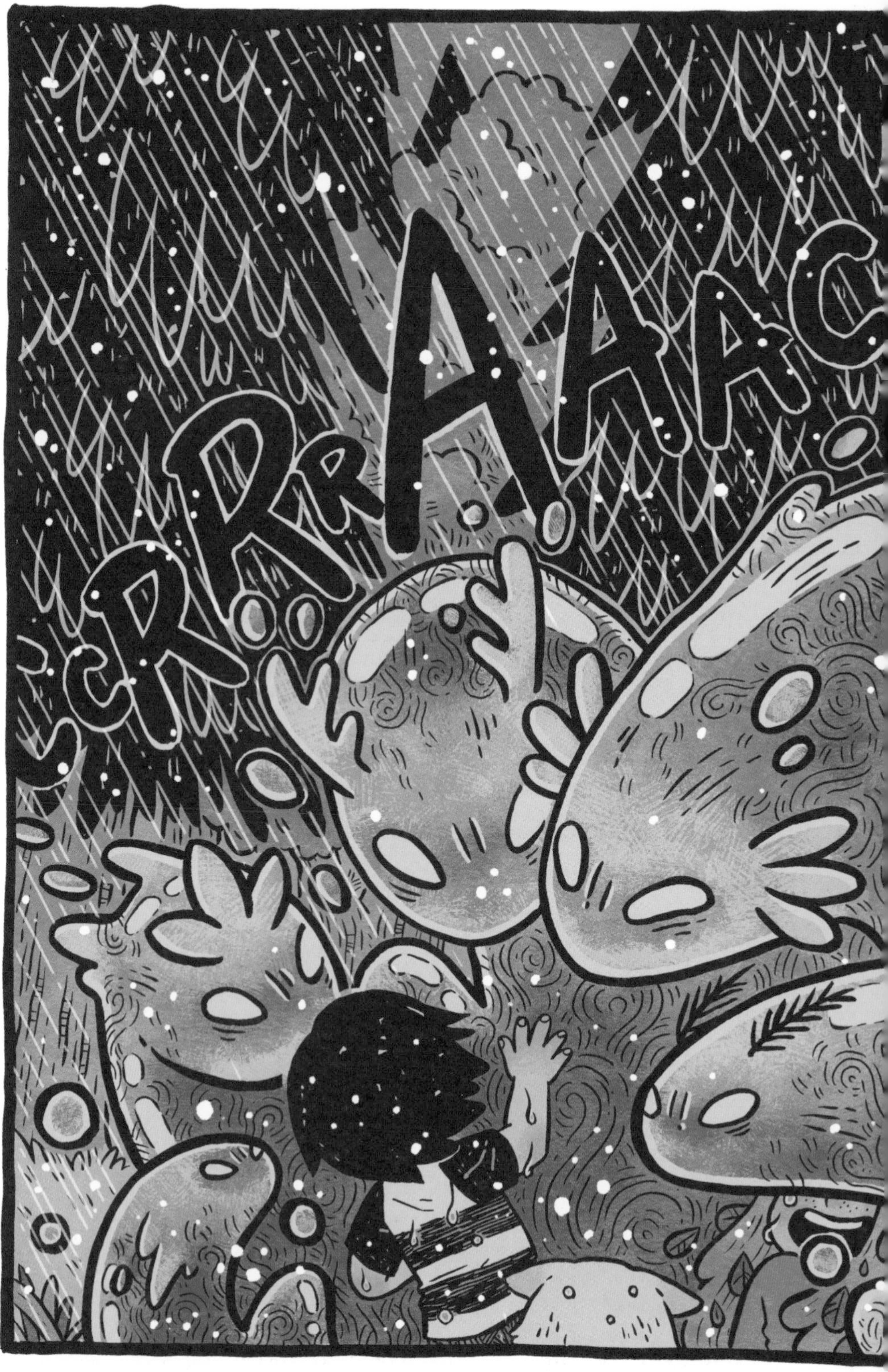
CRRRAAAC

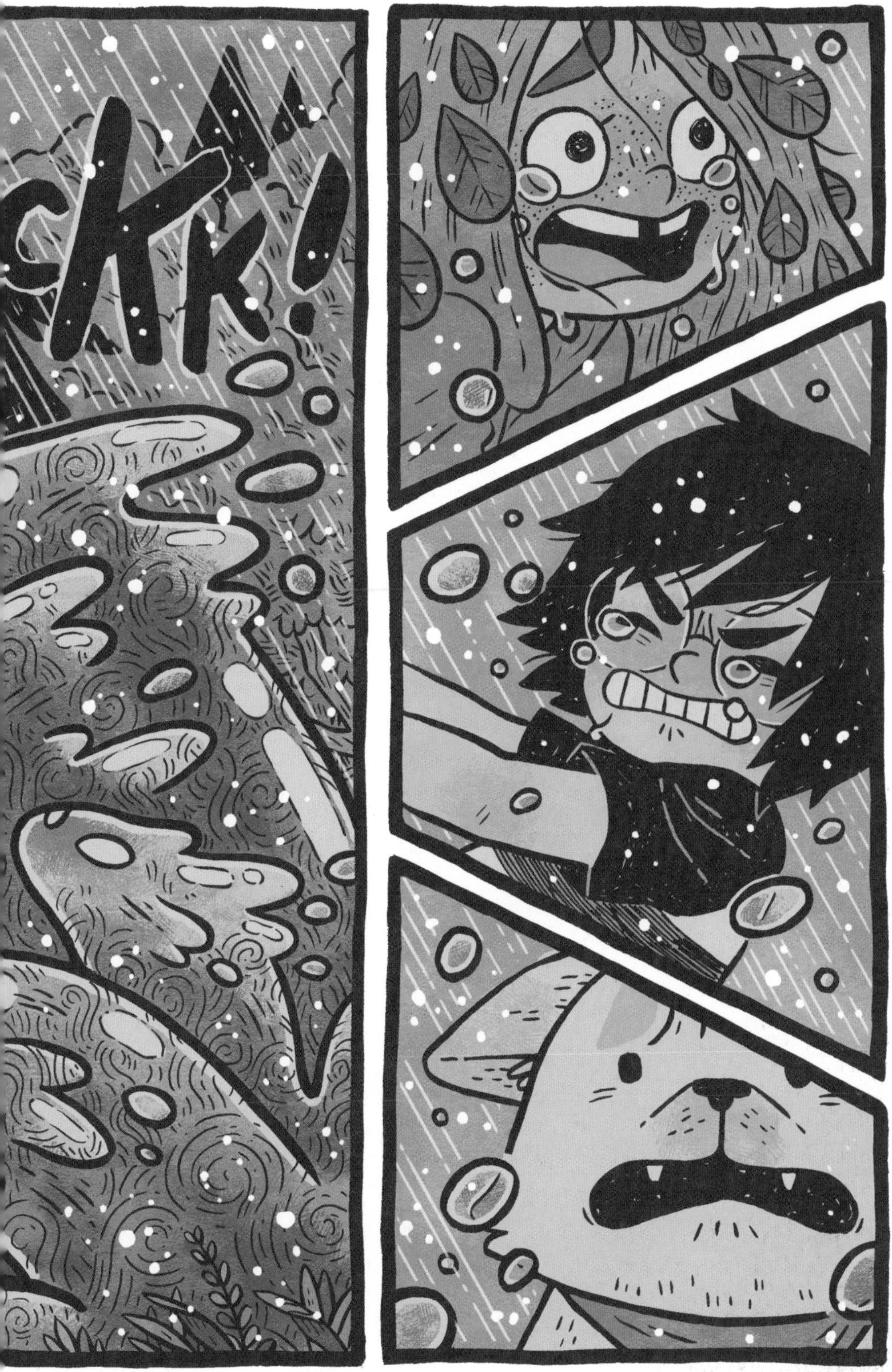
CKK!

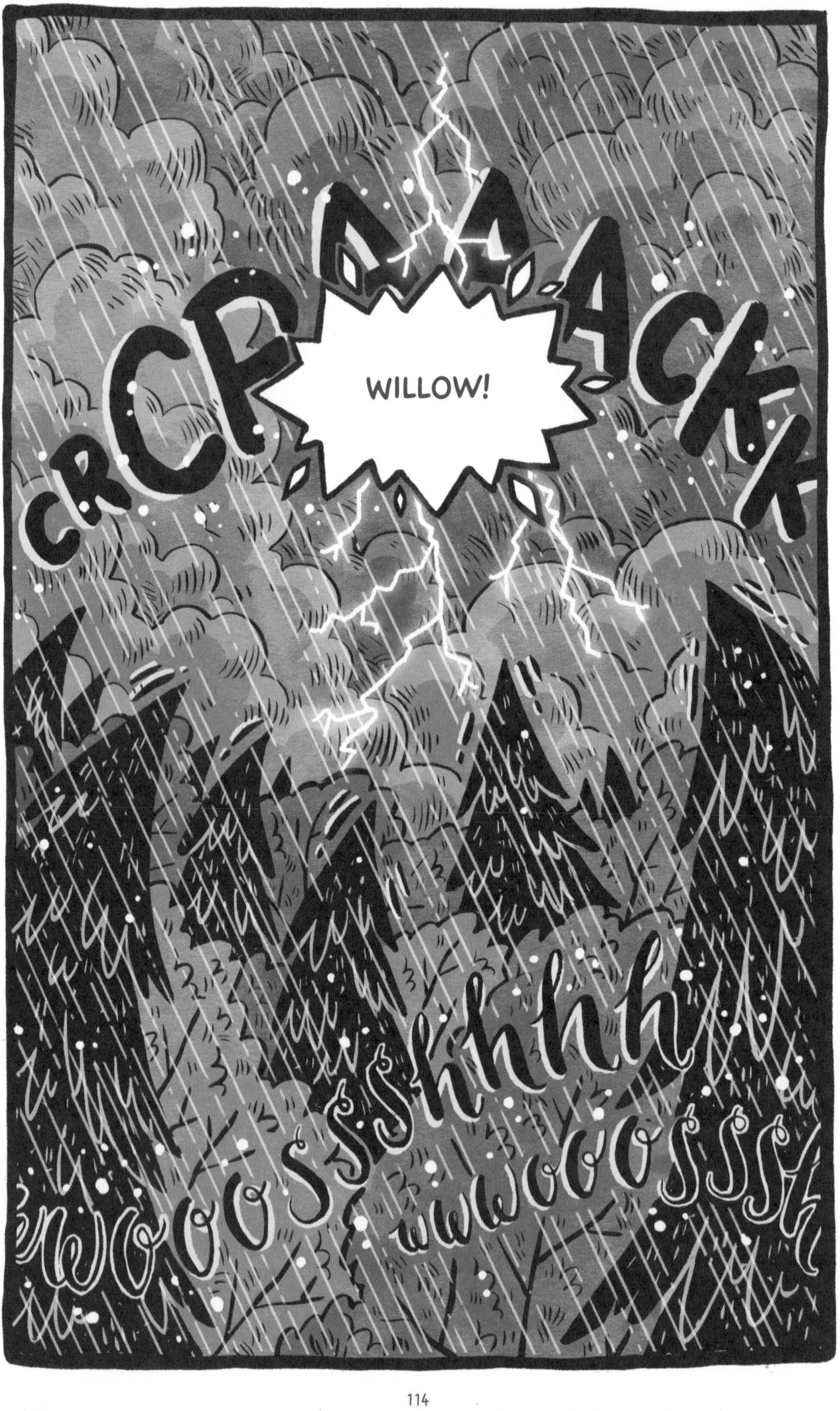
CRCRAAACKK
WILLOW!
WOOOSSShhhh
WWWOOOSSSH

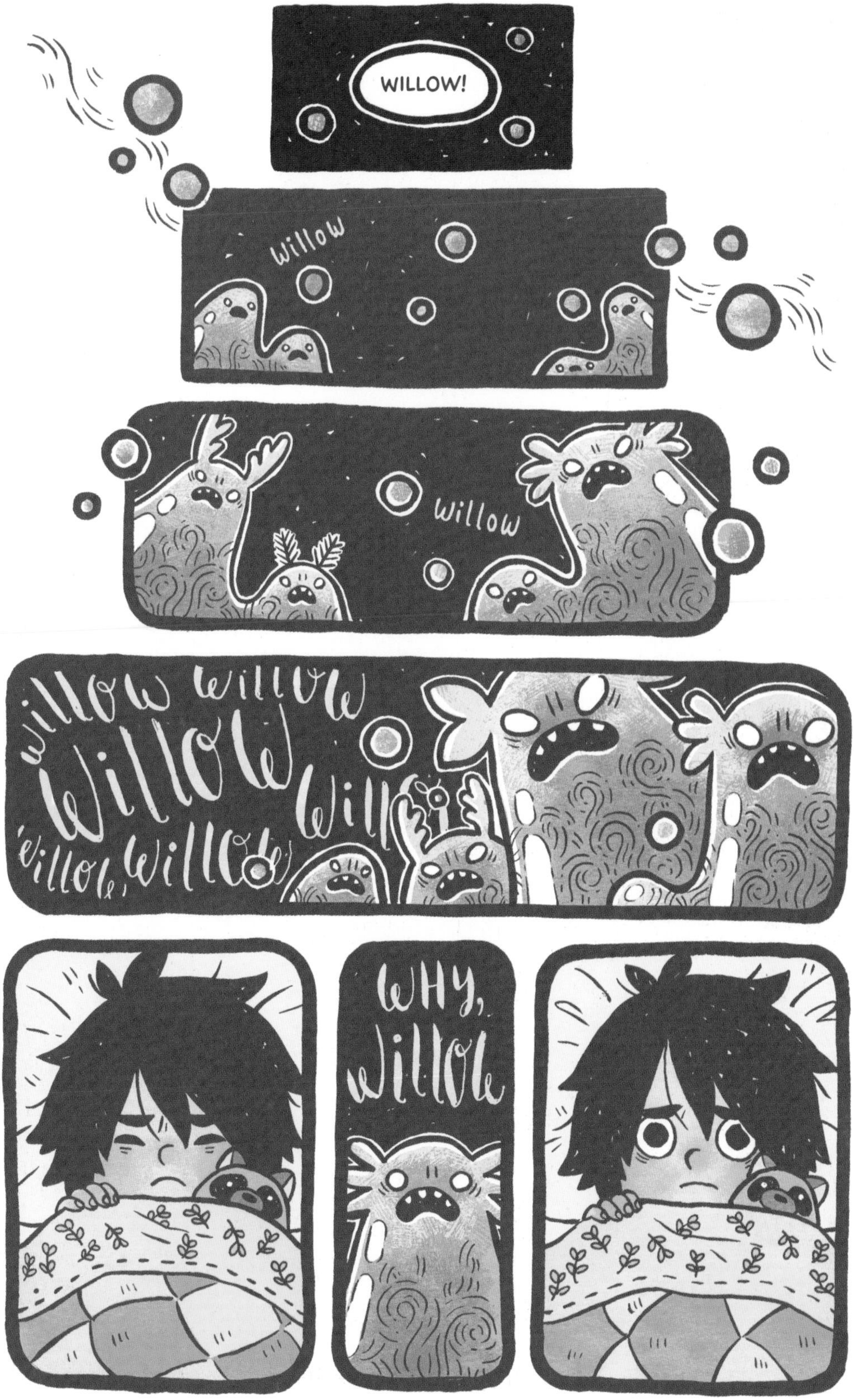
WILLOW!
willow
willow
willow willow
willow
willow, willow
WHY,
willow

116

118

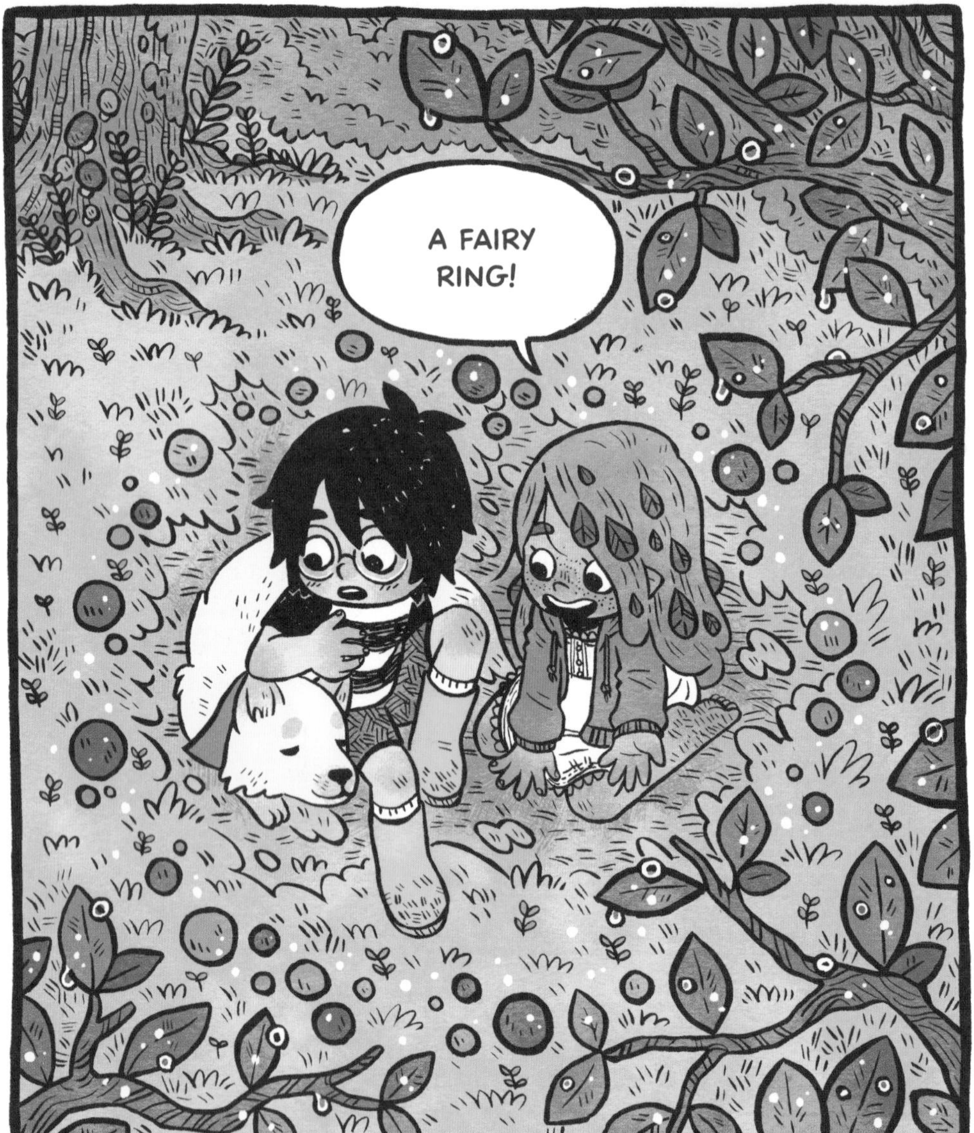
A FAIRY RING!

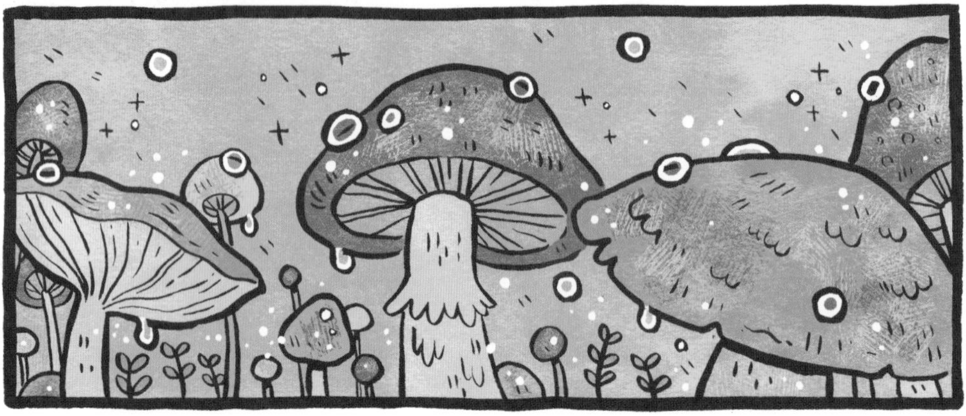

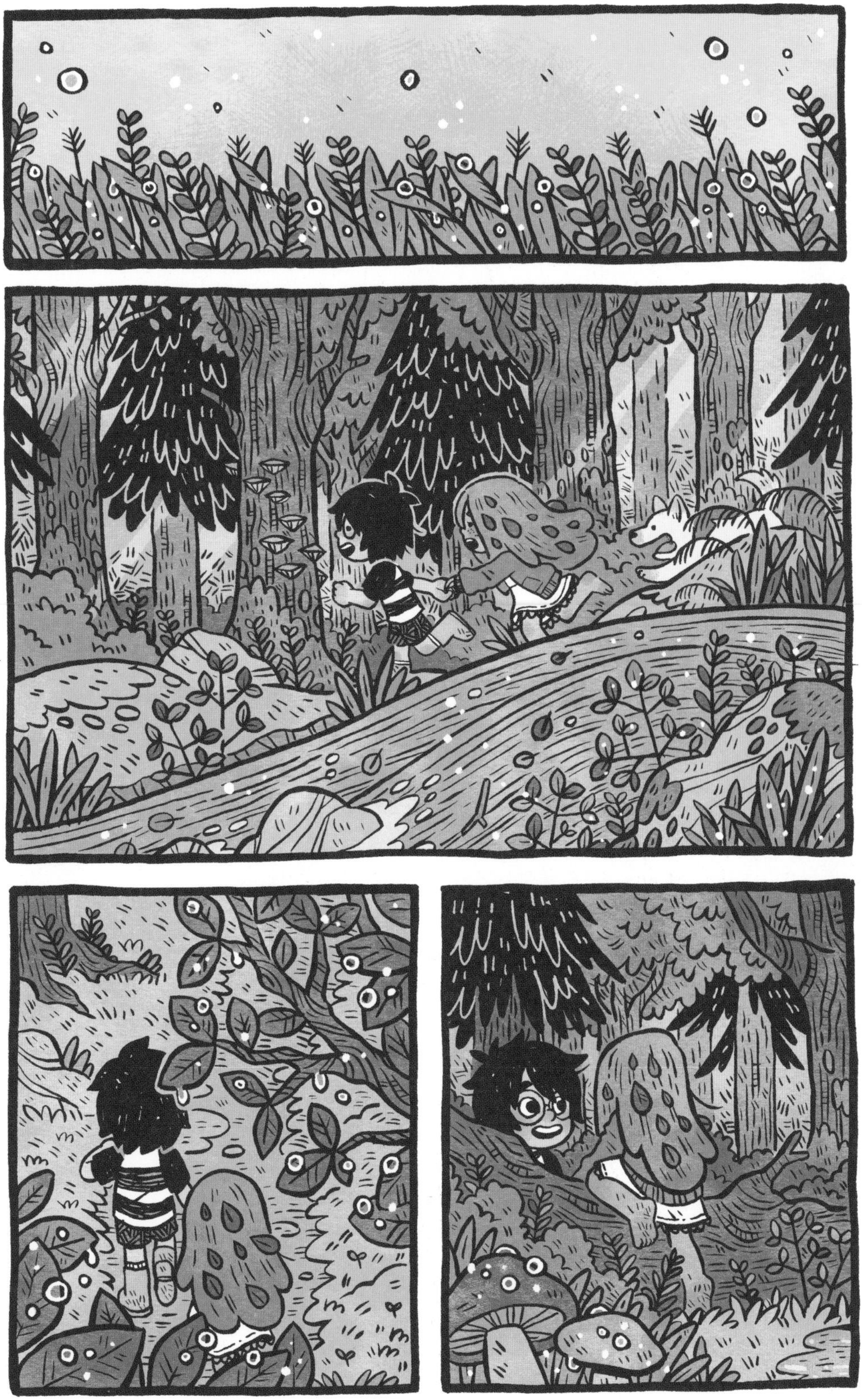

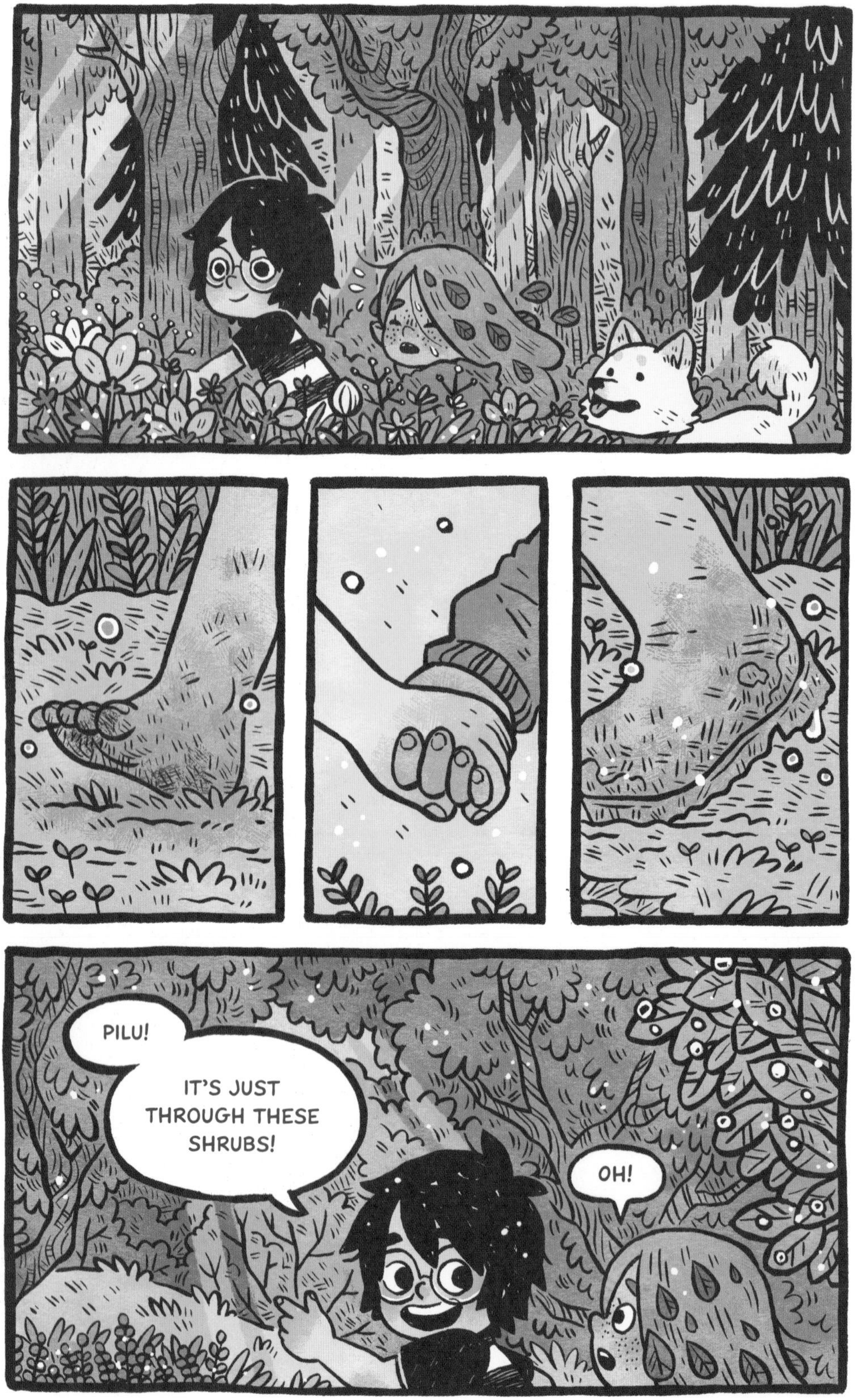
PILU!
IT'S JUST THROUGH THESE SHRUBS!
OH!

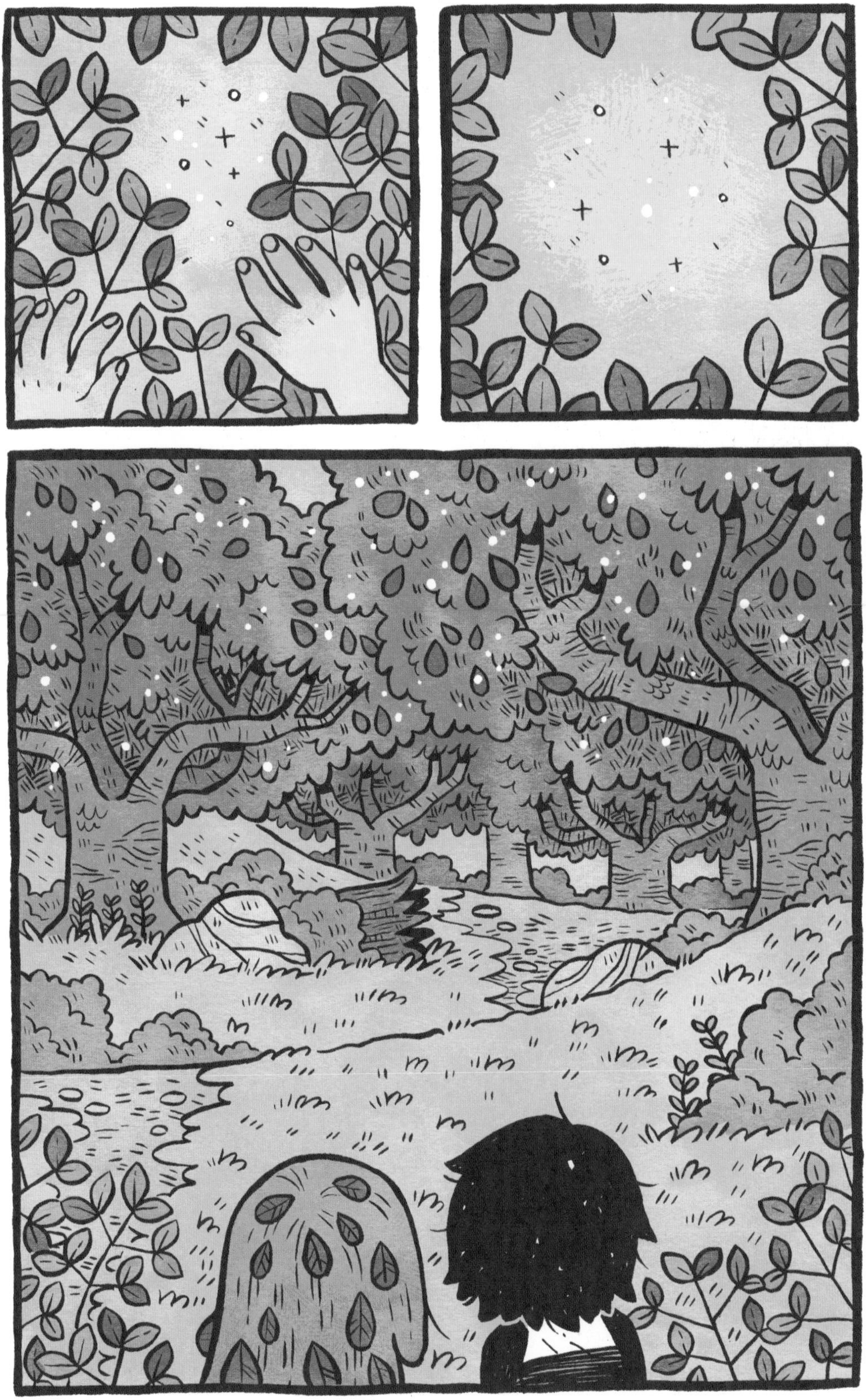

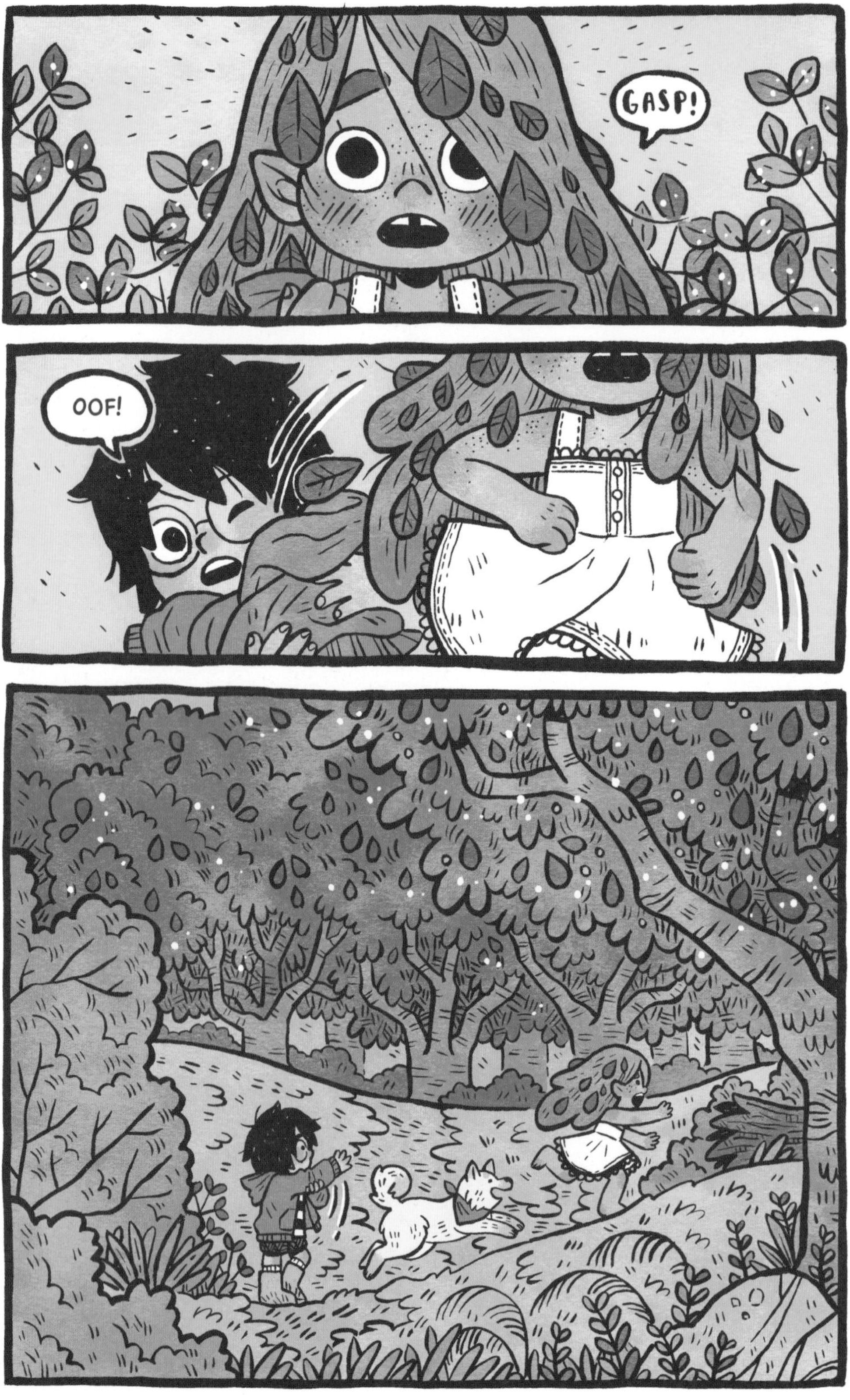
GASP!
OOF!

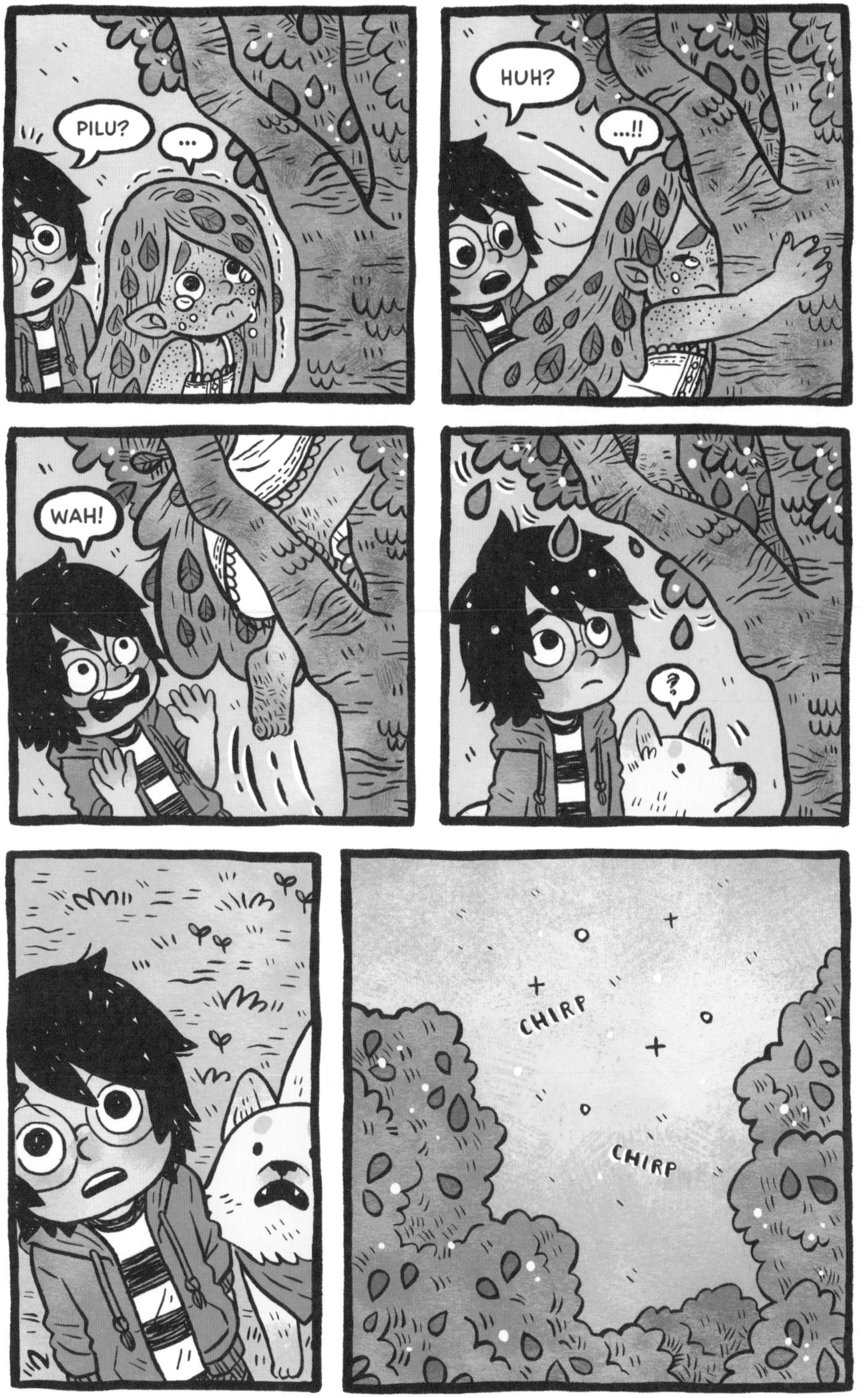
PILU?
...
HUH?
...!!
WAH!
?
CHIRP
CHIRP

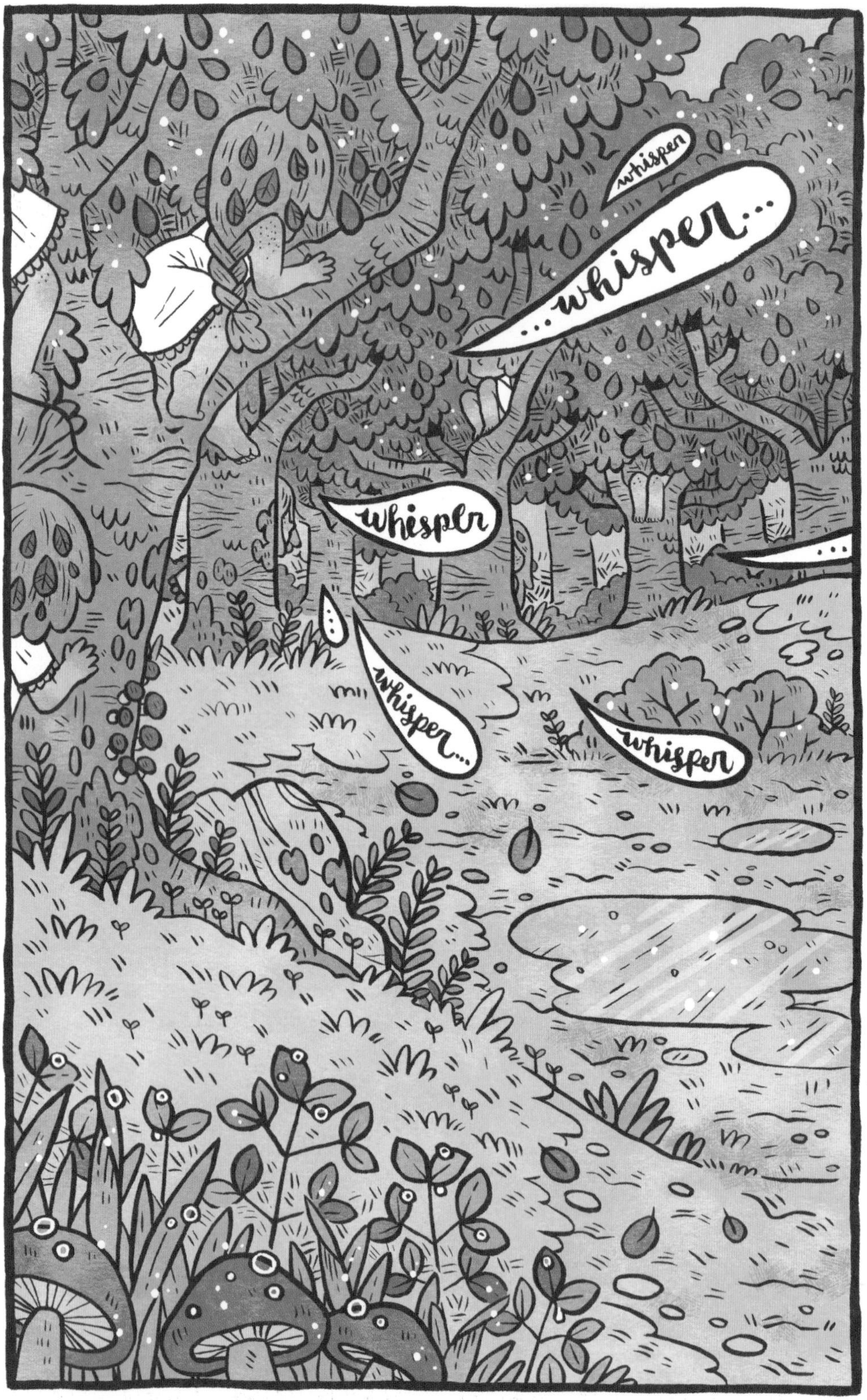
whisper
...whisper...
whisper
whisper...
whisper

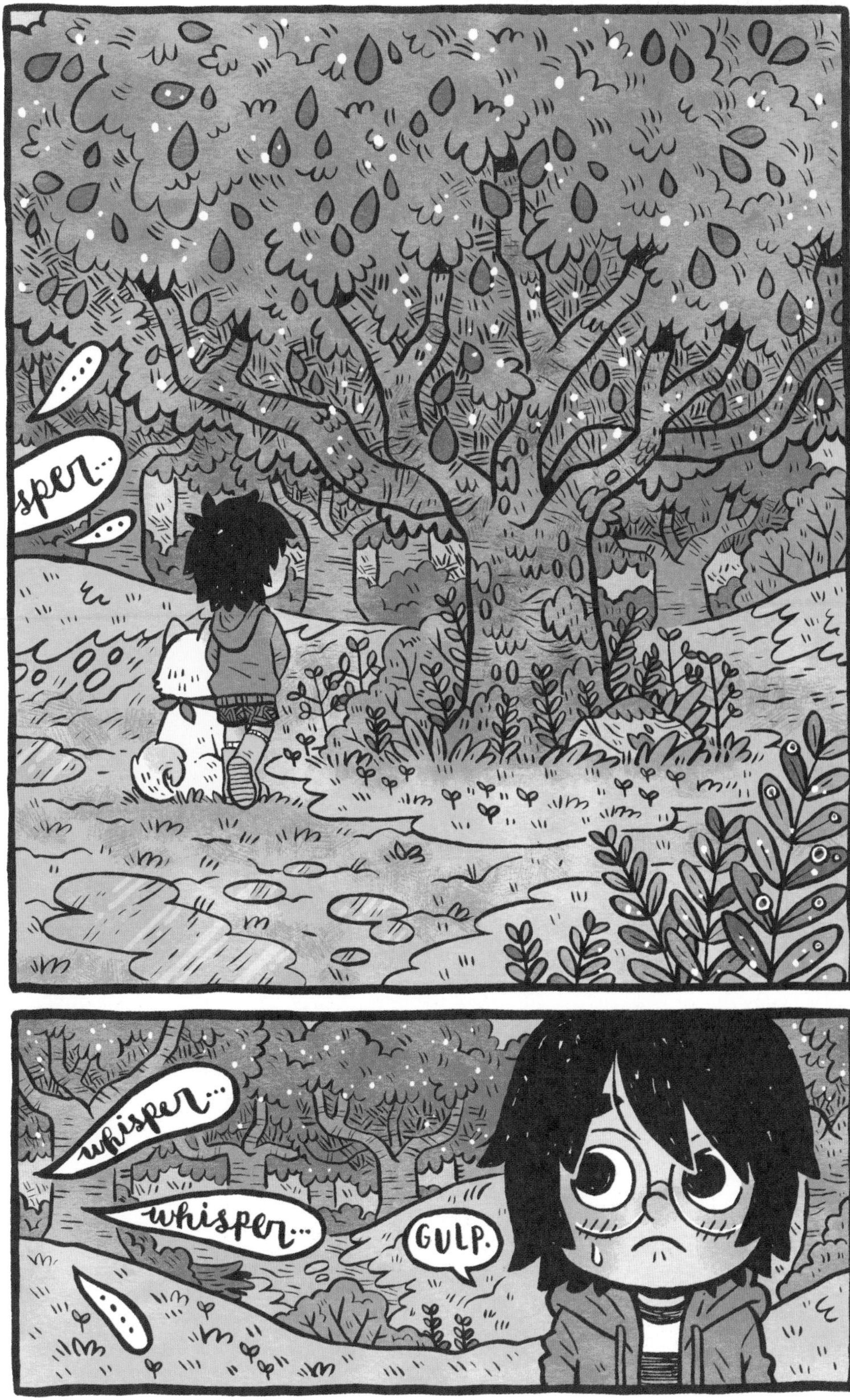
...
sper...
...
whisper...
whisper...
GULP.
...

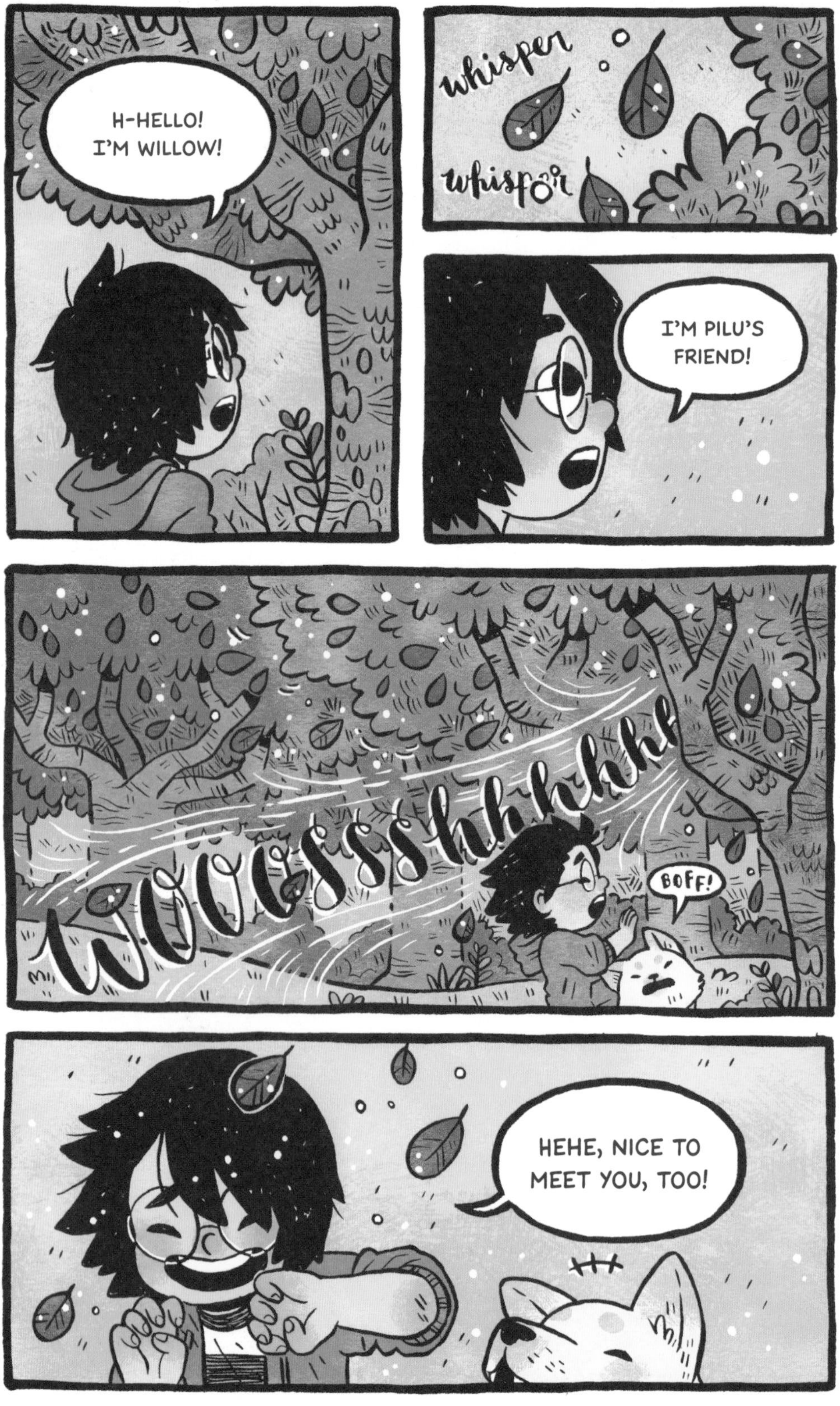
H-HELLO! I'M WILLOW!
whisper
whisper
I'M PILU'S FRIEND!
WOOOSSSHHHHHH
BOFF!
HEHE, NICE TO MEET YOU, TOO!

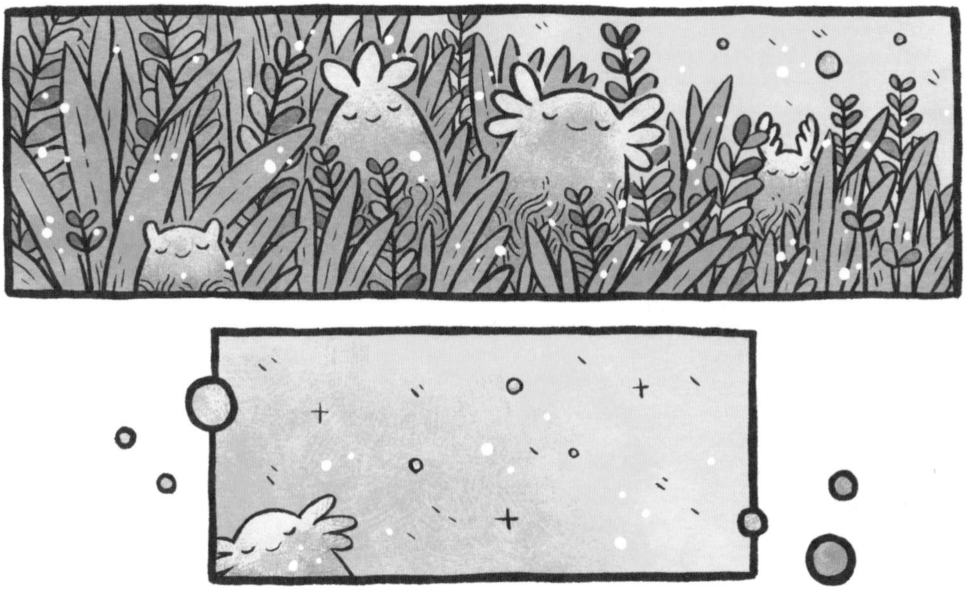

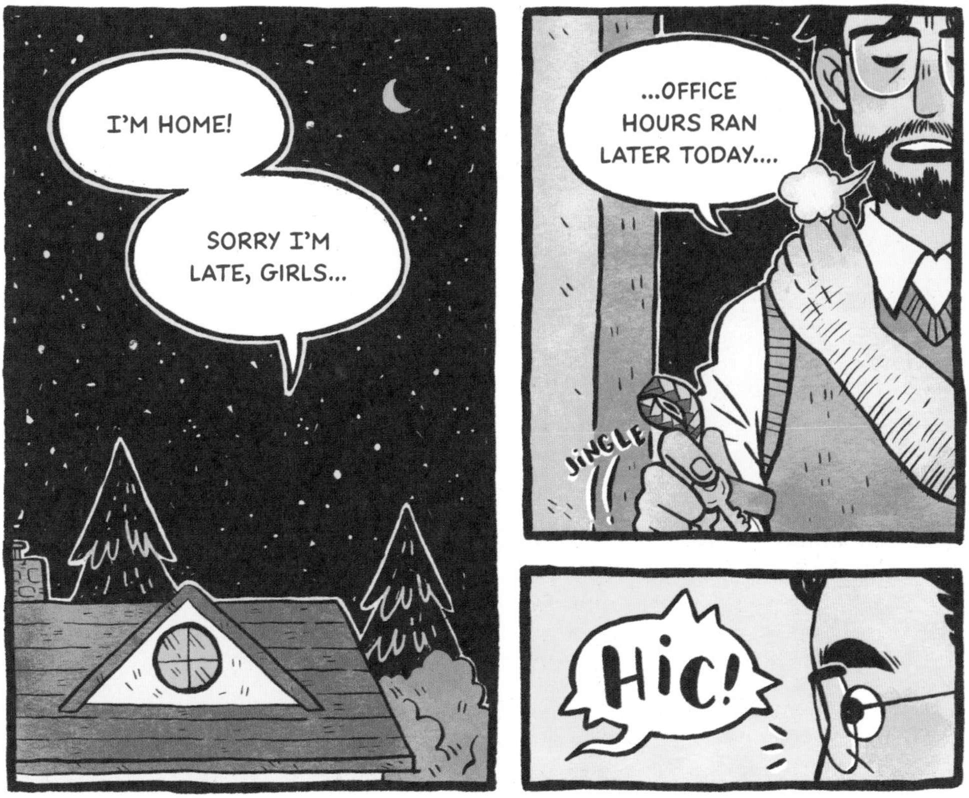
I'M HOME!
SORRY I'M LATE, GIRLS...
...OFFICE HOURS RAN LATER TODAY....
JINGLE
HIC!

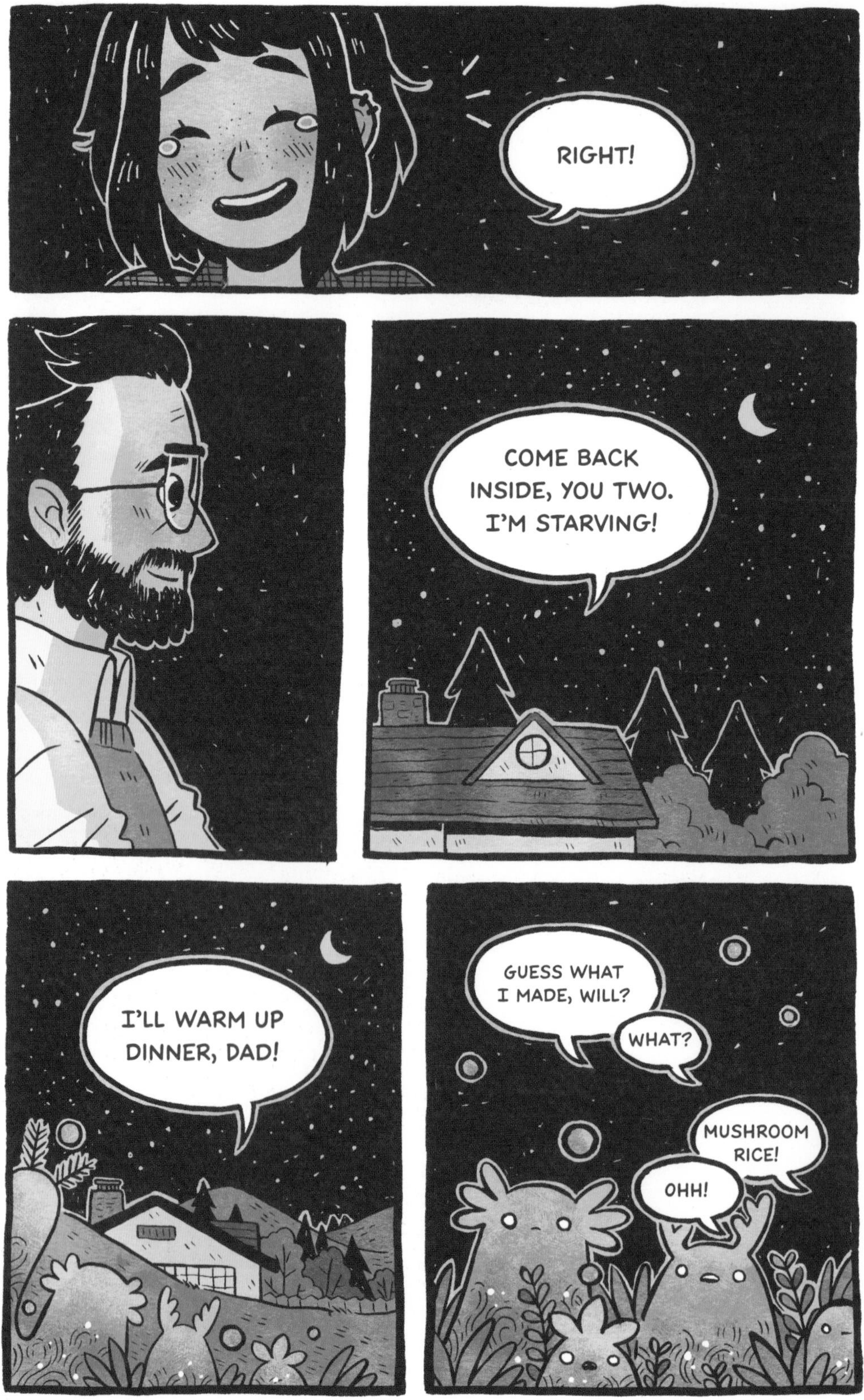
RIGHT!
COME BACK INSIDE, YOU TWO. I'M STARVING!
I'LL WARM UP DINNER, DAD!
GUESS WHAT I MADE, WILL?
WHAT?
MUSHROOM RICE!
OHH!

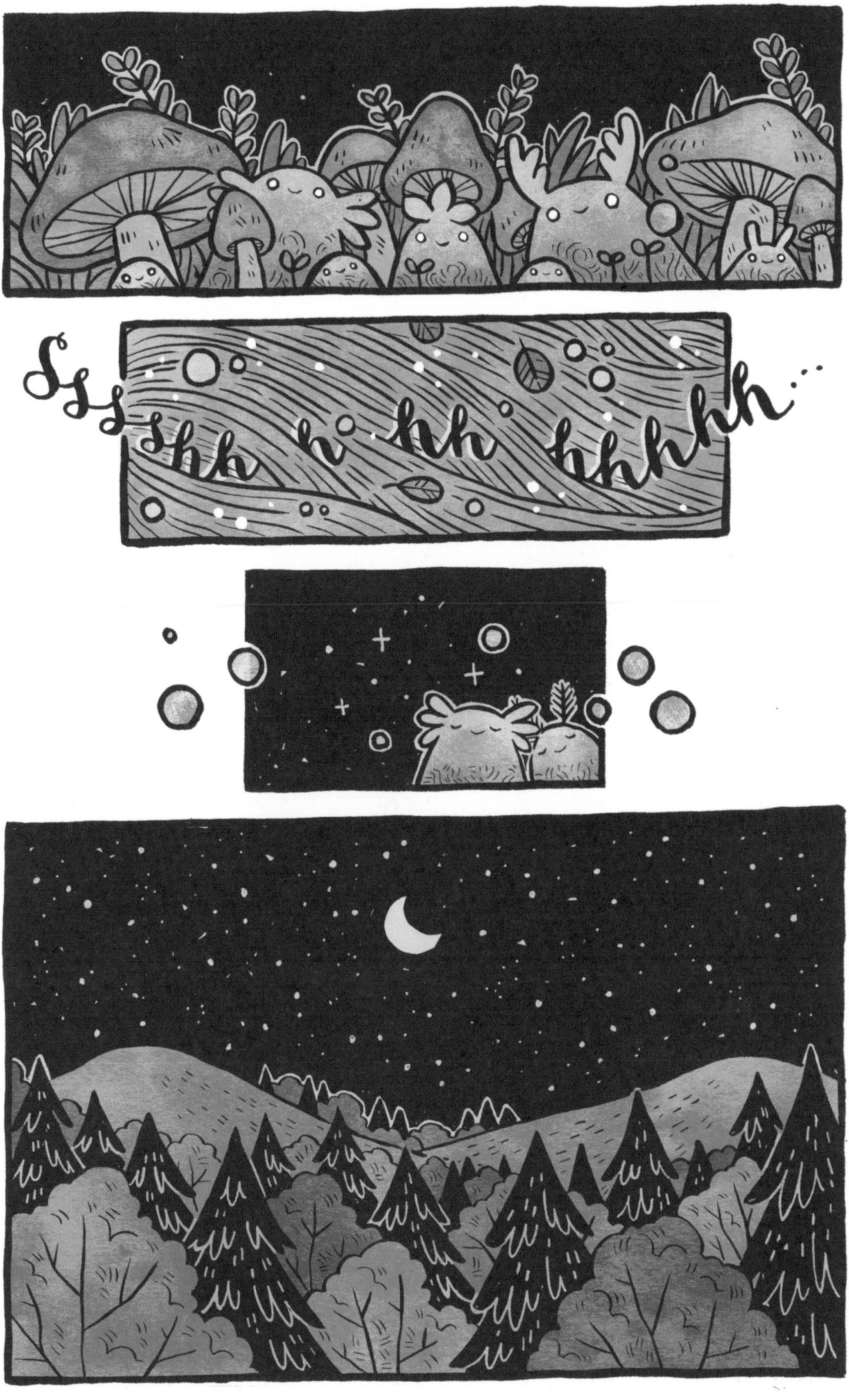
SSShh h hh hhhhh...

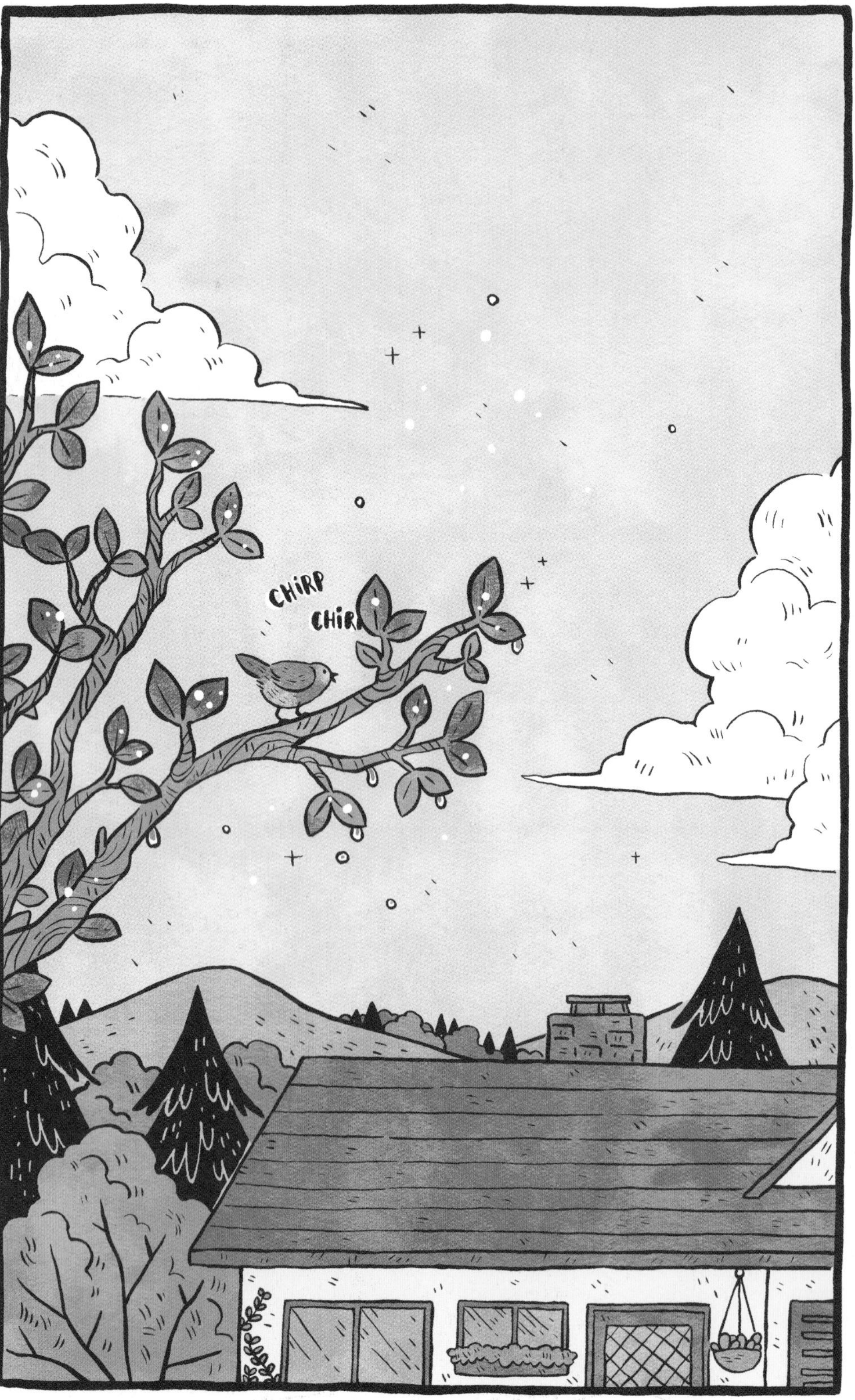
CHIRP
CHIR

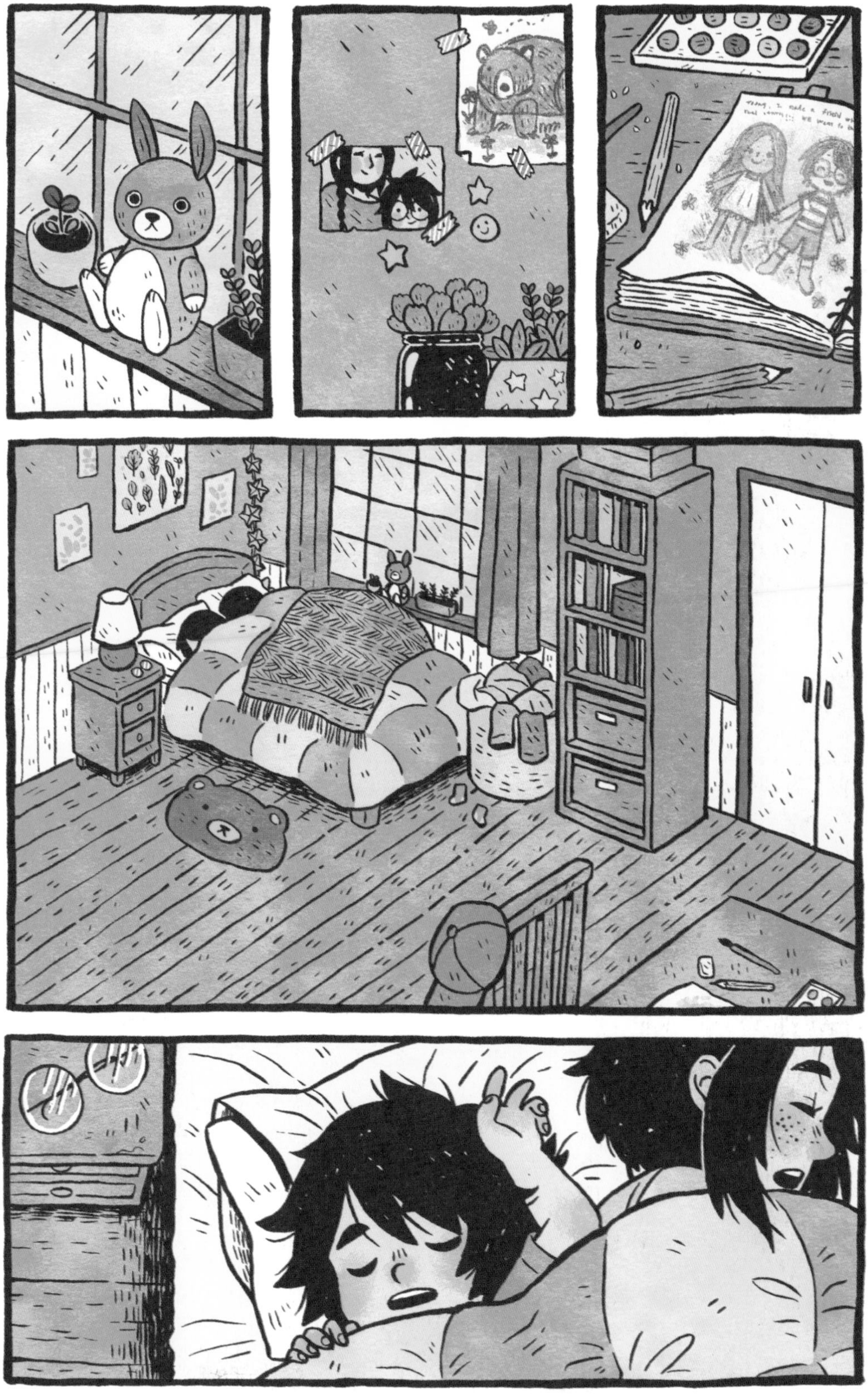

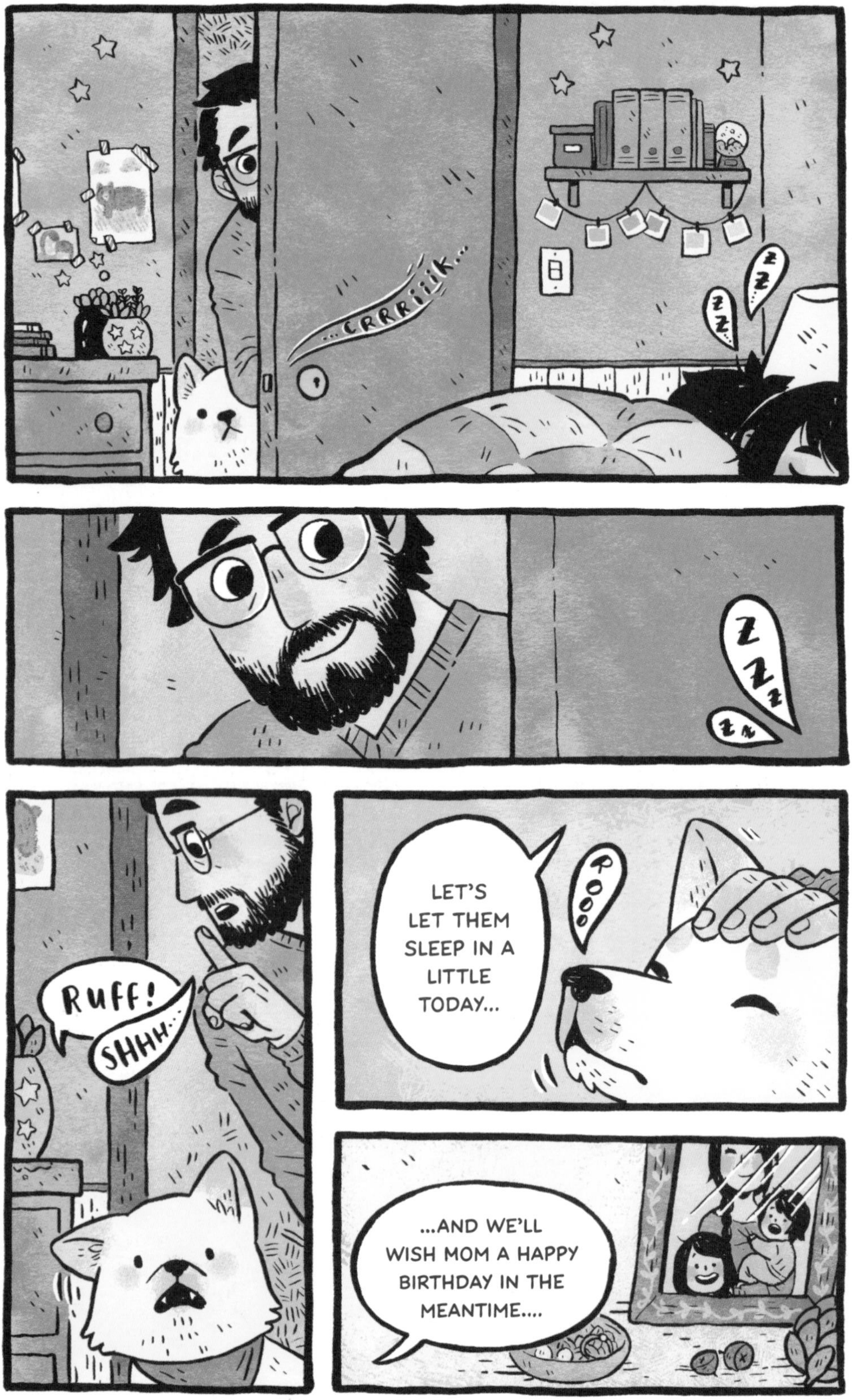
...CRRRiiik...
Z
Z
Z
Z
Z
Z
RUFF!
SHHH...
ROOO
LET'S LET THEM SLEEP IN A LITTLE TODAY...
...AND WE'LL WISH MOM A HAPPY BIRTHDAY IN THE MEANTIME....

NATURE JOURNAL

HERE'S A CHANCE FOR YOU TO RECORD THE THINGS YOU SEE IN NATURE, just like Willow does! WIllow loves to draw her favorite plants, flowers, and trees, and there are many other ways to interact with nature in your own journal. Use these pages as a jumping-off point.

Is there a plant, flower, tree, or animal that you see often in your daily life? Try drawing it here.

Try describing it here. What does it look like? If it's a plant, describe its smell. If it's an animal, describe the sounds it makes. What else can you describe about it?

_____

_____

_____

_____

_____

_____

Now, write about how it makes you feel. What memories do you associate with this plant or animal? What feelings does it give you? What other things does it remind you of?

_____

_____

_____

_____

_____

_____

_____

Go to your backyard, or a park, or another place where you can see a lot of nature. (The zoo counts!) List ten things you find in these places. You don't have to know the names of them, but you can make up descriptive names. (Like "Pretty Yellow Flower" or "Tall Tree Shaped like a Triangle.")

_____

_____

_____

_____

_____

_____

_____

_____

_____

_____

Look up at the sky. Clouds are a part of nature, too! What kind of clouds can you see? Again, you don't have to know the names.

_____

_____

_____

_____

_____

Are there plants and animals that don't exist where you live, but you want to know more about them anyway? What are they? Write them here. Find out where they can be found.

_____

_____

_____

_____

_____

Draw one item from the list you came up with on the previous page.
Draw while looking at it to try and get as accurate of a picture as possible.

Pick one small part of what you drew—an ear? A leaf? A petal?
—and draw it here, being as detailed as you can.

Draw one item from the list you came up with on the previous page from
memory. This means you are remembering what it looks like
instead of using your eyes to look at it. You can look at
your written descriptions, though.

: MOM'S :
MUSHROOM RICE
(KINOKO GOHAN)

2 CUPS OF RICE

250 G OF ENOKI AND SHITAKE MUSHROOMS

150 G OF SKINLESS CHICKEN THIGHS, CUT INTO BITE-SIZED PIECES

1/4 CARROT, SHREDDED OR DICED

1.5 CUPS OF BROTH, PLUS MORE

1 TBSP EACH OF SOY SAUCE AND COOKING SAKE

2 TBSP EACH OF SOY SAUCE, COOKING SAKE, AND MIRIN

½ TSP EACH OF SALT AND SUGAR

1 TBSP OF BUTTER

CHOPPED GREEN ONIONS

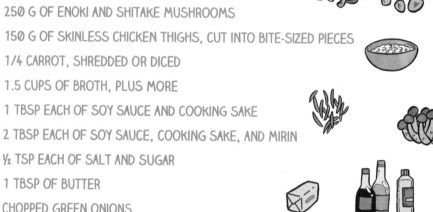

In a small bowl toss the chicken in 1 tbsp of soy sauce and 1 tbsp of cooking sake. Set aside.

Rinse 2 cups of rice until the water runs clear. Let it soak for 30 minutes (letting it soak will give you fluffier rice!). To ensure your rice is dry, put it in a sieve and let it drain for at least 15 minutes.

In a small pot, combine the chicken and carrots. Add 1.5 cups of broth (or enough to cover the chicken and carrots) and bring it to a boil. Lower the heat and let it simmer for about 10 minutes, skimming any foam.

Use a sieve to separate the chicken and carrots from the broth. Don't throw out the broth—we'll use it to cook the rice in!

In a heavy bottomed pot, combine the rice and 2 cups of chicken broth—
use the broth in step 3 and add regular chicken broth to make 2 cups.

Add 2 tbsp of cooking sake, 2 tbsp of mirin, 2 tbsp of soy sauce, 1/2 tsp of salt, and
1/2 tsp of sugar.

Add the mushrooms, chicken, carrots, and 1 tbsp of butter. Don't mix it!
Let everything sit on the rice.

Cover the pot and bring to a boil over
high heat. It's best to not lift the lid,
so try and listen for the clattering of
boiling water. Reduce the heat to low and
let the rice cook for about 12-13 minutes,
or until the water has been absorbed
(it's okay to take quick peeks).

Remove the pot from the heat with the lid, and let
it steam for about 10 more minutes. Lift the lid and
fluff the rice, making sure everything is evenly mixed.

Finally, add some of the chopped green onions and
enjoy your mushroom rice!

MAI K. NGUYEN is a comics maker, illustrator, and ice-cream enthusiast living in Northern California. She has previously self-published two short stories, *Coral and the King* and *Little Ghost*. When she's not doodling, she's hustling as a visual designer in San Francisco, watching too many true-crime documentaries, or dreaming about all the other comics she wants to make. Not unlike Willow, she loves feeling small amongst redwood trees and inhaling the salty-grassy smell of coastal bluffs.

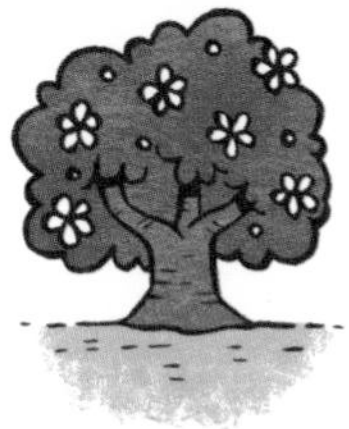

THANK YOU

FOR HELPING WILLOW & PILU FIND THEIR WAY HOME

ILA, who has been my favorite artist ever since I was little. This book wouldn't exist, like really really wouldn't exist, if it weren't for you pushing me to share my work with a bigger audience and to take my passion more seriously. Thank you for always finding time to look over my pitch, my script, my thumbnails, my sketches, and everything in between countless times.

AKSHAYA, for two years of dragging me to coffee shops every Thursday night to work on our books. You've been my accountability buddy, my tomato buddy, my compassion buddy, my wisdom buddy, and every other type of buddy. Thank you for reminding me every day of the importance of pursuing what you love with all your heart.

IAN, for always, always cheering me on. This book is better because you gave me honest and actionable feedback, helped me letter pages during crunch time, and scooped me up whenever I wallowed in too much self-doubt. Thank you for being the absolute best.

SHIRO, who kept me company during late night drawing sessions for most of the creation of this book, and who looks suspiciously like Chicory (or Chicory like Shiro?). I miss swiveling around in my chair to find you snoozing away.

MOCHA, because I learned to love drawing comics in middle school based on your angsty Fictionpress stories. At age 13, I thought, "When I publish my first real comic book, I'm gonna put Mocha's name in it somewhere." So here it is.

And last but not least, my first ever editor, **ROBIN** and the wonderful folks at **ONI PRESS,** who helped bring to life a little idea I had in 2012.

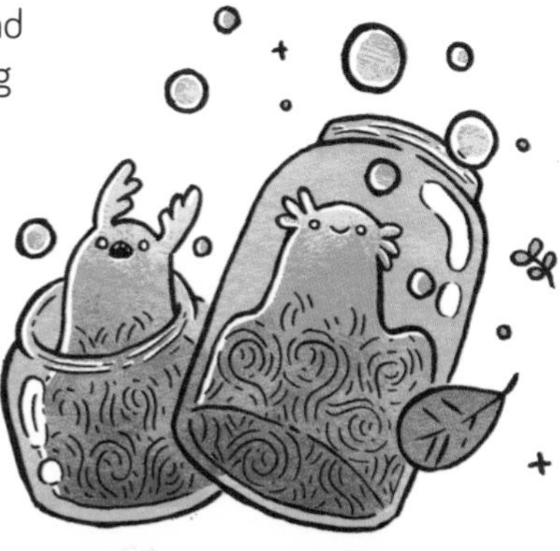

MORE FANTASTIC TITLES FROM ONI PRESS!

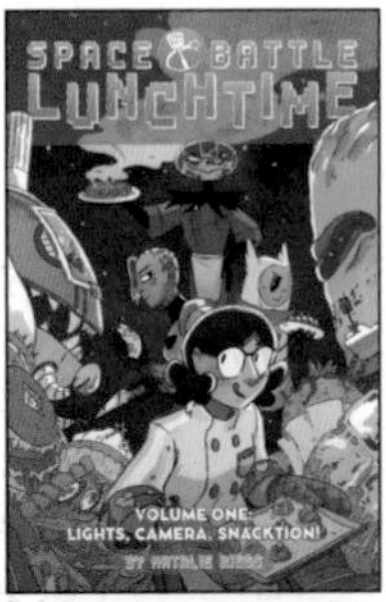
SPACE & BATTLE LUNCHTIME
VOLUME ONE: LIGHTS, CAMERA, SNACKTION!

SPACE BATTLE LUNCHTIME VOLUME 1: LIGHTS, CAMERA, SNACKTION!
BY NATALIE RIESS

Peony is a baker with big dreams! Can she make it through the universe's biggest reality cooking show?

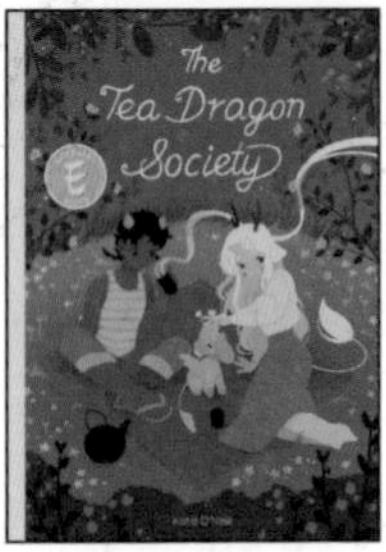
The Tea Dragon Society

THE TEA DRAGON SOCIETY
BY KATIE O'NEILL

When Greta finds a lost creature in the market, she learns about the nearly-forgotten art of Tea Dragon caretaking.

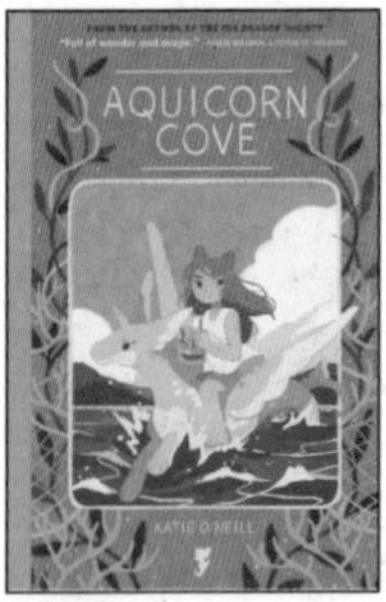
AQUICORN COVE

AQUICORN COVE
BY KATIE O'NEILL

Unable to rely on the adults in her storm-ravaged town, a young girl must protect a colony of magical creatures she discovers in the coral reef.

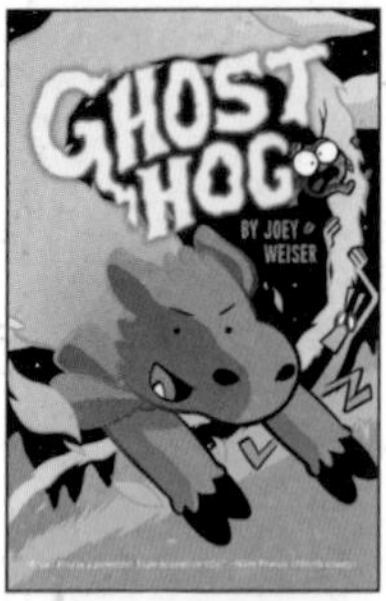
GHOST HOG
BY JOEY WEISER

GHOST HOG
BY JOEY WEISER

Truff, the ghost of a boar killed by a hunter, navigates her new afterlife as she seeks revenge.

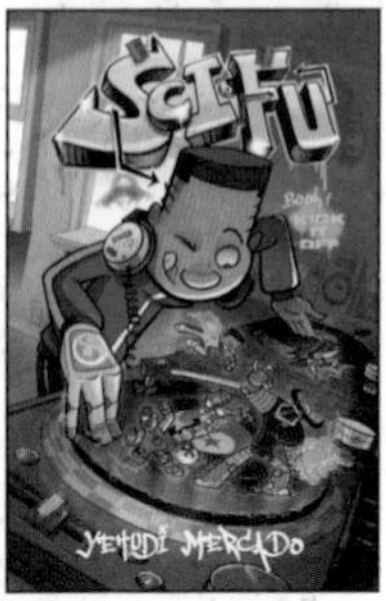
SCI-FU
YEHUDI MERCADO

SCI-FU BOOK 1: KICK IT OFF
BY YEHUDI MERCADO

Wax might be the greatest DJ in Brooklyn, but what happens when robot aliens expect him to save their planet, Discopia?